P9-AZX-358

The Bad Queen

A YOUNG ROYALS BOOK

THE BAD QUEEN

Rules and Instructions for
MARIE-ANTOINETTE

Carolyn Meyer

HARCOURT
HOUGHTON MIFFLIN HARCOURT
Boston New York 2010

Harcourt is an imprint of Houghton Mifflin Harcourt Publishing Company.

www.hmhbooks.com

Text set in Requiem Text
Designed by Regina Roff

Library of Congress Cataloging-in-Publication Data

Meyer, Carolyn, 1935–
The bad queen : rules and instructions for Marie-Antoinette / Carolyn Meyer.
p. cm. — (Young royals)
Summary: In eighteenth-century France, Marie-Antoinette rails against the rules of etiquette that govern her life even as she tries to fulfill her greatest obligation, giving birth to the next king, but she finds diversion in spending money on clothing, parties, and gambling despite her family's warnings and the whispers of courtiers.

ISBN 978-0-15-206376-4 (hardcover : alk. paper) 1. Marie-Antoinette, Queen, consort of Louis XVI, King of France, 1755–1793—Juvenile fiction. 2. Louis XVI, King of France, 1754–1793—Fiction. 3. France—History—Louis XVI, 1774–1793—Juvenile fiction. 4. France—History—Revolution, 1789–1799—Juvenile fiction. [1. Marie-Antoinette, Queen, consort of Louis XVI, King of France, 1755–1793—Fiction. 2. Louis XVI, King of France, 1754–1793—Fiction. 3. Kings, queens, rulers, etc.—Fiction. 4. Courts and courtiers—Fiction. 5. France—History—Louis XVI, 1774–1793—Fiction. 6. France—History—Revolution, 1789–1799—Fiction.] I. Title.
PZ7.M5685Bad 2010
[Fic]—dc22
2009019036

Manufactured in the United States of America
DOC 10 9 8 7 6 5 4 3 2 1
4500211454

In memory of Miss Mary Frankenberry,
the original Grammar Dragon

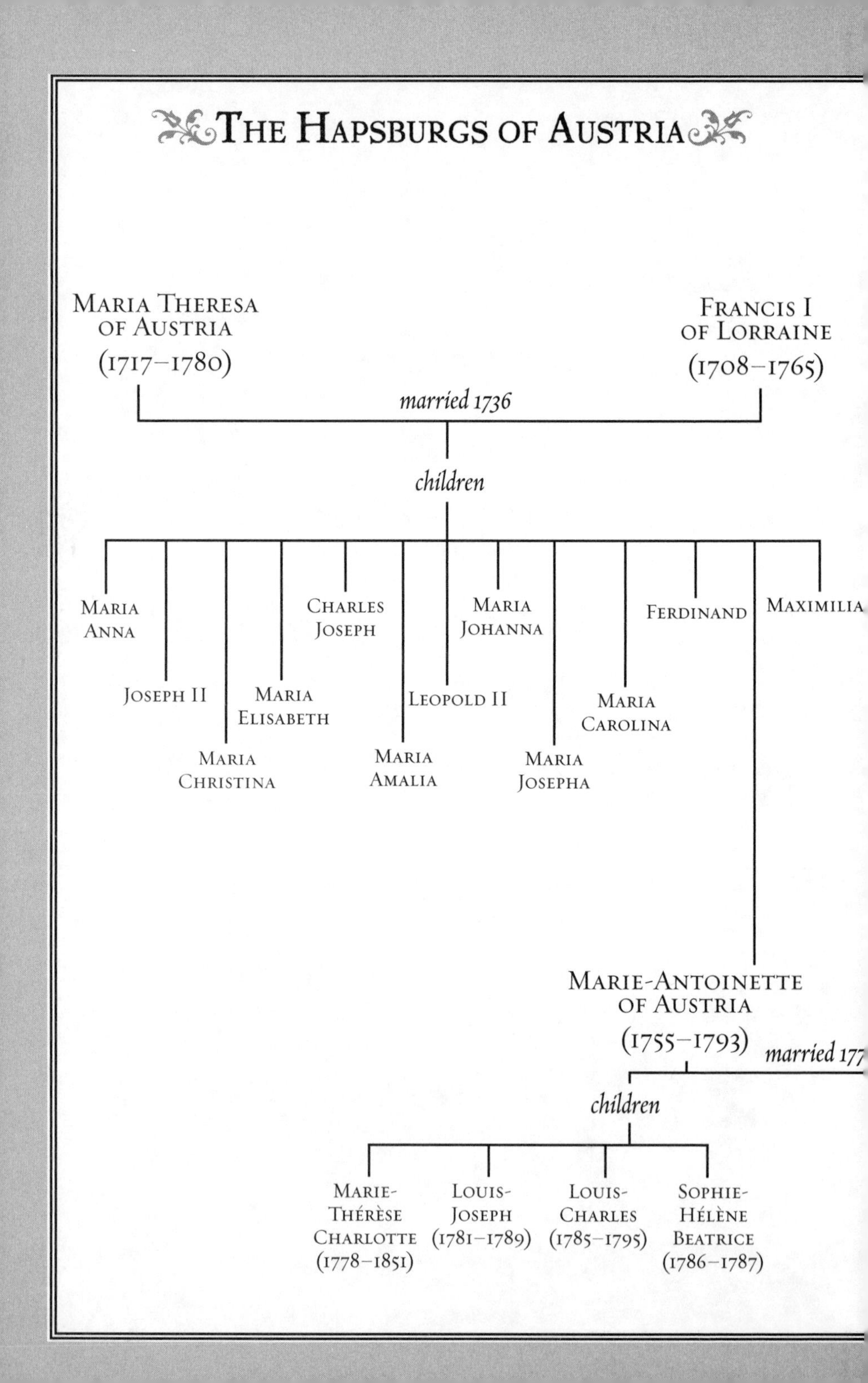
THE HAPSBURGS OF AUSTRIA
MARIA THERESA OF AUSTRIA (1717–1780)
FRANCIS I OF LORRAINE (1708–1765)
married 1736
children
MARIA ANNA
JOSEPH II
MARIA CHRISTINA
MARIA ELISABETH
CHARLES JOSEPH
MARIA AMALIA
LEOPOLD II
MARIA JOHANNA
MARIA JOSEPHA
MARIA CAROLINA
FERDINAND
MAXIMILIA
MARIE-ANTOINETTE OF AUSTRIA (1755–1793)
married 17
children
MARIE-THÉRÈSE CHARLOTTE (1778–1851)
LOUIS-JOSEPH (1781–1789)
LOUIS-CHARLES (1785–1795)
SOPHIE-HÉLÈNE BEATRICE (1786–1787)

The Bourbons of France

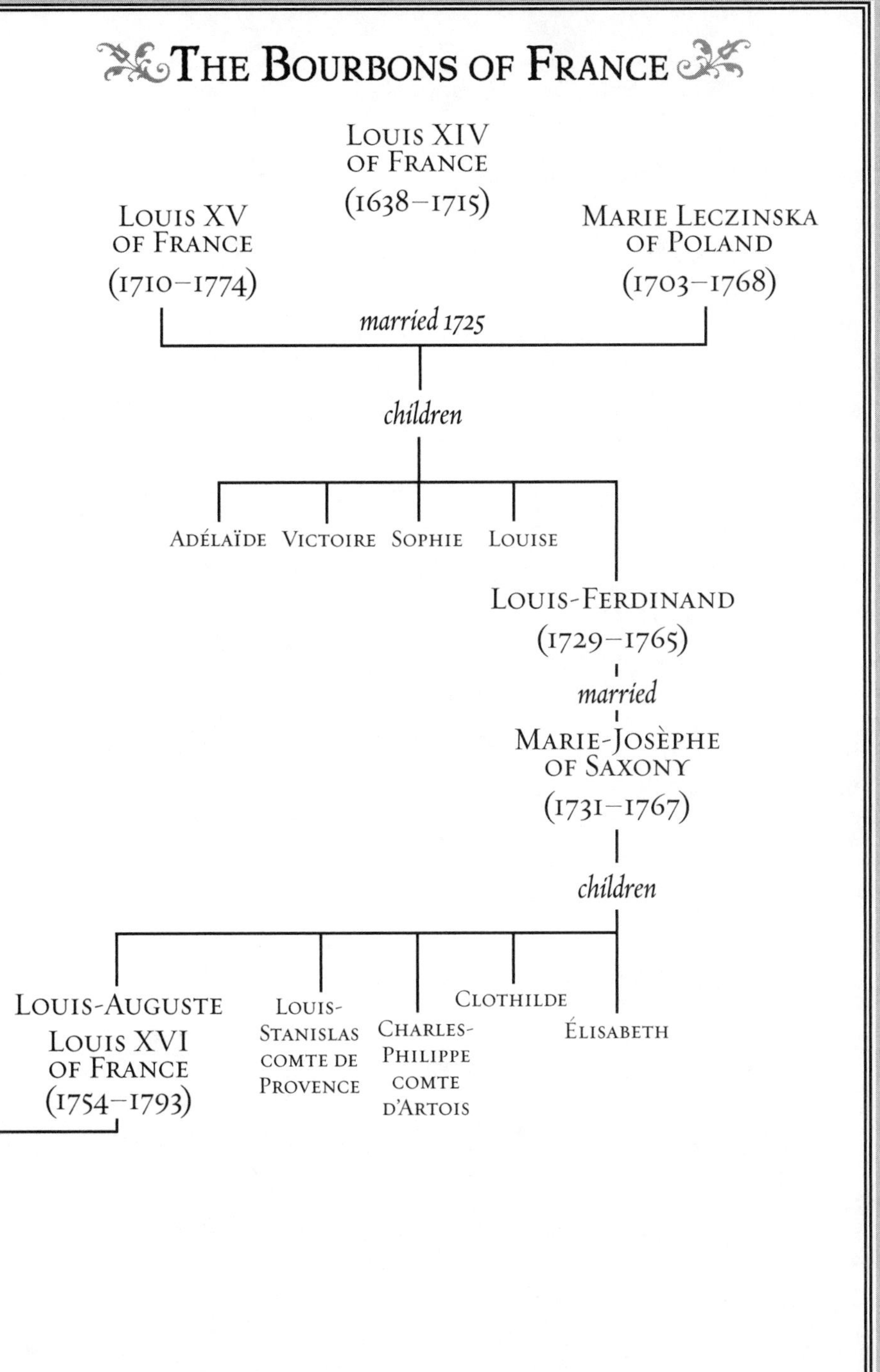

Louis XIV of France (1638–1715)
Louis XV of France (1710–1774)
Marie Leczinska of Poland (1703–1768)
married 1725
children
Adélaïde
Victoire
Sophie
Louise
Louis-Ferdinand (1729–1765)
married
Marie-Josèphe of Saxony (1731–1767)
children
Louis-Auguste Louis XVI of France (1754–1793)
Louis-Stanislas comte de Provence
Charles-Philippe comte d'Artois
Clothilde
Élisabeth

Part I

Rules for the Dauphine
1768

No. 1: Marry well

THE EMPRESS, my mother, studied me as if I were an unusual creature she'd thought of acquiring for the palace menagerie. I shivered under her critical gaze. It was like being bathed in snow.

"Still rather small, but I suppose she'll grow. Her sisters did," my mother said half to herself. She caught my eye. "No bosom yet, Antonia?"

I shook my head and stared down at my naked toes, pale as slugs. "No, Mama."

Swathed in widow's black, the empress frowned at me as if my flat chest were my own fault. "She's no beauty, certainly," she said, speaking to my governess, Countess Brandeis. "But pretty enough, I think, to marry the dauphin of France." She signaled me to turn around, which I did, slowly. "My dear countess, something must be done about her hair!" my mother declared. "The hairline is terrible—just look at it! And her teeth as well. The French foreign minister has already complained that the child's teeth are crooked. King Louis has made it quite clear that everything about my daughter must be perfect before he will agree to her marriage to his grandson."

Brandeis inclined her head. "Of course, Your Majesty."

"One thing more, Antonia," said my mother sharply. "You must learn to speak French—beautifully. And this too: from now on you are no longer Antonia. You are Antoine." She dismissed us with a wave and turned her attention to the pile of official papers on her desk.

Antoine? Even my name must change? I gasped and groped for an answer, but no answer came, just one dry sob. The countess rushed me out of the empress's chambers before I could burst into tears. That would have been unacceptable. Mama didn't allow her daughters to cry.

I've thought of this moment many times. And I think of it again, no longer attempting to hold back my tears after all that has happened to me since then.

My mother was known to all the world as Maria Theresa, Holy Roman Empress, archduchess of Austria, queen of Hungary and Bohemia, daughter of the Hapsburg family that had ruled most of Europe for centuries. Mama believed the best way to further the goals of her huge empire was not through conquest but through marriage. I'd heard her say it often: *Let other nations wage war—fortunate Austria marries well.* She used us, her children, to form alliances.

There were quite a lot of us to be married well. My mother had given birth to sixteen children—I was the fifteenth—and in 1768, the year in which this story begins, ten of us were still living. Three of my four brothers had been paired with suitable brides. The eldest, Joseph, emperor and co-ruler with our mother since Papa's death, was twenty-seven and had already been married and widowed twice. Both of his wives had been chosen by our mother. Joseph still mourned the first, Isabella of Parma, with whom he had been deeply in love, but not the second, a fat and pimply Bavarian princess whom he had detested from the very beginning. I was curious to see if Mama would make him marry well for a third time.

Next in line for the throne, Archduke Leopold was married to the daughter of the king of Spain. Then came my brother Ferdinand, thirteen, a year older than I, betrothed since he was just nine to an Italian heiress. No doubt he would soon marry her. The youngest archduke, chubby little Maximilian—we called him Fat Max—was not on Mama's list for a wife. He was supposed to become a priest and someday an archbishop.

Of my five older sisters, Maria Anna was crippled and would never have a husband, and dear Maria Elisabeth had retired to a convent after smallpox destroyed her beauty. (All of us archduchesses had been given the first name Maria—an old family tradition.) My other sisters had been found husbands of high enough ranks.

Maria Christina, called Mimi, was my mother's great favorite, and somehow she had been allowed to marry the man she adored, Prince Albert of Saxony. Lucky Mimi, one of the most selfish girls who ever lived!

Maria Amalia was madly in love with Prince Charles of Zweibrücken, but Mama opposed the match—he wasn't rich enough or important enough—and made Amalia promise to marry the duke of Parma. Amalia didn't like him at all, and she was furious with Mama.

"Mimi got to marry the man she loved, even though he has neither wealth nor position," Amalia stormed, "and Mama gave her a huge dowry to make up for it. So why can't I marry Charles?"

Silly question! We all knew she had no choice. Only Mimi could talk Mama into giving her whatever she wanted. Maria Carolina, the sister I loved best, had to marry King Ferdinand of Naples. This was the final chapter of a very sad story: two of our older sisters, first Maria Johanna and then Maria Josepha, had each in turn been betrothed to King Ferdinand. First Johanna and then Josepha had died of smallpox just before a wedding could take place. Ferdinand ended up with the next in line, Maria Carolina. He may have been satisfied with the change, but Carolina hadn't been.

"I hear he's an utter dolt!" Carolina had wailed as her trunks were being packed for the journey to Naples. She'd paced restlessly from room to room, wringing her pretty white hands. "And ugly as well. I can only hope he doesn't stink!"

It didn't matter if he stank. We had been brought up to do exactly as we were told, and Mama had a thousand rules. "You are born to obey, and you must learn to do so." (This rule did not apply to Mimi, of course.)

Though she was three years older than I, we had grown up together. We had also gotten into mischief together, breaking too many of Mama's rules (such as talking after nightly prayers and not paying attention to our studies), and our mother had decided we had to be separated. In April, when the time came for her to leave for Naples, Carolina cried and cried and even jumped out of her carriage at the last minute to embrace me tearfully one more time. I missed her terribly.

That left me, the youngest daughter, just twelve years old. I knew my mother had been searching for the best possible husband for me—best for *her* purposes; *my* wishes didn't count. Now she thought she had found him: the dauphin of France. The Austrian Hapsburgs would be united with the French Bourbons. But she also thought I didn't quite measure up.

After my mother's cold assessment, Brandeis led me, sobbing, through gloomy corridors back to my apartments in the vast Hofburg Palace in Vienna. She murmured soothing words as she helped me dress—I had appeared in only a thin shift for Mama's inspection—and announced that we would simply enjoy ourselves for the rest of the day.

"Plenty of time tomorrow for your lessons, my darling Antonia," the countess said and kissed me on my forehead. She hadn't yet begun to call me Antoine, and I was glad.

Her plan was fine with me. Neither Brandeis nor I shared much enthusiasm for my lessons. I disliked reading—I read poorly—and avoided it as much as I could. Brandeis saw no reason to force me. She agreed that my handwriting was nearly illegible—I left a trail of scattered inkblots—and allowed me to avoid practicing that as well. My previous governess had also given up the struggle, helpfully tracing out all the letters with a pencil so I had only to follow her tracings with pen and ink. When my mother discovered the trick, the lady was dismissed. Brandeis didn't resort to deception, but neither did she do much to correct my messy handwriting.

"You'll have scant use for such things," said my governess now. She shuffled a deck of cards and dealt a hand onto the game table. "You dance beautifully—who can forget your delightful performance in the ballet to celebrate your brother Joseph's wedding? Your needlework is exquisite, and your music tutor says you show a talent for the harp. What more will you need to know? A member of the court will read everything to you while you stitch your designs, and a secretary will write your letters for you. You won't even have to think about it. You'll have only to be charming and enjoy yourself, when you become the queen of France."

"Queen of France?" I exclaimed, a little surprised. I hadn't thought much beyond marrying the dauphin, whoever he was. "Am I truly to be queen of France, Brandeis?"

"You will someday, if everything goes according to plan. The young man your mother has chosen for you to marry is next in line for the throne. The future wife of the dauphin will be the dauphine, and when old King Louis the Fifteenth dies and his grandson the dauphin becomes king, you, my sweet Antonia, will become his queen." She smiled and sighed. "Everyone knows that Versailles is the most elegant court in all of Europe, and you shall be its shining glory!"

Queen! The idea thrilled me. My brothers and sisters had been matched with royalty from several other countries in Europe, but France was the most important—I understood that much—and that made *me* important, more important than my snobbish sister Mimi! Being married to the prince of Saxony wasn't much to brag about, compared to being queen of France. I pranced around my apartments with my nose in the air, as though I already wore the crown. Countess Brandeis swept her new sovereign a curtsy so deep that *her* nose almost touched the floor. I laughed and twirled and clapped my hands.

Then I remembered my mother's pronouncement: *everything must be perfect*. "Oh, dear Brandeis, what about my hair?" I cried. "And my teeth? Mama says they're not pleasing to the French king. And you're supposed to call me Antoine."

"I imagine a friseur will be sent to dress your hair," said Brandeis with a careless shrug, "though it looks fine enough to me—a mass of red-gold curls, what could be prettier? And I've heard that crooked teeth can be fixed as well as unruly locks. Meanwhile, I suggest you simply put all of this out of mind." She picked up her cards and arranged them. "Now, shall I draw first, or shall you?"

I did as my governess suggested and succeeded in winning a few *pfennig* from her. The next day we bundled ourselves in furs and rode through Vienna in a sleigh shaped like a swan and drawn by horses with bells jingling on their harnesses. We returned to my apartments in the Hofburg to sip hot chocolate and forget the unpleasant business of lessons and other worrisome matters. Brandeis always neglected to call me Antoine. I was still her dear Antonia—until one day when all our pleasant enjoyment came to an end.

No. 2: You must become fluent in French

I AWOKE ON A COLD winter morning at the beginning of 1769 to discover not my beloved Brandeis but a woman I scarcely knew sitting in the governess's chair near the porcelain stove. Her name was Countess Lerchenfeld, and she had once served as mistress of the robes for my older sisters.

"I have come to take charge of your education, Madame Antoine," she informed me. She had a high-arched nose and a wrinkled neck, and she did not disturb her sharp features by smiling. Brandeis always smiled.

"Brandeis does that," I told the woman airily.

"No longer," said Countess Lerchenfeld. "I have drawn up a schedule of your day so that you may know at every hour exactly what is expected of you."

She passed me a large sheet of vellum covered with writing. I puzzled over it for a moment or two before passing it back. "I want to see Brandeis," I said sullenly.

"Ce n'est pas possible, Madame Antoine." Suddenly this strange woman was speaking French. "It is not possible. Countess Brandeis is no longer here," she continued, still in French.

I gaped at her. I understood her—French was the language of the court, and in fact my dear papa had always spoken French to us. He was from Lorraine, which I knew was somewhere in France, and he'd never really learned to speak German. I think he didn't want to speak it, even though he was the emperor. But my sisters and I, and our brothers too, usually spoke German among ourselves. Brandeis spoke German sprinkled with French, or sometimes French sprinkled with German.

"Why are you speaking French to me?" I asked, frankly curious.

"Because, Madame Antoine, it is your mother's wish. From now on you and I will speak only French. You must become fluent in the language if you are to marry the dauphin of France." Impatiently she waved the sheet with my schedule on it. "You have already fallen behind. As soon as you are dressed and we have attended Mass in the chapel, and after you have eaten your breakfast, we shall begin our first lessons of the day."

I felt the tears well up in my eyes and spill down my cheeks.

"I want to see Countess Brandeis," I said thickly in German. The abominable Lerchenfeld pretended that I had not spoken. I tried again, this time in French. Lerchenfeld winced, as though she'd smelled something spoiled. She carefully gave me a long explanation, all in French, as to why I could not see her. I caught the gist of it. The answer was *non.*

My life changed completely. Brandeis, I discovered, had been dismissed because she hadn't taught me to read and write as well as Mama wanted. I grieved for her every day. I detested Countess Lerchenfeld, who was determined to cure me of all my faults and who punished me when I didn't study as hard as she insisted I must. Knowing how much I loved music and dancing and needlework, she did not allow me to play my harp, or dance, or embroider, or do any of the things I really liked until my lessons were completed to her satisfaction. There were no card games or sleigh rides, no cozy cups of hot chocolate. How could I possibly be fond of such a person?

Privately I called her Madame Sauerkraut. It suited her perfectly.

I questioned her relentlessly, searching for little nuggets of information about my future. I learned, for instance, that the dauphin's name was Louis-Auguste, that he was a year older than I, and that he was next in line for the throne because his father was dead and his two older brothers had died young.

"When am I supposed to marry him?" I asked.

"No date has been decided upon. Such matters are never simple or easy," Madame Sauerkraut lectured. "Many details remain to be worked out between the two countries. Before any agreement can go forward, the king insists on knowing exactly what you look like, and he is sending a portraitist to paint your likeness. Your mother, the empress, is most anxious that your teeth and hair be corrected by the time the painter arrives. The French foreign minister has dispatched a *dentiste* and a friseur to make the necessary changes. Then there is the matter of your bosom. The king is particularly concerned that you have lovely breasts to be displayed in the gowns now in fashion at the court of Versailles."

"Is the king sending someone to fix my bosom as well?" I demanded crossly. "I've not yet become a woman, you know."

Madame Sauerkraut pursed her thin lips. "Then, Madame Antoine, best you pray it happen soon," she advised. "I'm sure you're aware that your most important duty as dauphine will be to produce the next heir to the French throne."

I *was* aware of it, but I understood only vaguely how this important duty was to be accomplished. I assumed that I would receive instructions as I did in my other subjects, most of which I disliked. Maybe the instructions for producing an heir would prove more interesting than mathematics.

I was making little progress with the French language, always substituting German words when I couldn't think of the proper French words, and my accent was judged "intolerable." A French priest came to remedy that. Abbé de Vermond, a tall, thin man with sad, drooping eyes, spoke with an accent different from any I had ever heard. I could scarcely understand a word he said. The *abbé* would also tutor me in French history, of which I was completely ignorant. When my brother Joseph learned that I was equally ignorant of the history of my own country, he ordered that subject added to my studies.

"And you must read more, my dear sister," Joseph said, wagging a finger at me. "At least two hours a day."

Two hours a day! That was much too much. I detested reading! I nodded obediently but made a face as soon as his back was turned.

No. 3: Beauty must suffer

THE NEXT FRENCHMAN to introduce himself at the Hofburg Palace was the friseur who had been sent, Monsieur Larsenneur. He had me sit on a stool while he studied my hair from every angle. With a disdainful sniff he plucked off the woolen headband I wore to keep my hair away from my face, and my red-gold curls sprang out in every direction. Monsieur Larsenneur seized a handful of hair and produced a pair of scissors from his pocket.

"Very well, Madame Antoine," he said, "let us proceed."

I shut my eyes tight and listened to the click of the scissors. *Snip snip snip!* If he kept on, I would soon be bald. Presently he put a small mirror in my hand. *"Voilà, madame!"* he declared. "Open your eyes and tell me what you see."

The friseur had transformed a mountain of bushy hair into a pretty coif that hid my high forehead. He'd added a dusting of a white powder and had tucked a few little jewels among the tamed curls. "I call it the *coif à la Pompadour,*" he explained, "in honor of Madame de Pompadour, the late great friend of His Majesty, King Louis." He stepped back to admire his handiwork.

I had never heard of Madame de Pompadour, but I loved the way my hair looked. Everyone complimented me. Even Mama.

If only my teeth could have been so easily fixed!

The friseur was soon followed by the *dentiste,* Doctor Bourdet, who peered inside my mouth and poked my teeth with his fingers.

"The canines must be moved," he said and then muttered something about a pelican.

I thought the canines he talked about were probably dogs, and the pelican must be some exotic sea bird, and none of it made any sense to me. Then, without a word of warning, he placed a block of wood in my mouth to hold it open, gripped one of my upper teeth in the jaws of a dreadful instrument—this was the pelican—and forced the tooth into a new position. I let out a shriek of pain and terror, my arms and legs flailing. Several footmen rushed to pin me down and hold my head in place. While I howled, Doctor Bourdet repeated the horrible process on the remaining three canines—my pointed teeth, it turned out, and not dogs at all.

"Pas plus, je vous en prie!" I pleaded. "No more, I beg you!" But he ignored my cries and sobs and went on poking around in my mouth, tying each poor canine in its proper place with a leash of silk thread.

At last he put away his awful tools and wiped his bloody hands on a towel. "You have nothing more to fear, madame. The worst is over. We shall continue with additional adjustments when you've had time to heal." He tried to sound reassuring, but I was not reassured.

After he'd gone, Madame Sauerkraut rubbed a soothing medicine on my throbbing gums but offered little sympathy. "I remember well when your mother, the empress, endured a dental extraction with scarcely a murmur, just hours before the birth of your older brother," she reported. "The empress expects you to bear the moving of a few little teeth with the same resoluteness."

"I am not as brave as my mother," I said miserably. "And it hurt a lot. It still does."

For days my mouth pained me so much that I couldn't eat. The only good result to come of this wretchedness was that my French lessons had to be suspended because I could hardly speak. Instead, Abbé de Vermond had me begin to memorize the names and titles of the most important members of the French court and learn how they were related to one another. If it were possible to die of boredom, I would have expired immediately.

Eventually the pain went away, and Doctor Bourdet returned. I didn't trust him not to inflict more torture, and I kept my jaws firmly clamped shut and refused to let him peer inside my mouth. Madame Sauerkraut threatened to report my obstinate behavior to Mama, and the *dentiste* coaxed and promised there would be no more of the dread pelican. Finally I allowed him to do as he wished. What choice did I have?

He attached innocent-looking gold wires to my teeth. "See how simple?" he asked. "These little wires will guide your teeth in the direction they should go, the way one trains the branches of a tree. You are young, and they will move quite easily."

When he had finished, he brought me a little mirror. I grinned at my reflection. The gold wires, fastened to each tooth with a silk thread, gleamed back at me. I thought I looked ridiculous.

"A small adjustment now, madame," he said, and drew the wires tighter.

"Aïe!" I cried. "That hurts!"

"Only for a little while," Doctor Bourdet purred.

He lied, just as I had known he would.

Every day Doctor Bourdet inspected my mouth and made more adjustments, always twisting those gold wires a tiny bit tighter.

"Beauty must suffer," Madame Sauerkraut said pitilessly whenever I cried and pleaded to have the dreadful wires removed. But she did bring me sweet puddings and broth with soft noodles, assuring me the suffering would soon end. "Improvement is even more rapid than the *dentiste* expected," she said. "And you will be blessed with a lovely smile."

Meanwhile the king's portrait artist, Monsieur Ducreux, had reached Vienna. My mother invented one excuse after another to keep me hidden away until my transformation was complete. After three months Doctor Bourdet removed the hateful gold wires. Out came the mirror once more, which he handed me with a flourish. I smiled at my reflection, and the reflection that smiled back at me was beautiful indeed—my blue eyes, my unblemished complexion, my elegantly coiffed hair, and now my perfect smile.

I turned to the man who had created it and forgave him all the pain. "You may tell Monsieur Ducreux that I'm ready to sit for him," I informed Madame Sauerkraut.

Monsieur Ducreux believed the face told everything about a person. "Your heart and your soul are all reflected in your face, and that is what I must portray," said the painter. "But you must sit quietly for me, Madame Antoine, and think only the most beautiful thoughts."

I didn't like sitting quietly, but I did as Monsieur Ducreux asked. When the portrait was finished—Mama agreed it was all she'd wished for—the painter and the painting left for Versailles. Soon after Easter, our household moved to Schönbrunn Palace, on the outskirts of Vienna, for the summer months. My governess told me my portrait had arrived at Versailles and that King Louis XV was pleased. He sent his ambassador to deliver to the empress a formal proposal of marriage between the dauphin and me.

Mama was jubilant. "We have triumphed!" she announced when she got around to telling me that I would be married the following year.

No. 4: Perfection must be your goal

DURING MY MONTHS of seclusion away from society, while my teeth were in wires, there had been one bright spot: my mother had begun to assemble my bridal trousseau. The duc de Choiseul, the French foreign minister who had criticized my hair and teeth, now informed the empress that my Austrian wardrobe must be replaced by one made in the very best French style. The most elaborate gown, the *grand habit de cour,* was reserved for great court occasions, while the *robe à la française* was required for most public events. I needed several of each, as well as a variety of morning dresses and afternoon gowns for less formal times. Velvets and heavy brocades were prescribed for the winter season, lighter silks for summer. Certain colors could be worn on some days but not on others.

Everything must be the work of the finest seamstresses and cobblers, furriers and silkwomen, glovemakers and milliners to be found in the city of Paris.

"I have agreed to it all," Mama informed me. "You must be perfectly dressed for every occasion, Antoine, and I am willing to spend a fortune to be sure that you are."

Soon dozens of *poupées du mode,* wooden fashion dolls, began to arrive from Paris. Each doll was dressed in a miniature version of a particular robe or gown that had been proposed for my wardrobe. I had always loved to play with dolls, and though I was too old for that now, I exclaimed over their beautiful clothes—clothes that would soon be mine.

The delivery to the palace of a new trunkful of *poupées du mode* always caused excitement. Each time one arrived, Madame Sauerkraut allowed me to interrupt my dull studies, and I sent for my two best friends, Charlotte and Louise, the princesses of Hesse-Darmstadt, telling them to drop whatever they were doing and rush to my boudoir. My little niece Maria Teresa, Joseph's daughter, pouted if I forgot to send for her as well. My maidservants reverently unpacked the dolls, which were dressed in gowns of silk.

"Oh, how lovely!" Charlotte sighed rapturously.

"Exquisite," Louise murmured.

My niece carefully touched the smooth silk. Even Madame Sauerkraut allowed herself to admire the delicious colors and rich embroidery.

After a few months the actual gowns arrived for fittings by our royal seamstresses. Fittings were tedious, but I didn't protest about the long hours I had to stand still while the seamstresses pinned and tucked. The gowns were laden with lace and ribbons and flowers and feathers and beads and fringe, and they sparkled with jewels. Austrian ladies never wore anything like these gowns, with the enormous skirts draped over gigantic panniers—hoops—tied on either side of the hips.

Emperor Joseph disliked the style. "Women look like donkeys carrying baskets of chickens to market," my brother had remarked ungallantly, and he opposed such ornate costumes at our Viennese court.

I thought the French gowns were brilliant. Those wide skirts—wider than three or four men standing side by side—showed off a tightly laced waist easily encircled by two hands. But the dramatic fashion did present problems. The skirts were hard to maneuver through narrow doorways, and it was almost impossible to sit down in them.

Monsieur Noverre, dancing master to the imperial court, had been summoned to teach me the French dances I would be expected to perform flawlessly at the court of Versailles. I had to learn not only the steps of the minuet and several other dances but also the exact manner in which to walk, stand, and sit while wearing those awkward gowns.

"You must hold your head erect and your body upright, without affectation or boldness," he explained.

"Then it will be said, 'There goes a fine lady.' You must remain poised at all times, and yet you must appear entirely natural."

This made no sense to me, but I nodded agreeably.

Monsieur Noverre explained how to make an obeisance: with my feet well turned out, as I was taught when I danced in the ballet with my brothers, I had to keep my body upright, bend my knees slightly, and lower my gaze. "As dauphine, you will find yourself making such gestures at every moment, though yours will, in the main, be an acknowledgment of a person of lesser rank. Still, you will be expected to make this acknowledgment whenever someone hands you something, or enters your chamber, or leaves it, or greets you, or takes leave of you—"

"How dreadfully tiresome it all is!" I cried. I had been practicing this little movement, the obeisance, for what seemed like hours.

"But absolutely necessary, madame," Monsieur Noverre continued patiently. "It has been thus for at least a hundred years, since the reign of King Louis the Fourteenth. Perfection must be your goal."

Now the dancing master tried to teach me how to walk properly. I was sure I already knew how to walk properly. What could be simpler?

I was wrong.

"It is necessary for the dauphine of France to walk gracefully in high-heeled slippers and the heavy *robe à la française,* with its wide skirts and long train. You see, madame, that you must not walk heel to toe, as one does normally, but with many tiny steps made quickly while balancing forward on one's toes, so that one gives the impression of skimming just above the surface of the ground without touching it, as though one weighs no more than a cloud. This is well known as the Versailles glide."

Rising on my toes, I lurched across the floor of the hall where we practiced the court dances. Monsieur Noverre watched, shaking his head. "Float, madame, float! *Comme ceci,*" he cried. "Like this." He demonstrated, and I tried to copy him. *"Encore, madame, s'il vous plaît,"* he said with utmost patience. "Again, madame, if you please."

Monsieur Noverre was very exacting, and so I did it again and again, first in my usual flat slippers, later in shoes with high heels. My legs began to ache. "Why would anyone want to *do* this?" I asked, weary and tearful.

"No one *wishes* to do it, Madame Antoine, but one is *expected* to do it, as in all things at the court of Versailles. As you shall see for yourself very soon."

Grimly I practiced until I finally mastered the Versailles glide and could sweep gracefully across the hall without a stumble.

"And now you must learn to do it while wearing the *robe à la française,*" said the dancing master.

Someone had had the wisdom to order a practice version of the royal court dress; it was made of heavy brocade and weighted down with fake jewels and cheap embroidery and lace. "This thing weighs almost as much as I do!"

I complained after my ladies had fastened the two huge panniers on my hips, maneuvered me into the gown that now extended far out on each side, and attached the heavy train at my back. Tightly laced stays bit into my flesh. I could hardly breathe. When I tried to step into my high-heeled slippers, I realized that I should have put them on *before* I'd gotten into the gown. It was out of the question either to sit down or to balance in this enormous creation. My friends Princess Charlotte and her younger sister, Princess Louise, supported me while my little niece Teresa crept under the voluminous skirt and managed to get a slipper on each foot. All of us veered between giddy laughter and helpless tears.

I teetered uncertainly for a moment. Then I lifted my chin, shifted the weight of my body onto my toes—and glided gracefully across the floor. My friends applauded.

My dancing teacher stepped forward, bowed, and raised my hand to his lips. "Believe me, Madame Antoine," said Monsieur Noverre, "you will enchant everyone who sets eyes upon you."

On the eve of my name day, the Feast of Saint Anthony, June 13, my mother, the empress, invited hundreds of people to Schloss Laxenburg, my favorite country palace, for a celebration of my betrothal to the dauphin. I wore a beautiful gown of embroidered rose-colored silk (at my brother's insistence, the panniers under my skirts were much smaller than those I would wear in Paris). My hair was done in the *coif à la Pompadour,* and I smiled my beautiful new smile. Guests dined on our good German food and danced our good German dances. I adored being the center of attention and gave no thought to the fact that in less than a year I would be eating French food and dancing French dances. A year seemed like a very long time—almost forever.

No. 5: You are born to obey, and you must learn to do so

It was Amalia's turn to leave. In July, Joseph would escort my sister over the Alps to marry Ferdinand, the duke of Parma. For a while no one had been sure which Ferdinand—the one from Parma or the one from Naples—was going to marry which sister, Carolina or Amalia. But the king of Naples, who had lost first Johanna and then Josepha, chose Carolina. That left Amalia stuck with the duke of Parma, the brother of Joseph's first wife, Isabella. Even that was a complicated story: Joseph had been violently in love with Isabella, but Isabella was not in love with *him*—she was in love with our sister Mimi! My older sisters gossiped about that, sometimes forgetting I was around when they talked about how Mimi and Isabella were always together, holding hands and kissing, and how Joseph flew into jealous rages. Now it was Amalia who was in a rage as she prepared to marry a man she was ready to hate.

"Duke Ferdinand is weak-minded, did you know that?" Amalia said to me. "Joseph let it slip. And he's only sixteen—six years younger than I am! It's all too revolting." She paused in our conversation to scream at the maidservants who were packing her trunks for the journey. "I know why Joseph is making the journey with me," she went on. "He's afraid I'll try to run away. And I'd do it if I could." Her hands were balled into fists, and she pounded on the lid of a trunk until the maids scurried away in a fright. "Oh, I despise them all, Antonia!" she cried. "Mama and Joseph for forcing my dear Charles to leave Austria, and that spoiled brat Mimi for being able to get whatever she wants, and the dimwitted clod I'm to marry! But I promise you this, Antonia, once I'm there, I shall do exactly as I want! I'll sleep with whomever I please, and there's nothing Ferdinand or Mama or Joseph or anyone else can do to stop me!"

I burst into tears because I was so shocked at her anger and her threats that I truly didn't know what to say. *You are born to obey.* I could scarcely imagine having the courage to defy Mama's rules, but I had not the slightest doubt Amalia would do as she threatened. A part of me envied her determination.

The very next day she was gone. I stood in the courtyard of Schönbrunn, waving and waving as her carriage drove away, but Amalia stared grimly straight ahead and never looked back.

No. 6: Never behave in a manner to shock anyone

SCARCELY A MONTH after Amalia left to marry her awful duke, Mama decided to take me on a pilgrimage to Mariazell, a long day's journey west of Vienna. She wanted to visit the church where she had received her First Communion. This plan surprised me, for we had never before gone on a religious retreat—or anywhere else—together. The empress was usually too busy conducting the business of the empire to spend time alone with me. Sometimes I didn't see my mother at all for days on end, or I encountered her only on formal state occasions. Now that Amalia and Carolina were gone and Mimi lived in Pressburg, a few hours' journey down the Danube, maybe Mama would have more time for me. I would never be her favorite—that would always be Mimi—but I did look forward to the pilgrimage.

I hoped we would have a good talk as the carriage rolled through the countryside, but Mama said we must spend the time in silent meditation, and so we did. Once in Mariazell, we knelt in prayer for hours before the shrine in the basilica. I thought the paintings on the ceiling were beautiful, but whenever Mama noticed my attention wandering, she tapped me on the arm. Later, when we'd finally stopped praying, she began to speak to me of serious matters. She was worried, she said, about how I would maintain my faith in God and remain virtuous at the court of Versailles. Everyone knew the French court was completely lacking in Christian virtue!

"You must be obedient," Mama said. "You must learn the customs of the French court and follow them meticulously. You must not do anything unusual or show any initiative but always ask for guidance. Never behave in a manner to shock or upset anyone. Never forget your private devotions. You must not read any books that haven't been approved by your confessor. At the same time, my dear Antoine, you must remain a good German and remember always to put your country first."

"*Ja,* Mama." I agreed to whatever she said but without any clear idea of what I must do or how I should do it.

"You will walk a fine line," she concluded. "But I have great confidence that you will accomplish it to perfection."

Before we retired on our last night at Mariazell, my

mother announced that she wished to speak to me about marriage. *At last!* I thought.

"Love between husband and wife is the highest blessing bestowed by God on human beings," she said. "My greatest wish for you is the kind of fulfilling marriage I enjoyed with your dear father." She began weeping, as she always did when she talked about Papa. "Your father was the best of all husbands," she said tearfully.

I murmured, "*Ja,* Mama," and "Of course, Mama," but I found this quite confusing, not at all the practical advice I'd hoped for.

I had loved my father dearly. He always showed his affection for me far more openly than my mother did. After his death, five years earlier, my mother had cut off her long, thick hair, put away all her jewels, dressed in black, and draped her imperial apartments in somber black velvet. Nothing had changed since then. She was still in mourning. Yet I remembered the gossip I'd overheard while Papa was alive. Servants who must have thought I was deaf or too young to understand whispered about his many mistresses, especially a certain young Princess Auersperg, whom they said he loved unrestrainedly and my mother hated with all her heart.

I understood that having a mistress was a man's privilege and a wife's burden. I thought it likely my own future husband would exercise that privilege as well. But what about Amalia, angrily declaring that she was going to sleep with as many men as she wanted? Did women usually sleep with men who were not their husbands? I wondered. I didn't know, and it certainly wasn't a question I could ask Mama—especially during a pilgrimage to the Blessed Virgin!

"I must ask you again, dear child," she whispered now confidentially. "Have you yet had a visit from Général Krottendorf?"

I shook my head. *Général Krottendorf* was the term my sisters used to refer to the monthly cycle. I had no idea where that name had come from. But I had not yet become a woman, and so there had been no visit from the *général.*

Mama sighed. "You must tell me immediately, of course, for there can be no wedding until you have reached that critical milestone. The French will insist the marriage be delayed until you are ready to bear children. Remember, it is your sacred duty to provide a male heir to the throne of France."

"I understand," I said and leaned forward eagerly, hoping that since we were on the subject, or at least close to it, Mama would tell me in plain words what was expected of me once I was a wife. I was still completely ignorant of the process of conceiving—Madame Sauerkraut had so far not been helpful—and I had only the vaguest notion of what was involved in performing my sacred duty. I assumed that my future husband would know, but I wanted to be informed as well.

When my mother said nothing more, I decided to press on. "My dearest Mama," I began, "I know nothing of the mysteries of . . ."—I searched for the right words—"of the marriage bed. Perhaps you could explain it to me?"

"The time is not yet right, my sweet Antoine," she said, drawing away from me a little. "If I revealed these mysteries to you now, months before your wedding, it would only give you time to wonder about them. Once you've become a woman, then you shall receive a frank explanation. In the meantime, I would advise you to direct your prayers to the Blessed Virgin. I've always found her sympathetic."

Mama folded her hands and closed her eyes, and that was the end of the discussion.

No. 7: Learn to concentrate

I TURNED FOURTEEN on November 2, All Souls' Day. Because that date was an occasion observed somberly by the church, the gala celebration of my birthday was held on its eve, All Saints' Day. Four thousand people were invited to attend a masked ball. It seemed that everybody in Vienna wanted to have a glimpse of the archduchess who would soon become the dauphine of France and someday its queen. Engravings made of my portrait began to appear all over Vienna. The best gift of all was from Joseph, who gave me a little pug dog I called Mops. Mops followed me everywhere, getting in the way and leaving his messes wherever he went.

I was busy now from morning till night. When Abbé de Vermond discovered that I couldn't perform simple arithmetic or find my own country or the city of Paris on a map, he added some mathematics and a smattering of geography to my lessons.

"You think I'm stupid, don't you, Abbé?" I asked him one day when he had grown so impatient with me that he had to leave the room for a while.

"*Non,* Madame Antoine, I do not think you are stupid. Not at all! In fact, I find you very clever. But you must learn to concentrate. You are like a *papillon,* a beautiful butterfly, your mind flitting first here, then there, then somewhere else. Am I right, madame?"

"Completely," I said, pleased that he understood. "There are lots of things that interest me much more than reading and writing. And now adding up those silly numbers and multiplying and dividing! And why must I learn to read a map when I may go only where I am taken? What's the use of any of it? Better just to have fun and enjoy oneself, wouldn't you agree?"

Abbé de Vermond frowned and wrinkled his brow as he tried to think of a way to persuade me to be more serious about my studies. I leaned toward him with my brightest smile. "Don't worry, Abbé," I said. "I won't embarrass you, I promise. I'll learn just what I need to know. And no more!"

The *abbé* didn't smile back at me. "At the very least, you must continue with your study of French," he said.

"I like to speak French," I said. "But, *mon cher abbé,* you know how much I hate to write! You yourself have complained that I write so slowly you're afraid we'll both grow old before I finish a letter. And reading is such a bore! Won't it do just as well to have you read to me?"

The *abbé* sighed. "*Comme vous voulez, madame*—as you wish," he said. He gave me a courtly bow—and stepped into one of Mops's messes.

No. 8: Master the rules for their gambling games

THE FRENCH ambassador, the marquis de Durfort, rode in from Versailles in January of 1770, carrying a small golden coffer ornamented with jewels. Inside the coffer was my engagement ring, set with pleasingly large diamonds and pearls. On a Sunday morning after Mass at the Church of the Augustinian Friars, the archbishop blessed the ring. Accompanied by Princess Charlotte, Princess Louise, and my little niece Teresa, I approached the altar. As proxy for the dauphin, my dashing older brother Ferdinand stepped forward and slipped the ring on my finger. The choir sang, trumpeters blew a fanfare as I walked up the aisle, and all eyes were upon me. After years of being the generally ignored fifteenth child, I loved being the center of attention.

But the occasion was marred by tragedy. That very night at a festive dinner my niece fell ill and had to be taken away by her governess. Two days later, Teresa died. Emperor Joseph was devastated.

"Dear God in heaven, restore me to my daughter!" my brother sobbed at the child's funeral. Courts all over Europe went into mourning, ending the festivities in my honor for a time. But the little body in its small coffin had scarcely been removed to the burial vault before my governess and my tutor insisted I return to my studies.

Then, just as suddenly, there was another crisis. For some time Countess Lerchenfeld had complained of pain in her leg. I paid hardly any attention, for Madame Sauerkraut complained a great deal about a great many things. She was absent for a few days, and, glad to be free of her constant criticism, I barely thought of her until Abbé de Vermond brought me the startling news: Madame Sauerkraut was dead. I'm sorry to say I did not mourn her passing, although naturally I put on the proper grieving face and attended the countess's Requiem Mass with my mother.

I wondered, but did not ask, who would now become my governess. The answer, announced a few days later, was Madame Sauerkraut's sister-in-law, Countess Trautmansdorf. A smiling woman with cheeks as round as apples, she asked me to call her Madame Lulu. She bustled into my apartments to take over her duties on the same day as the longed-for arrival of Général Krottendorf. I had become a woman.

I rushed to tell Mama the good news myself. She embraced me with tears in her eyes and immediately sent word to the French ambassador, who dispatched a courier on a fast horse to Versailles. The appearance of the *général* changed everything. Plans for my wedding could now go forward. Maybe my bosom would soon grow large enough to please the king. And I would receive the promised explanation of the mysteries of the marriage bed, I hoped.

Madame Lulu undertook to tutor me in a subject she considered of even greater importance, or at least one that needed more detailed instruction. I must learn to play *jeu de cavagnole,* an Italian game of chance popular at the French court. "Everyone at Versailles loves to gamble," said the countess, "and you will be expected to preside over the gaming tables."

I liked to play games, but I thought *jeu de cavagnole* was tiresome—almost as tedious as my studies. Dozens of subtle rules governed the game and the players. "You are expected to master them all," said Madame Lulu, ignoring my complaints.

So day after day I practiced diligently, and night after night I persuaded various members of the Viennese court to play, and eventually I could manage the game and the side bets as effortlessly as I glided across the marble floors of the Hofburg.

But still I learned nothing about what I was to expect on my wedding night.

No. 9: You must submit bravely

One day, soon after Madame Lulu had moved into Madame Sauerkraut's old quarters, I received a letter from my sister Carolina. We hadn't corresponded much since she'd left to marry King Ferdinand of Naples, but I loved to receive letters almost as much as I hated to write them. Eagerly I broke the seal. In handwriting so much clearer and neater than mine, she began with congratulations and kind wishes for my future, having heard—from Mama, I supposed—of my engagement to the dauphin. I expected to read news of her life at court, but instead I found something quite different.

Oh, my dear little Antonia, I do hope that someone—other than Mama!—will undertake to prepare you for marriage. I found it a terrifying experience. I was just fifteen, as you'll recall, a little older than you will be when you marry the dauphin. I was ill-prepared for the painful separation from the ladies, even Lerchenfeld, who accompanied me on my journey to Naples. I was even less prepared to meet my future husband. Why had Lerchenfeld not spoken to me of the wedding night, except to caution me to "think about God"? Death would have been preferable to what I had to endure.

My legs grew weak, and I had to sit down before they gave way completely. My hands were shaking, but I couldn't stop reading:

One suffers real martyrdom, which is all the greater because one must pretend to be happy. I would rather die than endure again what I had to suffer for eight days after the wedding. It was an earthly hell. I live in dread now of what you, dearest Antonia, will have to suffer. I shall shed many tears when you face this situation in a few short months, for I do believe all men are brutes, at least until one learns to tame them.

Madame Lulu found me collapsed on my bed, sobbing. Without a word I handed her Carolina's letter and buried my face in my pillow.

"Oh, my poor darling." Madame Lulu sighed. "It's not as bad as all that, I promise you. Now dry your tears and let's have a little talk, for I can see that your sister has frightened you badly."

Once I was calmer, the dear lady tried to explain the differences between men and women in very general terms, and she expressed the hope that the dauphin would be kind and gentle, that any unpleasantness would be gotten over quickly—it sounded like something I'd endured with the pelican—and that with time and patience I could learn to enjoy what she called "the act."

"But you must always keep in mind that your principal duty as the dauphine—some would say your sole duty—is to give birth to the Children of France. For that, you must submit bravely to the act."

"Oui, je comprends," I murmured. "I understand."

I understood my duty—I'd certainly heard it often enough—but I still did not understand the act. When I asked Madame Lulu to describe it in more precise terms, she blushed deeply and finally managed to whisper, "Two beloved bodies become one."

I would have to be content with that explanation of the great mystery.

Another mystery was the dauphin himself. I wore his ring. I had received a letter from him, written in Latin—the *abbé* translated it for me—pledging his honor and respect. But I still had no idea what he looked like. I had heard his grandfather King Louis XV described as the handsomest man at the French court. But what about Louis-Auguste?

By the time Général Krottendorf had made his second visit, two portraits of Louis-Auguste had arrived from Versailles. I gazed at the portraits, one a miniature of the other. Here was a young man with thick, dark eyebrows, a small mouth, and heavy-lidded eyes that seemed to be peering at something far away. I had the larger portrait hung in my boudoir and wore the miniature pinned to my waist, and every day I studied the pictures, trying to imagine what it would be like to speak to him, to sit beside him, to touch him. I could not.

I showed the portrait to my friend Princess Charlotte, who was always very honest when asked her opinion. "What do you think?" I asked. "Speak truthfully."

"It doesn't matter what I think," she said, glancing at the painted image and then at my face. "It only matters what *you* think."

"He's not exactly handsome, is he?"

"But he's not ugly," Charlotte said. "In fact, I think he looks interesting."

"Yes," I agreed. "Interesting."

Madame Lulu found me contemplating the portrait one day. A silent tear rolled down my cheek, followed by another, and another. "What is it, my child? Why this sadness? This is a time for rejoicing!"

"Oh, Lulu, what if I just can't bear him?" I asked.

"You must remember that the goodness in his heart will doubtless far outweigh any other quality," she said thoughtfully. "Remember too that love begets love. The dauphin cannot help but fall deeply in love with you, and his love will blind you to any other faults he might have."

I hoped she was right. If she was wrong, I was surely doomed to misery.

No. 10: All eyes are upon you—there can be no mistakes

EASTER FELL on April 15 in 1770, and though it was the custom of the imperial court to move from the Hofburg to my mother's favorite palace, Schönbrunn, during the week after Easter, she had decided to postpone the move until after I left for Versailles.

April was a turbulent month for me and, no doubt, for everyone in my household. I endured an unsettling mix of excitement, fear, and sadness. I now spoke French easily, and a French actor was polishing my accent. I had mastered the Versailles glide and was pronounced a most elegant dancer by my dancing teacher. Trunk after trunk of robes and gowns arrived every week from France to be fitted by our royal seamstresses, along with countless boxes of thin slippers with high heels, silk stockings, delicately embroidered underthings, furs and feathers. My mother had spared no expense for my trousseau—four hundred thousand *livres,* more than she'd spent on all of my sisters put together! I hoped Mimi heard *that* little piece of news!

The French ambassador, the duc de Choiseul, and Count Mercy d'Argenteau, the Austrian ambassador, were making preparations for my bridal journey from Vienna to Paris; I was to be accompanied by members of the Viennese court as far as the border between Germany and France.

Two days after Easter I signed papers giving up all my claims to the crown of the Holy Roman Empire. It was a symbolic act, for I had two brothers whose claims were ahead of mine anyway, but the signing became the occasion for a grand celebration. Though Joseph was still mourning the loss of his precious child, my brother set aside his grief in order to provide a magnificent supper for more than a thousand guests. Hundreds more attended a masked ball that lasted until daybreak. That was just the first of many celebrations; night after night the whole city of Vienna was aglow with lanterns. The sky blazed with fireworks as my wedding day drew near. Not since before my dear papa's death had the people of Vienna enjoyed such spectacles.

On April 19, at six o'clock in the evening, I entered the Church of the Augustinian Friars next to the Hofburg. My mother and my brother Joseph, empress and emperor, led me down the aisle. Madame Lulu walked proudly behind me, carrying my train. My beautiful gown of cloth of silver shimmered in the candlelight. As was the custom, my future husband was not present for the ceremony, but my brother Archduke Ferdinand stood in his place. I was not in the least nervous, for I was surrounded by people who loved me. I felt very elegant, from head to toe a princess.

After the prayers and the blessing of rings, I said my vows in Latin with hardly any bad mistakes, and Ferdinand repeated the dauphin's vows. Trumpets sounded a triumphant fanfare. Outside the church, the guns of the Hofburg boomed again and again. I was now officially Madame la Dauphine.

Though I tried not to think about it, the time for my departure was quite near, and my mother and I had the last of our long talks. She presented me with a list of rules that she'd drawn up, had copied onto parchment, and placed in a leather case ornamented with pearls and gold. "I beg you to read them once a month," Mama said. "They will guide you."

Then she gave me a tiny gold pendant watch as a keepsake and looked over my shoulder as I struggled to write a proper letter to King Louis. She kept offering bits of advice she thought I'd need, and she repeated the reminder that I must be a perfect Frenchwoman but at the same time remain a good Austrian and always put my country first. "You may be marrying a Bourbon, but you will always be a Hapsburg." Count Mercy d'Argenteau would be there to advise me. I hoped he could explain how I was to do all that.

"Remember," she said, "all eyes will be upon you—there can be no mistakes."

No. 11: The perfection of Versailles demands perfection of its residents

A LEADEN SKY pressed ominously over the city, and rain seemed likely. Dressed in one of my fine brocade gowns and carrying Mops, my little dog, I descended to the courtyard early in the morning of April 21. A splendid carriage waited there. The berline, specially built for me by order of King Louis, was made almost entirely of glass with a roof of solid gold and ornaments of hammered-gold garlands and flower bouquets. Eight white horses wearing feather plumes and golden harnesses stood motionless as statues.

I had already said my formal goodbyes and given tokens of remembrance to my friends Charlotte and Louise, to Madame Lulu, and to my servants and tutors. Now all these dear friends joined the rest of my family for a last farewell. Mama drew me to her breast for a final embrace. She was weeping, though she hardly ever wept unless she was speaking of Papa.

"God bless you, my dearest child," she said. "We are to be separated by a great distance, and only God knows when we shall see each other again." I clung to her, trembling. "I am sending them an angel," she murmured, the words catching in her throat, and she firmly pushed me away.

My brother Ferdinand handed me into the berline. Mops licked the tears that streamed down my cheeks. The princesse de Paar, an old friend of Mama's who would be my companion, climbed in after me. The doors were closed and latched, an order given, and the berline rolled forward. I turned in my seat for a final glimpse of my family and my home. For the next hour I was crying too hard to see much of anything at all.

Once we'd passed beyond Vienna's ancient city walls, my carriage joined the rest of the cortege bound for the place of the *remise.* The princesse de Paar, who'd been silent so far, suddenly came to life. As the wife of the gentleman responsible for the organization of the cortege, she had every important number at her fingertips. There were, she said, 132 members of the imperial court traveling with us, and three times as many servants. Fifty-seven carriages were needed to transport all these people. The prince de Paar had arranged for a change of horses for each carriage at each post stop, every fifteen miles or so, in order to keep the procession moving steadily during the daylight hours.

"That's twenty thousand horses all told, madame!" Princesse de Paar exclaimed. "Can you imagine?"

I yawned. I had always found numbers uninteresting.

The interior of the berline was exquisitely appointed with every luxury. Velvet cushions were embroidered with scenes representing the four seasons, but the elegance of the carriage and all those cushions didn't make up for the rough roads that we jolted over, hour after hour. A cold rain began to fall. Nevertheless, my mother's subjects turned out in droves to wait in the downpour for a glimpse of the gold and glass berline, and of me, the archduchess on her way to France to marry the dauphin. I waved and smiled as we passed.

None of the ladies except for the princesse de Paar had ever been to France or visited Versailles, and we plied her with questions.

"It is the most beautiful palace in the world!" she declared.

"More beautiful than Schönbrunn?" I asked.

She hesitated for a moment. "More opulent," she said. "Schönbrunn is delightful—utterly charming! But Versailles is luxurious; its grandeur exceeds all others. Wait until you see the Hall of Mirrors, and the royal chapel, and the king's apartments. Their beauty is quite overwhelming!" On and on she went, describing brocade and gilding and vast paintings and gardens filled with statuary.

Finally she ended with this: "The perfection of Versailles will demand equal perfection from its dauphine."

I had begun to wonder how I would live up to all these expectations of perfection.

After a few days my heart began to ache a little less. Except for the pilgrimage I'd made with Mama to Mariazell, I had never before traveled beyond the outskirts of Vienna, and I felt as though I had embarked on a great adventure. To relieve the tedium of the long hours, the ladies of the court took turns riding in my carriage and did their best to amuse me. We played card games. Sometimes they sang, and I joined in the singing, or they told stories. Occasionally I slept.

Arrangements had been made for me and my attendants to spend each night in a castle or monastery. After we had dined—sometimes sumptuously, sometimes austerely—and I had retired to the chamber my hosts had taken pains to prepare for me, I took out the miniature portrait of my future husband and studied it.

Night after night I spoke to the portrait of Louis-Auguste and imagined what he might say to me. I decided that he was surely intelligent and amusing. No doubt he danced well—Monsieur Noverre had told me that Frenchmen were by nature graceful dancers. Probably the dauphin was fond of music and would enjoy listening as I played the harp, which I had been practicing faithfully. He probably loved animals and would take at once to my dear little Mops. He would be impressed that I had learned to speak French so well and had mastered the customs of the French court so completely. Maybe he would beg me to tell him about my life in Austria, and I would teach him a few phrases of German, just to amuse him. I would do my best to please my dear Louis-Auguste—that's how I always addressed him in my imaginary conversations—and he in turn would go out of his way to please me.

After each imagined conversation I wished my future husband a good night's rest, kissed his picture and placed it beneath my pillow, and slept soundly until I was awakened the next morning to continue my journey.

But the hours soon turned monotonous. I was sick of card games and the silly stories the ladies told, and we still had a very long way to travel. After two weeks I thought I could not bear to climb back into my berline, which had once seemed so luxurious but had become a glass prison. Even the princesse de Paar seemed exhausted.

Finally, fifteen days after leaving the Hofburg, we dragged ourselves into the Benedictine abbey where I would pass my last night as an Austrian in my mother's empire. The *remise*—the ceremony of the hand-over, when I would officially leave Austria and all things Austrian behind and become a Frenchwoman—would take place the next day.

I lay awake in my vast bedchamber listening to the nighttime sounds. On a pallet beside my bed a maidservant coughed. An owl hooted outside my window. I slipped out from under a thick coverlet, crept barefoot across the cold stone floor, and knelt on a hard ledge beneath the window. The rain that had fallen throughout most of the day had stopped, and an almost full moon glided through scraps of ragged clouds, spilling patches of pale silvery light on the wet ground. The owl fell silent.

Tomorrow, I thought, *I'll be in France. I'll look up at this same moon, but everything will have changed.*

A small hare loped out of the shadows and into a swath of moonlight. Suddenly the owl's silhouette blotted out the moon, and the startled hare raced for cover. Too late: the owl plunged silently, seized the luckless hare in its talons, and flew off, its great dark wings beating the air. Shivering, I rushed back to my bed and pulled the coverlet over my head. It was a long time before I slept.

No. 12: An outward display of emotion violates all the rules of etiquette

I HAD NO IDEA what to expect.

Prince Starhemberg, the empress's special ambassador in charge of the *remise,* had vaguely described the ceremony. It would take place in a pavilion, built just for this occasion, on a tiny island in the middle of the Rhine, halfway between the German town of Kehl on the east bank of the river and the French town of Strasbourg on the west. An argument about whose signature would appear first on the official documents, the Austrian ambassador's or the French ambassador's, had finally been settled: two sets of papers were drawn up, identical except that the Austrian would sign first on one set and the Frenchman first on the other.

I paid no attention to the arguments or the compromises and didn't even think too much about my part in the ceremony. My thoughts were already racing one week ahead to my meeting with Louis-Auguste: *What is he really like? Will he find me pleasing? Will the conversations I've been having every day with his miniature portrait match the real ones?*

On the morning of May 7 I slipped into a dainty chemise of fine batiste and then drew on a pair of silk stockings, sheer as spider webs and embroidered with gold thread. My ladies helped me into a pair of satin slippers, tightened the stays that squeezed my waist to a span easily encircled by two hands, and fastened two huge panniers on my hips. Once I was dressed in the *grand habit de cour,* the friseur added sparkling jewels to my coif. I was ready.

I maneuvered my skirts into the berline for the short ride to the pavilion. Since I couldn't sit down, I teetered on a tall stool. Prince Starhemberg, carrying Mops, managed to cram himself into the carriage with me and my gigantic skirts. "I'm not sure exactly what I'm supposed to do," I confessed to the prince, suddenly worried. At home such public events were always rehearsed, and I'd never had such a big role.

The prince's eyebrows shot up when he realized that I really *didn't* know. "You will enter the great hall of the pavilion from the Austrian side," he explained. "There you will bid farewell to the ladies and gentlemen of the empress's court. After the signing of the official documents, you will depart from the French side, no longer an Austrian but a Frenchwoman. Is it clear so far?"

I said it was, and the prince continued. "The comtesse de Noailles, wife of one of King Louis's ambassadors, has been appointed your *dame d'honneur* and will serve in future as mistress of the household. She is said to know everything there is to know about court etiquette to the smallest detail. I'm sure she'll tell you just what to do," he added and patted my hand.

I already knew the countess's name and position, the result of Abbé de Vermond's endless drilling. My carriage rolled to a stop, its front wheels on the bridge to the island, its back wheels still in German territory. The bridge was narrow, my skirts were wide, and my passage from carriage to pavilion extremely awkward.

Members of the French court crowded into the pavilion. The great hall was elegantly furnished with gilded chairs and dark tapestries, but it was also very cold and damp. I began to tremble, partly from the chill but mostly from nervousness. The time had come to bid farewell to the members of my suite, who were now about to leave me and turn back to Vienna. I embraced each one and wept more than a few tears with each goodbye. I held tight to my little dog to calm myself, but suddenly a servant appeared and snatched Mops out of my arms. I gasped, barely managing not to cry out. I could hear the dear little creature whimpering as he was carried away.

The French ambassador chose that moment to present an unsmiling woman with a sharp nose, a cruel mouth, and a chilly manner. "Madame la Comtesse de Noailles!"

The countess swept me a deep curtsy and then eyed me critically—even more critically than my mother had done. "Now, Madame la Dauphine," she said in a voice as hard as marble, "shall we begin the ritual undressing?"

I nodded, choking back tears. I felt a little sick to my stomach. *What if I throw up?*

Several ladies of the French court stepped forward and, smiling grimly, proceeded to remove my *grand habit.* I had been told this would happen, but I hadn't really understood. "The bride must retain nothing belonging to a foreign court," the countess explained as the ladies worked. The gown had been made for me in France by French seamstresses in a design provided by the French mistress of the wardrobe, but because I had worn it as I entered from Germany, it now represented the life I was leaving behind. It had to go.

The ladies removed the train and the tight-fitting bodice and the enormous skirts, arguing in French among themselves over who should now take possession of this bejeweled costume. I thought this was outrageous. Did they think I could not understand them? But I dared not speak up.

I waited for them to bring the new *grand habit* to replace the one taken from me. But I was in for a shock. They had not yet finished undressing me. Piece by piece, every item I wore—panniers, stays, slippers, stockings, even my chemise—was removed and claimed by the ladies of the French court. Only by thinking quickly did I manage to hide the tiny gold watch my mother had given me, tucking it into my coiffure. Now I stood completely naked before a crowd of strangers, Frenchmen and Frenchwomen, who stared and whispered. I heard the men remarking on my bosom, which had in fact grown more generous in the months since the first visit of Général Krottendorf. They commented on every part of my person.

Outside, the rain beat down and the wind whistled through the cracks in the pavilion. I shivered with an ugly mixture of fear, cold, and utter humiliation.

I closed my eyes while they stared, praying that my mortification would soon end. Then, piece by piece, I was dressed once more from the skin out in everything new—chemise, stockings, panniers, and a *grand habit* of cloth of gold laden with quantities of lace and ribbon and dozens of glittering gems. A new friseur appeared and dusted my coiffure with powder; the watch remained safely hidden under a pile of curls. The ladies coated my face with a white paste and painted my cheeks with large circles of red rouge. I was now completely French, from the jewels in my hair to the diamond buckles on my high-heeled shoes. I wondered what I looked like with all that rouge.

The ladies of the court escorted me into the damp and drafty *grande salle* of the pavilion. Row upon row of the highest-ranking members of the French court waited to be presented. One after another, the gentlemen bowed low over my hand and the ladies dropped into deep curtsies. Aloud they pledged their loyalty, but their eyes were hard and their smiles seemed empty and false. I heard the whispers behind the jeweled fans: "*L'Autrichienne* . . . the Austrian girl," but I couldn't fail to notice how they pronounced the second part, *chienne,* with special emphasis: *chienne,* the French word for a female dog, a bitch. What else were they saying about me?

The pain of leaving my mother and my home forever, the weariness of the long journey, the sadness of bidding farewell to all those who had accompanied me, the loss of my beloved Mops, the embarrassment of standing naked in front of strangers, the unfriendly whispers—all of it was suddenly overwhelming. My composure deserted me, and I began to sob. I threw myself into the rigid arms of my *dame d'honneur,* the comtesse de Noailles.

That was a serious error.

The countess shuddered and drew back from my helpless embrace with a look of pure disgust, as though I were covered in horse dung. "Madame la Dauphine," she said, her voice as cold and brittle as an icicle, "such an outward display of emotion by a member of the royal family is unseemly and in violation of all the rules of etiquette."

One last sob caught in my throat. I knew I had made a significant mistake by letting my feelings overcome me, and I told myself sternly that I would never, *ever* allow that to happen again. "I beg your pardon, madame," I said. My voice was now calm and steady. "And I ask you to forgive the tears I have just shed for my family and for my homeland. From this moment on I shall never forget that I am a Frenchwoman."

The *comtesse*'s eyelids fluttered, her nostrils flared, and her frigid expression betrayed exactly how she felt about my breaking of a basic rule of etiquette. "Excellent," she said.

The roof of the pavilion had begun to leak. Water dripped down on the silks and velvets and the complicated coiffures of the ladies and gentlemen. In a few minutes, I thought, the women who judged me would all look like drowning rats. The notion made me smile.

Still smiling and with my head held high, I swept out of the pavilion and climbed into my berline, which had been brought around from the German side. The order was given, trumpets sounded, and the grand procession crossed the Rhine. I had entered France.

No. 13: Our sovereign is never to be the object of humor

CHURCH BELLS rang out across Strasbourg. Little girls shyly presented me with bouquets of flowers and scattered petals under my feet as I walked. The mayor greeted me in German, no doubt intending to please me, but I interrupted him in French. "Monsieur le Maire, do not speak to me in German, *s'il vous plaît.* From now on I want to hear only French."

That brought cheers from the crowd. Instead of insulting whispers of *"l'Autrichienne,"* there were cries of "How beautiful is our dear dauphine!" My heart lifted with the warmth of the welcome, so different from the chill of the *remise.* I smiled until my face ached. That night I slept soundly for the first time since I had left Vienna and without dreams to disturb my rest. The next morning we began the last stage of my bridal journey, to my first meeting with King Louis XV and my husband, the dauphin. In a few days I would no longer need to depend on invented conversations with the miniature portrait of Louis-Auguste. I would meet my husband face to face.

At midafternoon on Monday, May 14, my cortege rolled slowly into a great forest near Compiègne.

"This is the dauphin's favorite place to hunt," said Prince Starhemberg, who must have been as relieved as I was that the journey was nearing its end. The responsibility for my safe delivery to the king of France was about to be taken off the prince's shoulders. "And there is the king's carriage," he added.

I giggled—loudly, I'm afraid. "Who else would ride in such an elaborate carriage surrounded by such a crowd of courtiers?" I asked.

Comtesse de Noailles, who hovered at my elbow, always ready to correct and admonish, said severely, "Our sovereign is never to be the object of humor."

"I meant no offense, madame," I murmured.

A tall, distinguished-looking man was advancing toward my berline. "Here comes the duc de Choiseul, the French foreign minister," Starhemberg said. "He's the man who persuaded King Louis you'd be the perfect bride for his grandson."

A pair of footmen unrolled a thick red carpet over the uneven ground, and a third footman opened the carriage door with a flourish. Prince Starhemberg alighted first and turned to hand me down. "Madame la Dauphine, may I present the duc de Choiseul," announced the prince.

The duke bowed, murmuring polite phrases.

"My dear sir," I said—in French, of course—as his lips barely grazed my hand, "I shall never forget that you are the author of my happiness!"

"And the happiness of France," the duke replied with a gracious smile.

An old man—certainly much older than my mother—climbed down stiffly from the royal carriage and made his way toward me. *The king,* I thought. *He walks as though he is always the center of all eyes.* He was followed by three shapeless ladies nearly buried under their unfashionable gowns. Behind them stumbled a large, awkward boy who might have fallen flat if he hadn't been steadied by one of the courtiers. *Could that be—?*

There was no time to speculate. The king halted and leaned on his jeweled walking stick, looking me over intently from my coiffure to my slippers, and gazing with undisguised interest at my bosom. I tried to ignore that stare as the first gentleman of the bedchamber presented me, and I prepared to sink into my deepest curtsy. But at the last moment I dropped to both knees at the feet of King Louis. *"Mon très cher grand-père,"* I said. "My very dear grandfather."

That was the right thing to do, even though it surely wasn't in the comtesse de Noailles's rulebook. Beaming, the king raised me up, this time looking at my face instead of my bosom. I knew by his smile that I had charmed him. I'd heard him described as the handsomest man at court, and maybe he was—thirty years earlier. His fine dark eyes gleamed with good humor. He bent down and kissed me on first one cheek and then the other. Etiquette required the dauphin to do the same, and the large, awkward boy who I assumed was my husband shuffled forward and stopped short. Unlike his grandfather, he did not look at my bosom or at my face. He stared at the patch of red carpet between us.

I did try to find something attractive about Louis-Auguste, but to be truthful, I could find nothing. I felt nearly ill with disappointment. Could this ungainly fellow be the boy in the painting, the agreeable boy my imagination had been engaging in lively conversations for weeks, the suave young man who was already my husband by law and in another day or two would become my husband in the eyes of God? His chin was heavily jowled. His mouth turned down in a sulk. And he appeared clumsy, probably because he was fat—very fat. I smiled encouragingly at him, but he looked resolutely away, as though the last thing he wanted to do was meet my eyes, let alone kiss me. He seemed so miserable that I felt a little sorry for him.

One of the courtiers leaned close to the dauphin and

murmured something in his ear. Louis-Auguste took a tentative step forward, placed his chubby hands on my shoulders, brushed his lips against one cheek and then the other, and released me quickly, almost pushing me away. My smile was wasted. He still wouldn't look at me.

Maybe he's just shy, I thought. *Surely he'll get over it.*

I took a deep breath and turned my attention to the three dowdy ladies who stood glaring at me—one quite fierce, one quite stout, and one quite ugly. Thanks to Abbé de Vermond's tutoring I knew who they were: Mesdames Tantes, the daughters of King Louis. "Very important ladies," the *abbé* had told me. "You will surely become intimately acquainted with the dauphin's three unmarried aunts, Madame Adélaïde, Madame Victoire, and Madame Sophie. Since the death of the dauphin's mother and father, the boy has been devoted to his aunts." A fourth aunt, he'd said, had become a nun. I mustered another gracious smile and greeted them. They never stopped glowering. And then, thank God, that part was over.

That night we dined at the palace near the forest, and I met one distinguished—and almost indistinguishable—member of the court after another: this prince and princess, that duke and duchess, some other count and countess. There were the elegantly dressed duc de Chartres, who was the king's cousin, and the dauphin's two younger brothers, Louis-Stanislas-Xavier, the comte de Provence, who was at least as fat as Louis-Auguste but boisterous and not at all shy, and Charles-Philippe, the comte d'Artois, a handsome (and still thin) boy of twelve. Abbé de Vermond had been beyond despair to discover that I had no head for numbers and detested reading and writing, but I had easily memorized his chart. Everyone was impressed by my ability to remember names and titles. The dinner lasted a long time.

The following day we traveled to La Muette, a chateau that had once been a royal hunting lodge on the outskirts of Paris. That evening the king was the host at another dinner. Among the guests I noticed a lady who was not on the *abbé*'s chart, a strikingly handsome woman with enormous blue eyes. Her breasts were nested like a pair of plump white doves in the shockingly revealing décolletage of her gown. Though she spoiled the effect with a voice as harsh as a crow's, she commanded the king's full attention.

I turned to the comtesse de Noailles and whispered, "Who is that lady?"

The countess gave me that look again, as though an unpleasant scent had been detected by her long, thin nose. "The comtesse Du Barry." She sniffed. "She is here to amuse the king."

Abbé de Vermond had not mentioned her. Unusual, I thought, but I brushed off the omission and replied innocently, "Then I shall be her rival, for I too wish to amuse the king."

The comtesse de Noailles rapidly fluttered her jeweled fan but said no more. How naive I was! I would learn later that Madame Du Barry was the king's mistress.

In the excitement of the coming wedding celebration I forgot about Madame Du Barry. But I should not have forgotten her, for she, sensing a rival, had already begun to plot my downfall. I just didn't know it then.

No. 14: You must be without blemish on this day of all days

WEDNESDAY, MAY 16, 1770: my wedding day.

I was awakened at dawn to make the three-hour journey from La Muette to the Chateau de Versailles. It was still early morning as my berline, cleaned and polished after its long and arduous journey halfway across Europe, rolled through the great iron gates. I was wide awake, and I was thrilled. Who would not have been? Here at last was the splendid palace I'd heard about for so long. At a distance Versailles appeared much grander than Schönbrunn, much less gloomy than the Hofburg. But as we drew closer, I noticed that though the palace was imposing, it was not well kept—the fountains weren't playing; statues lay broken; the grounds were littered with trash.

No *Austrian* empress would have allowed such disorder—certainly not Maria Theresa.

The comtesse de Noailles led me to my quarters on the ground floor. The rooms were dark, but not so dark that I didn't notice the worn and shabby furniture and the thick film of dust that lay over everything. Crowds of people had already gathered for the wedding, and they pressed their faces against the windows, trying to peer inside. This was not at all what the princesse de Paar had described.

The countess must have recognized the look of dismay on my face, and she murmured an apology. "This is only temporary, of course. These rooms were once the home of the dauphin's mother," she explained, "and no one has lived in them since she died. Your new rooms will soon be ready. But they aren't ready yet."

Why not? I wondered. *They've known for months I was coming. If I had time to have my teeth rearranged and to learn all the complicated court dances, couldn't somebody have found the time to dust?*

At that moment two young girls appeared. One was so fat she seemed wider than she was tall, barely able to drop a curtsy without toppling over. The other, a pretty six-year-old, had not yet begun to grow plump. Madame de Noailles introduced the children, Madame Clothilde and Madame Élisabeth, the dauphin's sisters.

"Because of their tender ages, by the rules of etiquette you may receive them before you have put on your *grand habit de cour,*" the countess informed me.

I rolled my eyes. These tedious rules of etiquette

were obviously going to govern my life. I would just have to get used to it.

The little girls charmed me, but they were soon sent away, for the time had come for me to begin my toilette. A parade of high-ranking ladies now began to undress me. Some I had met at dinner the previous evening at La Muette, and some I had never seen before. The toilette felt very much like the *remise,* something I'd hoped I would never have to endure again. According to some order of precedence that I didn't even try to understand, the ladies took their turns, removing each item of clothing until, for the second time since I left home, I stood naked and completely exposed. Each item was then replaced with a new one. After heavily powdering my hair, coating my face with white paste and rouge, and putting on my stays and panniers, the ladies presented the *grand habit de cour,* shimmering white cloth of silver stitched with hundreds of diamonds—my wedding gown.

But the splendid gown did not fit! The bodice was far too small. No matter how the ladies tugged and pulled, they could not close it in back. Everyone would see the lacings of my stays as I walked down the aisle of the royal chapel. There was nothing to be done. The clock was ticking toward one o'clock, when I must make my appearance. The train attached to my shoulders would help to disguise the gap. But it would not be perfect, and those who were searching for flaws in my appearance and deportment would definitely be pleased.

The comtesse de Noailles was much more upset than I was. *"Ce n'est pas possible!"* she moaned. "This is not possible! You must be without blemish on this day of all days, and you are not!"

The clock chimed the hour, the doors swung open, and the countess led me to the king's apartments. I'm certain she wished I were more distressed. But surely the gown was not my fault. I would simply have to make the best of it.

King Louis, the dauphin, his brothers and sisters, the aunts, and other members of the royal family, mostly cousins known as the princes and princesses of the blood, stood ready. The procession began to move. Louis-Auguste, looking ill with anxiety, shuffled along beside me, eyes downcast. Behind us came the comtesse de Noailles, keeping her hawk's eye on the young pages carrying my heavy train. Various princes of the blood followed my new brothers-in-law, the comte d'Artois and the comte de Provence, the king, fat Clothilde, and sober little Élisabeth. Mesdames Tantes—Adélaïde, Sophie, and Victoire—came last.

At least six thousand people had crowded into the chateau that day. Women dressed in the formal *grand habits de cour* and men wearing the required ceremonial swords jammed into the grand Galerie des Glaces, the Hall of Mirrors. Tall, arched mirrors—I later counted seventeen of them—lined one wall of the long, narrow arcade, each mirror matched by a window on the opposite wall. The

Galerie des Glaces, at least, lived up to the princesse de Paar's description. The day had been brilliantly sunny when we arrived at nine o'clock, but by noon the sun had disappeared behind a heavy curtain of clouds. Now rain threatened, and thunder rumbled in the distance. The lack of sunlight didn't matter, for thousands of candles blazed in the crystal chandeliers. The effect was dazzling.

I tried to draw a deep breath, but alas! my stays were drawn too tight to allow it. With my left hand resting lightly on the dauphin's right, I began the long walk through the magnificent hall, nodding and smiling, acknowledging people I had met or who I somehow sensed were important. Orange trees in silver planters placed among the marble statues released a sweet scent. Solemn chords poured from the great organ in the royal chapel. I remembered my dancing teacher's admonitions to glide along the polished parquet floors. When we reached the chapel, the organ fell silent. Drums and flutes announced our entrance. Everyone rose. With measured steps we continued down the aisle. At the high altar, Louis-Auguste and I knelt beneath a silver canopy. The archbishop of Rheims began to intone the words of the ceremony in Latin, his deep voice filling the chapel.

I glanced at the dauphin. His gleaming gold wedding suit was too tight—possibly as tight as my stays—and strained at every seam. Beads of sweat rolled from under his wig and down his round cheeks, and his hands were shaking. My poor Louis-Auguste! I smiled at him, trying to reassure him: *everything will be fine.* We were both used to public ceremonies. Hadn't we grown up with them?

Yet he continued to tremble, and his breathing was hard and irregular, as though he'd just run a race. When the time came for him to slip the wedding ring on my finger, his face turned a bright red. He still avoided looking at me, as he had since I first stepped out of my berline.

The Mass went on at great length, interrupted often by bursts from the choir. When it finally ended, we stepped over to the book in which we were meant to inscribe our names. The king signed first, simply *Louis.* The dauphin signed next, *Louis-Auguste.* When it was my turn, I dropped a blot of black ink beside the name by which I would now officially be known: *Marie-Antoinette-Josèphe-Jeanne.* I had never signed it that way before, and the blot was there, beside the second *J.* A bad omen, but there was no way to fix it.

Oboes, cornets, and trumpets blew a fanfare, the organ began a triumphal march, and Louis-Auguste and I left the chapel side by side. Perhaps when we were finally alone together, he would look at me and speak my name. I was sure I could put him at ease. We returned to the king's apartments. But the day was far from over.

No. 15: Do not speak of how things are done in Austria

KING LOUIS HAD a surprise for me. With a flourish he opened the doors of an enormous cabinet, as long as a coffin but much wider and covered in red velvet. Inside were dozens of compartments and drawers of different sizes, each lined with pale blue silk and holding a piece of jewelry. He waved aside his servant and lifted out each piece and presented it to me himself: a diamond necklace, a collar of pearls, earrings set with emeralds, hair ornaments made of precious gems.

"The jewels belonged to the former queen of France," he explained. "And now they belong to you."

There was more to come: a diamond-encrusted fan and several diamond bracelets with my monogram, *MA,* on the clasps. It was not as though I needed any more jewels to add to the many I had brought from Vienna as part of my dowry.

"Ah, *mon cher grand-père, merci, merci!*" I said. I'm sure my pleasure showed in my face, for I was very fond of jewels.

Afterward, I returned to my gloomy apartments—they must have used up all the candles at the wedding—and I was again undressed and dressed once more by a succession of ladies. In a different *grand habit de cour,* with my hair rearranged and the red splotches on my cheeks redone, I was ready for the next event, the presentation of those who would serve me.

A tall, armless chair was brought—the panniers got in the way, of course, but I was grateful to be sitting down as the most tedious of ceremonies followed. Hundreds of people were involved in preparing my food, caring for my gowns, dressing my hair, maintaining my carriage, feeding my carriage horses, and rendering every other kind of service, and every single one of them came forth to kneel before me and swear an oath of loyalty. I thought it would never end.

I wondered what Louis-Auguste and his family were doing as I endured this ritual. I longed for everyone to go away and leave me for a little while, but I realized this was not going to happen. I was tired, and I was hungry too—I'd had nothing to eat since a small breakfast early in the morning. My husband's stomach had rumbled through much of the wedding ceremony.

When the ceremony ended at last, I hurried off in search of the family and found them all playing *jeu de cavagnole.* No one else seemed tired or even hungry. Had they eaten while I was smiling at all those servants? And what about my husband? Louis-Auguste had disappeared. Just when I thought I might do the same, the wedding supper was announced and Louis-Auguste reappeared.

"The *salle de spectacles* was built only weeks ago," the king told me as we entered the opera house. "With you in mind, my dear," he added.

Every inch seemed to be covered in gold that gleamed in the light of a thousand candles. The upper loges were already crowded with row upon row of people eager to watch the royal festivities below. The king took his place alone at the head of the long table. I was seated on his left, Louis-Auguste on his right. The rest of the royal guests—Artois and Provence, Mesdames Tantes, the princes of the blood, and a few favored courtiers, including the grand huntsman and his daughter-in-law—were seated below us according to rank. There was a roll of drums, the first gentleman on duty waved his silver wand and called, "The king's meat!," and the parade of delicacies began.

Hungry as I was, I passed up nearly all of the dishes I was offered. My stays dug mercilessly into my flesh—it was painful when I stood, more painful when I was sitting. Most of the food was unfamiliar to me, except for the strawberries. I loved strawberries.

The dauphin attacked his food with gusto. I watched

him finish one plateful after another. He did have a huge appetite. If he had been nervous during our wedding ceremony, his nerves seemed remarkably steadied by the presence of food. *No wonder he's so fat,* I thought, *if he eats like this at every meal.*

The king was watching him too. "Don't have too full a stomach for tonight!" he whispered loud enough for me to hear, though I pretended I hadn't.

The dauphin glanced up from yet another plate. "But I always sleep better when I've eaten well." He returned to his meal.

I was nibbling another strawberry when suddenly the sound of the dauphin's voice from across the table startled me. "The strawberries are from the king's garden," he said.

It was the first time my husband had spoken to me without prompting. Our conversation to this point had been limited to *"Oui, madame,"* and "*Si vous voulez*—if you wish, madame," in reply to something I had said in one of my attempts to start a conversation. So his remark about strawberries came as a surprise.

"Pardonnez-moi?" I said. "Pardon me?"

"The strawberries. They're from the king's garden. It's early for them, but they're grown in special glasshouses."

"Oh," I said. "They're delicious."

"I'm fond of them myself."

"At home we use them to whiten the skin," I said, an attempt to keep our little conversation going. Then I realized I'd committed a blunder. *Home* was not to be mentioned. My mother had warned me not to mention how we do things in Austria. The comtesse de Noailles would have been shocked if she'd been close enough to hear. I corrected myself. "I meant to say, I've been told that women sometimes use crushed strawberries to improve their complexions."

"Your complexion would require no improvement, madame," said the dauphin. I was delighted that he had said something nice to me.

But we couldn't discuss the uses of strawberries for long. Supper was to be followed by dancing, followed—if it didn't rain—by fireworks, and then the final ritual of the very long day: the wedding night. I didn't want to think about that. Not yet.

The king, who'd been observing us fondly, signaled that the meal had ended and dancing would now begin. Louis-Auguste, fairly calm a moment earlier, became nervous again. "It's the *danse à deux,*" he muttered as we waited for the table to be carried away. "I hate to dance."

I had spent many weeks with Monsieur Noverre preparing for this moment, when the dauphin and I, the highest-ranking people in the great *salle de spectacles* except for the king, were expected to perform the minuet alone. My mother had told me often, "Every eye will be upon you," and that was certainly true now.

All eyes were also upon Louis-Auguste. He bowed stiffly, the music started, and together we began to move through the prescribed steps. Despite my husband's clumsiness, we managed not to make any serious mistakes. Our places were taken by the next-ranking couple and others joined them. I would have been happy to dance all night. I was tired, but I knew quite well that my true test was coming: *first the wedding, then the bedding.*

And then a sudden downpour canceled the fireworks. There would be no further delays.

No. 16: This is how it has always been done

To be truthful, I was frightened.

I wished, certainly not for the first time, that I had received some practical instruction in what was to follow. All of my mother's concern for the visits from Général Krottendorf as a sign of my readiness for marriage had given me no information. Just as unhelpful was Madame Lulu's explanation of "the act": *two beloved bodies become one.* I told myself that my husband would surely have received more specific instructions. But from the little I had observed of him since we'd met, just one day earlier, I wasn't the least bit confident.

I wished my sister Carolina were here. She'd comfort me. Or even Amalia. She'd have practical advice. Not Mimi, though—Mimi, who married the man she loved and climbed into bed every night with him. He was probably a wonderful lover. Mimi, who had everything.

Now here I was, caught again in a web of etiquette. A long procession of high-ranking gentlemen and ladies, led by the archbishop of Rheims and his attendants, seemed to be required to convey us for the *coucher*—the bedding. A flock of ladies with their huge panniers crowded into my dressing room and began to unlace and unfasten and remove the several layers of my wedding finery. Someone plucked the jewels and feathers out of my coiffure and let my hair tumble down over my shoulders. Someone wiped off my ghastly makeup. Finally they dressed me in a delicately embroidered sleeping shift and led me to the bridal chamber, where my husband and I were expected to get into bed together in front of the horde of people jostling for position.

"They are here because they have the right of entry, depending upon their rank and position," murmured the comtesse de Noailles. "This is how it has always been done."

The archbishop blessed the huge bed, sprinkling holy water every which way, and my husband and I climbed into it from opposite sides while the old king watched us, grinning and gleefully rubbing his hands. A coverlet was pulled over us, all those present bowed or curtsied and finally left, and a pair of attendants drew the curtains around the great bed.

Now, I thought, *it's going to happen. Two bodies will become one.* I wondered if it was better to shut my eyes or keep them open.

Suddenly the curtains flew apart, and there stood the king, for one last look. The curtains were drawn for a second time. The great door closed with a thump, and everything grew quiet. I held my breath, waiting.

But nothing happened. Nothing at all. *"Bonne nuit, madame,"* said Louis-Auguste. "Good night."

He rolled over on his side, away from me, and within minutes he was snoring lightly. I lay staring into the darkness until I too fell asleep.

When I awoke the next morning, the bed was empty. My husband was gone.

"Hunting," the footman reported soberly. I believe that behind his expressionless face the servant was laughing.

No. 17: You may not reach for anything yourself

FOR NINE DAYS and nine nights, ballets and operas were performed, balls and feasts were held, and gambling went on at all hours, all to celebrate the wedding. I was at the center of it, dressed in one gorgeous gown after another, coiffed and made up and decorated with jewels like a real-life *poupée du mode.*

But every night ended in the same puzzling way: After the ritual undressing, my husband and I climbed into the marriage bed, and our attendants closed the curtains around us and left the chamber. Then, just as he had each night since our wedding, Louis-Auguste said, *"Bonne nuit, madame,"* rolled over, and fell asleep. Every morning I woke up alone.

On the last night of the celebration, a brilliant display

of fireworks danced across the sky. Then, as we watched from the windows of the Galerie des Glaces, the grand canal, extending westward to the horizon, was gradually illuminated, until the canal became a river of light stretching as far as the eye could see. That thrilling display marked the end of the wedding festivities.

Again that night nothing happened, and my husband left to go hunting before I woke up in the morning. It was the last night he came to sleep in my bed. From then on he ignored me, in public as well as in private. I had no idea what was going on, I had no one to ask, and so I simply smiled and pretended everything was fine. With all the rules I was expected to learn and to follow precisely, I had plenty to worry about. But Louis-Auguste's behavior toward me worried me more than anything.

The earliest hours of the day weren't too difficult: I put on a dressing gown, said my morning prayers, and ate a little breakfast—a bowl of broth and a small roll. But after that, I had no more privacy for the rest of the day. The *lever,* the first official ceremony of the day, brought an audience of strangers crowding into my apartments to watch me at my toilette.

King Louis had appointed a dozen highborn ladies to be my companions, and sixteen more ladies of lesser birth to serve as women of the bedchamber. Most were old. Over them all loomed the mistress of the household, the comtesse de Noailles. How I wished there were someone close to my age to be my friend! But there was not.

By eleven o'clock, when Monsieur Larsenneur, the friseur, arrived to arrange my coiffure, the ladies had gathered in my boudoir. The friseur pomaded my hair, curled it with hot irons, and piled the curls on wire frames and cotton wool. While two ladies held a mask over my face, the friseur used a bellows to blow white powder over his creation. Two more ladies whisked away the peignoir I'd been wearing to protect my dressing gown. At this moment the doors to my boudoir opened, and any ladies—gentlemen too—whose ranks entitled them to right of entry squeezed in to watch the next unavoidable part of the ritual: rouging my cheeks. The first lady of the bedchamber stepped forward with a pot of rouge and proceeded with her task.

When my sisters and I were growing up, Mama did not permit us to wear rouge, but reddened cheeks were required of aristocratic ladies in the French court. (Women who weren't members of the court were forbidden to use rouge.) I thought it looked ridiculous, but I too had to submit to having the hideous red circles painted on my face. That done, the gentlemen withdrew, the doors were closed, and the most irksome ritual began: getting dressed. It was unbelievably complicated. The comtesse de Noailles laid out the rules.

"You may not reach for anything yourself. Each item must be presented to you by the person designated for that duty."

Should I get thirsty, I couldn't just help myself to a

glass of water. If the lady in charge of pouring my water didn't happen to be present at that parched moment, I would have to stay thirsty until she arrived. Then the servant of the chamber would hand a silver-gilt salver with a covered goblet and a decanter to the lady of the proper rank, who would place the salver on a side table and pour the water into the goblet. At that point I might be allowed to drink—if I hadn't already fainted from thirst.

I was required to change my gown at least three times in the course of a single day. The gown I was supposed to wear on any particular occasion and all that was to go with it were selected by the mistress of the robes and carried to my boudoir in baskets covered with green taffeta. ("Why green?" I wondered aloud. "Because it has always been green," I was told. "That's the Bourbon color.") The first lady of the bedchamber laid out the gown. Then the second lady of the bedchamber removed my dressing gown. The mistress of the household—that was the comtesse de Noailles—poured water into a basin for me to wash my hands and handed me a small towel from a special basket to dry them. My underthings had been brought in by the wardrobe woman in charge of my linens. Now the countess was ready to present me with my chemise.

Sometimes this tiresome procedure went fairly smoothly, but often it didn't. One morning, having had my dressing gown removed, I stood completely naked, waiting. The comtesse de Noailles had stripped off her glove when a scratching at the door—for some reason, the ladies did not knock or even tap but *scratched*—signaled the arrival of another privileged lady. As it happened, the new arrival was a princess of the blood and ranked higher than the countess, therefore *she* had the right to hand me my underthings. No sooner had the princess removed *her* glove and picked up my chemise than we heard another scratching, and yet another princess entered, one who ranked even higher than the first princess. The first princess now had to yield the privilege—and the chemise on its silver salver—to the second princess.

I wanted to scream! There I stood, naked and shivering, my arms crossed over my chest, praying that no one else would arrive and throw everything out of order again. What could be the point of all this? When I was a child, I'd always had help dressing, but I surely didn't need that kind of help now. I understood that these great ladies weren't interested in serving me but in proving who was more important in the court and more deserving of the privilege. If it hadn't been so maddening, it might have been amusing.

Someday I'll have to write to Carolina about this, I thought. *She won't believe it. She'll think I'm making it up.*

After I had been tightly laced into my stays and arrayed in my *robe à la française* and the chosen jewels, my toilette was complete. At one o'clock, my husband and his gentlemen emerged from his apartments, where I assumed he had endured a similar ritual after a morning of hunting, and we all proceeded to the royal chapel to hear

Mass. From there our procession moved to the anteroom outside the royal apartments for the *grand couvert*—the "great table." The midday meal was always eaten in public, and anyone who was properly dressed—ceremonial swords required for the gentlemen—was allowed to stand nearby and watch us eat. Course followed course as vast amounts of food were presented: at least two soups; roast veal and either mutton or beef; roast chickens and partridges and hare; and a number of smaller dishes. Four ladies assisted the comtesse de Noailles, who knelt in front of me to serve me each bite of food, each sip of water. With hordes of people gaping, I was supposed to eat my main meal of the day. I promptly lost all desire for food.

Having an audience didn't dampen Louis-Auguste's appetite the least bit. It wasn't unusual for him to consume several cutlets, a whole chicken, a plateful of veal, and half a dozen boiled eggs, washing all of it down with a bottle or two of champagne. And that was before he attacked the sweetmeats arranged on a towering *épergne,* each silver arm laden with pastries and preserved fruit. The dauphin ate as though eating were his solemn duty, and he gave it his entire attention. There was no conversation. My husband was in love with his food.

No. 18: Show your subjects the proper recognition

I HADN'T EXPECTED my life at Versailles to be so wearisome. Surrounded by much older ladies and expected to learn so many dreadfully dull little ceremonies, I felt trapped.

The comtesse de Noailles nipped at my heels in a most annoying way, tirelessly correcting everything I did, down to the smallest gesture. For instance, I must not incline my head too much when greeting someone who was not of a rank deserving such recognition. And I must *seem* to be about to rise but *not actually rise* when a princess of the blood entered the chamber. The absurd rules went on and on and on. But without the countess hovering at my elbow to coach me, I would no doubt have committed countless crimes of etiquette, bringing gasps of disapproval. Behind her back I called her Madame Etiquette. I grew sick of the very sight of her.

Three times each day I had to visit Mesdames Tantes, my husband's three fusty old aunts. These visits were required because the aunts were the king's daughters, officially known as the Children of France, though they were certainly no longer children. The eldest, Madame Adélaïde, was clearly in charge of her sisters. She liked to talk about her gowns and jewels and to boast about her beauty as a young girl—she was now anything but beautiful—and she pointedly told me she had refused many offers of marriage in her day because none of her suitors was worthy of an Enfant de France. Madame Victoire, a placid woman, had pretty features buried beneath layers of fat. The youngest, Madame Sophie, was horridly ugly, nervous, and high-strung. All three aunts wore billowing black gowns that hid their shapeless bodies. Their father called *les mesdames* by childish nicknames I would have found humiliating: Adélaïde was known as Rag, Victoire was called Piggy, and Sophie was Grub. Peculiar as these ladies were, they always greeted me warmly and treated me in a motherly fashion, often correcting me, but in a kindly way. The aunts truly seemed to care about me—no one else did—and I became fond of them.

"Ah, my dear Madame Antoinette!" Madame Adélaïde called out each time I entered their apartments. "How delightful to see you!" As though I hadn't visited them two hours earlier.

One day, not long after my arrival at Versailles, I settled into what had become my usual chair, and the aunts picked up the well-worn threads of their conversation—gossip, as usual.

"She sat on the arm of his chair again, the strumpet!" Madame Sophie announced shrilly. Her sisters nodded vigorously.

I didn't need to ask who "she" was. The ladies were discussing the comtesse Du Barry, the king's mistress. "His chair" was, of course, the chair belonging to their father, King Louis. On each visit to Mesdames Tantes I learned a little more about the strumpet. I was expected to show stern disapproval of Madame Du Barry and whatever she said, did, or wore.

The scandalous story of the king's favorite began when she was born, the illegitimate daughter of a seamstress. "Her father was a monk!" shrieked Madame Victoire, pale with shock at the thought. Her name then was Jeanne Bécu, and though she worked for a time as a shop girl, she soon found that she could earn more money in a brothel. One of her customers was a man named Du Barry.

There Madame Adélaïde took up the story. "That evil man introduced her to our father, who was not yet recovered from the death of his previous mistress Madame Pompadour."

"Pompadour was indecent, but not half so indecent as Bécu," declared Madame Victoire.

"Father has an uncontrollable weakness," sighed Madame Adélaïde. "We pray for him daily."

"Several times daily," amended Madame Sophie, rolling her eyes upward toward heaven.

"The evil man married off Bécu to his brother, who was a count, and suddenly the harlot had a title! She had become the comtesse Du Barry!"

"At first our father installed her in a house in Compiègne, where she stayed hidden all day. At midnight a sedan chair arrived with two liveried servants to escort her to the palace. At daybreak she left Father's apartments and returned to her house."

All three of the aunts pulled out handkerchiefs and began to weep. "At least she didn't embarrass us. But then our foolish father had his new mistress presented at court!"

"In she walked, flaunting jewels worth a hundred thousand *lívres*!"

"Diamonds by the score on the heels of her shoes!"

"It was the scandal of the century!"

"Our father, the king, has given her a lovely little chateau, Louveciennes. There is nothing he won't do for her. And you can see for yourself how vulgarly she behaves and how loudly she speaks!"

"She's barely out of the gutter." Madame Sophie sobbed. "And she should certainly go back there."

I agreed: the situation was scandalous. The comtesse Du Barry created a sensation as she paraded through the halls of the chateau trailed by her Bengali page dressed in pink velvet with a turban on his head, turned-up toes on his shoes, and a little jeweled sword fastened to his belt. Wherever the king was, there was Du Barry, the two of them riding through the park in the king's carriage, with the curtains drawn, or gliding along the grand canal on warm summer evenings in a magnificent gondola while musicians played and the rays of the setting sun gilded the calm waters.

"It's hard to ignore her presence," I told the aunts.

"You could refuse to recognize her, Madame Antoinette," Madame Adélaïde suggested with a conspiratorial look. "Simply pretend not to see her, as though she didn't exist! That would put her in her place! Not so difficult, is it, my dear child?"

True—it would not be difficult at all.

The aunts smiled at me approvingly and patted my hand. They called for pastries to be brought, which they consumed with great relish, and I returned to my apartments until it was time for the next visit.

No. 19: You cannot change the rules of etiquette

TWO EVENTS occurred that pleased me very much. One was the return of my adored and adoring Mops. Of all the things that had been stripped away from me when I left Austria, the loss of my little dog had been most upsetting. "You may have as many French dogs as you wish," the comtesse de Noailles had assured me, but it was Mops I longed for.

Now, through the gracious efforts of Count Mercy d'Argenteau, the Austrian ambassador, my little pug arrived in the arms of my former tutor Abbé de Vermond. Although I had several priests in my service, at my request Vermond had been appointed my confessor. I felt a little less lonely now, knowing that neither dog nor priest would repeat the most private thoughts and secrets I confided to them.

I usually worked on my embroidery while I waited for the *abbé* to arrive for his regular afternoon visit. I had begun making a vest for the king, but progress was slow. One day, when we'd finished praying together and I had resumed my embroidery, I suddenly burst out, "Why am I subjected to these tedious rules of etiquette? They make no sense to me. We certainly didn't have all these ridiculous habits in Austria." And there I was, breaking one of Mama's rules: *Do not talk about how things are done in Austria.*

"Austria is not France, Madame Antoinette," the priest reminded me gently. "It all goes back to King Louis the Fourteenth, great-grandfather of our King Louis the Fifteenth, great-great-great-grandfather of your dear husband, the dauphin."

"The Sun King," I said, remembering the history the *abbé* had managed to stuff into my head. "Ruled France for seventy-two years, if I'm not mistaken." I absently picked out a few wayward stitches from the king's vest.

"Indeed. Louis the Fourteenth invented all of these rules of etiquette that you find so annoying simply in order to control the noblemen of his court. The King Louis of a hundred years ago wanted to be worshiped, and worshiping him kept an army of people fully occupied. The custom of courtiers wearing shoes with *talons rouges*—red heels—was an easy way for him to tell at a glance which men belonged at court and which did not. When he died in 1715, our own dear Louis was next in line, at the age of five. There was no one else alive to do it."

"Then I wish he'd get rid of the silly rules," I said.

"But he will not, and believe me, Madame la Dauphine, there's nothing *you* can do to change them. I understand that you dislike having the whole world watching everything you do." He pulled his lower lip thoughtfully. "The comtesse de Noailles tells me you insist upon getting into your bath while wearing your shift."

"Because I can't bear having all those people stare at me!" I cried.

"And that you refuse to give up your habit of bathing several times a week."

"That's what we did at home!"

"But this is your home now, madame. You must not forget that."

I threw aside my needlework and began to cry. "I have not forgotten, Abbé!" I sobbed. I could not stop.

"Is something else bothering you, daughter?" the priest asked.

The truth burst out of me, unrestrained. "*Oui, c'est vrai!* It's true! My husband has not yet made me his real wife; people are talking about it, and I don't know what to do!"

The priest sighed and tugged again at his lip. "I've heard the rumor. Naturally, your mother is much concerned. So is King Louis. Everyone has a different idea. It has been suggested by the ambassador that your husband may be suffering from some, uh, physical problem. The king, on the other hand, thinks it's just a matter of shyness and that the dauphin will get over it in his own good time."

"And my mother blames me!" I said unhappily. "She lectures me in every letter, telling me I'm not doing enough."

The hour ended disappointingly, with nothing concluded. Did I really expect my priest to tell me what to do? Now I had to prepare for my music lesson. It was the day for either the harp teacher or the singing teacher to come to my apartments—I couldn't remember which.

When the weather was fair I was allowed to go for a walk after the lesson, accompanied by some of my ladies. In the evenings—after a third required visit to the aunts—I was expected to preside over card games. *Jeu de cavagnole* was as dull a game as I had ever encountered, but many of the courtiers seemed to enjoy it and won and lost a good many *livres.* By the time we ate supper—the *petit couvert*—at nine or ten o'clock, I was starving. This was not a public dinner, and finally I could relax a bit. Sometimes King Louis joined us, though mostly he preferred to have an intimate supper with his favorite, Madame Du Barry.

The whole day was exhausting, and I could hardly wait until the ceremony of the *coucher* was over and I was undressed; then I'd fall into bed and wonder if this night would be different and my husband would come to me at last.

But each night was the same as the one before.

No. 20: Your sole task is to please your husband

I WAS STILL NOT a real dauphine, and everyone seemed to know it. Chambermaids inspected the bed linens each morning to see if the dauphin had finally performed his marital duty. Certain members of the court were willing to pay handsomely for such a piece of information. Hundreds of minor aristocrats milled around Versailles with not much to occupy them but spying and gossiping. I was embarrassed to be the subject of such speculation, but all I could do was pretend to ignore it and smile, smile, smile.

Once my sisters and I were married, my mother had instructed us to report to her each visit of Général Krottendorf, as well as all marital activity, to assure her we were fulfilling our duty. She arranged for a secret courier to carry my letter to her at the beginning of each month, ensuring that anything I told her would not fall into the hands of spies. Mama was not pleased to learn that all was not going according to her plan.

I didn't feel that Louis-Auguste disliked me or found me objectionable in any way. He was not like my brother Joseph, who couldn't bring himself to make love to his second wife, the Bavarian princess cursed with a dark mustache and lots of pimples. I believed that Louis-Auguste was frightened—not of *me,* but of what was expected of him. I felt sorry for him. He really didn't know how to behave. I made up my mind to be his friend and to win him over, little by little. But how could I be his friend if he wouldn't speak to me, or even look at me? All I could do was wait.

One night a few weeks after the wedding Louis-Auguste appeared in my bedchamber. "My grandfather has ordered me to visit your bed," he explained and crept timidly under the coverlet.

Almost immediately he rolled over and was about to fall asleep when I reached out, very carefully, and rested my hand on his shoulder. Through the thin cloth of his nightshirt I felt him grow tense, as though he actually believed I might do him harm. I thought of my little Mops, who'd been frightened and nervous at first until I'd scratched his back. After that, my dog had quickly come to adore me. I decided to try the same technique on the dauphin.

Starting near his neck, I began to scratch my husband's back, lightly at first until his shoulders slowly relaxed. I scratched a little harder, my fingers working their way carefully down his spine. "Ahhhh," he sighed.

And then he fell asleep.

He was back again the next night. "Scratch my back, *s'il vous plaît, madame,*" he said, rolling on his side. I began scratching. When I was making circles and figure eights somewhere below his shoulders, he murmured, "I enjoy what you're doing almost as much as I enjoy making locks."

"Making *locks?*" I was glad to learn that he enjoyed something besides eating and hunting. I switched hands and continued scratching.

"*Oui, madame,* making locks," he said. "Every evening I'm at my forge. I'm a good locksmith. Someday I'll make a lock for you. Now, if you would be so kind, madame, a little to the left."

In minutes he was snoring softly. Before I awoke the next morning, he was gone.

Nearly three months had passed since my wedding. Though my husband still mostly ignored me in public, and we exchanged only a few words at the *grand couvert*—whatever he said then almost always had to do with the food—we were slowly becoming friends. I believed he was beginning to trust me.

But this was not what my mother wanted to hear—that he liked to have his back scratched and that he preferred making locks to making love.

How painful it was to confess in my letters that nothing had changed between us: I had not been made a real dauphine. I was no longer living in the shabby apartments that had once belonged to my husband's dead mother but had been moved to new and very pretty quarters that, unfortunately, were far from my husband's apartments. If he wanted to visit me to have his back scratched, he had to make his way there with everyone watching. Anyone who happened to be present knew exactly where he was going. This was too much for poor, shy Louis-Auguste.

Mama was outraged.

Surely, Antoinette, you are at fault here. Why are you not sharing the same bed as we do here?

Dearest Mama, I wrote, *the French sleep not only in separate beds but in separate apartments. It is the custom here.*

That custom of separate beds is most peculiar. You must do whatever is necessary to change it, she replied.

Mama's advice on the subject was confusing, because all along she had preached that I must be obedient and follow the rules of court etiquette without question, take care to do everything exactly as it was done at Versailles, and never behave in a manner to shock or upset anyone.

Now her letters were filled with harsh criticism and blame. *Everything depends on the wife,* she wrote sternly. *She must be willing, sweet, and amusing. It is up to you to cajole him endlessly. Redouble your caresses! Your sole task is to please your husband. Do not forget that!*

I wanted to scream, *I am willing, I am sweet, and I try my best to be amusing, I caress and cajole as much as he will allow, but still my husband does not want to make love to me!*

I must confess that I was not overcome with passion for my husband. He certainly wasn't handsome, as I'd dreamed he would be, but neither was he ugly or disgusting—just fat and clumsy. And he wasn't rude or unpleasant—just awkward and reticent. I understood well my duty to produce the future kings and queens of France. My reputation at court depended on my success—indeed, my whole future depended on it. But I couldn't do it without Louis-Auguste's cooperation. Back scratching had made him my friend, but it hadn't made him my lover. I had no idea what would.

I decided that at the first opportunity I would speak openly to him about this serious matter. Then one day early in August, after the dauphin had plowed through his usual mountainous meal at the *grand couvert,* he turned to me and said, "*S'il vous plaît, madame,* visit me this afternoon, when it is convenient for you to do so."

I was surprised and delighted—he had never before invited me to come to his apartments. *At last,* I thought, *this is my chance.*

Once the required visit to the aunts was finished, I hurried to the dauphin's apartments. As usual, the duc de La Vauguyon, my husband's longtime tutor, was hovering nearby. I absolutely detested this man. As governor of the

Children of France, La Vauguyon had made it clear all along to Louis-Auguste and his brothers that they must not trust anyone of Austrian blood. I was sure La Vauguyon had been a bad influence and might even have poisoned the dauphin's mind against me. I swept past the duke without acknowledging him and was ushered into my husband's library.

Louis-Auguste peered at me through a pair of jeweled spectacles that I had never before seen him use. The dauphin was very shortsighted, but etiquette forbade him to wear spectacles in public. "I'm glad you're here madame," he said, blushing, and invited me to sit on a pretty chair elaborately carved and covered in embroidered silk. "I had this chair made just for your visits." That pleased me.

He dismissed his roomful of attendants—he had even more of them than I did—and finally we were alone. I waited to find out what he wanted to discuss. Maybe he was thinking of the same thing I was. How much simpler that would make my task!

He struggled to begin, unable to look at me directly, and put away his spectacles. Maybe it would be easier if he couldn't see me clearly. Trying to make him feel more at ease, I reached for his hand. It was cold and damp. "Dear husband, *je vous en prie*—I beg you—feel free to speak your mind openly and with confidence that I will understand."

"What I've been wanting to say to you is that—" He

paused, coughed, dropped my hand as if it were something hot, and began again. Finally he blurted it out: "It would mean a lot to me if you . . . that is to say . . . I . . . I want very much for you to join my hunting party!"

It must have cost him a great deal to choke out these words, which could not have been more different from what I was thinking. I wanted to laugh, but somehow I managed to reply in the same serious tone, "Monsieur, I've never hunted. I've never ridden a horse."

"But you could learn, I'm sure," he said earnestly. "Hunting is what I love best. I go hunting nearly every day, first thing in the morning."

"Then I shall learn," I promised. "But, my dear monsieur, I think we have more to discuss than hunting. May I speak frankly?"

He got that frightened-rabbit expression, but he did give me one quick nod before he looked away and began to study his thumbs. He may have suspected what I was going to say.

I reminded him gently that it was our solemn duty as the future king and queen of France to produce children. With my sweetest smile I asked, "Is there something I can do to help to make that possible?" I was sure Mama would call that *cajoling.*

The dauphin blushed and stammered and rubbed his eyes until they were pink. At last he admitted in a strangled voice that he knew very well of what I spoke but that he suffered greatly from shyness. Then he seemed to collect himself and said with some determination, "I have come to an important decision, Antoinette." This was the first time he had called me by my given name, and I took it as a good sign. "On the twenty-third of August—just two weeks from today—I'll observe my sixteenth birthday at Compiègne. That's my favorite palace—the hunting in the forest there is fantastic! At that time I promise you I shall begin to live with you in the kind of intimacy our union requires."

I was thrilled! This formal speech was, for Louis-Auguste, a great show of courage. For half a minute I believed he was actually going to kiss me—he still had not done even *that,* except for the ceremonial kiss on both cheeks at our first meeting. And maybe he would have, if we hadn't both heard an odd noise at the door of his library. In two swift strides he crossed the room and flung open the door. There, trapped behind the door, was the duc de La Vauguyon. He'd obviously been listening to every word.

"What is it you want, sir?" the dauphin demanded.

This was the first time I had seen my husband angry, but La Vauguyon didn't even seem disconcerted. "The king, your grandfather, has asked me to review several documents with you, Monsieur le Dauphin," said the duke, glancing at me through slitted eyes.

Louis-Auguste looked at me and shrugged. I rose and swept haughtily out of his apartments. I hated having our important conversation end that way, and I wondered how much the detestable La Vauguyon had managed to hear at the keyhole and would find a way to use to his advantage. But at least I had my husband's promise to make me a real dauphine on his birthday, in two weeks. And I had promised him I'd learn to hunt.

My confidence grew that my husband was ready to love me fully. I wrote at once to my mother with the good news, and I even confided excitedly in Mesdames Tantes. They'd fallen into the habit of asking me every morning if Louis-Auguste had visited my bed the night before, and I'd always had to admit that he had not. Even direct orders from his grandfather had had no effect. I was sure the aunts would be delighted to hear that their dear nephew was about to get over his timidity and prove his manhood.

"I've told him quite sternly that he must be about it," Madame Adélaïde declared triumphantly. "At last he's listening to me."

Next I went to King Louis, first making sure that the vulgar Madame Du Barry was not present. The king, as always, seemed pleased to see me.

"Dear Grandpapa King," I said, "I find my cherished husband becoming more and more lovable each day, and my greatest wish is to please him in every way possible." I knew the king would understand that little hint. "Therefore, I ask your kind permission to allow me to learn to ride so that I may accompany him on the royal hunts."

The king gazed at me. "Not everyone approves of young ladies riding horses," he said, rubbing his chin thoughtfully. "It is said to be ruinous to the complexion and injurious to the figure, perhaps even dangerous to women under thirty."

"I will take every care, dear Grandpapa King. But I know it would please my husband greatly. He has told me so."

The king seemed to think it over. *"Eh bíen, ma chère Antoinette,"* he replied at last. "I compliment you for your desire to please your husband. I shall have the equerries find some donkeys of a sweet and tranquil nature for you to ride."

"*Donkeys,* Grandpapa?"

"Much safer for you, *ma chère,* and surely as enjoyable."

It wasn't quite what I wanted, but I thanked him and kissed his hands and fairly skipped out of his chambers. Everything was at last going my way.

Louis-Auguste's sixteenth birthday arrived, and I prepared for his visit to my bed at Compiègne. I wasn't even frightened anymore. In fact, I looked forward to this new adventure. But he spent the whole day out hunting, and when he returned very late, muddy and completely exhausted, I wondered if he would do what he had promised.

Alas, he did not.

No. 21: You must wear the grand corps at all times

I WAS IN THE FOURTH month of my marriage, and I was doing everything exactly as I was supposed to. Madame Etiquette no longer corrected me a hundred times a day—a dozen times was enough. King Louis seemed pleased with me. My husband made a point of seeking out my company whenever he was not hunting or working at his forge. But he still had not made love to me.

I was worried. Whom could I trust? I had no one but the aunts, and they were mainly interested in gossiping about Madame Du Barry. "You must not recognize her or give her the slightest satisfaction," they told me over and over.

I completely agreed with them and followed their advice. Mesdames Tantes were my friends, weren't they?

And they wanted the best for me, didn't they? It had never occurred to me that being a dauphine would shut me off from everyone else. I had never in my life been lonely. Now loneliness gnawed at me, eating me from the inside out.

Then King Louis kept his promise and sent me a dozen donkeys and a riding master to instruct me. I chose one of the sweetly braying little animals and named her Fleur, and within days I was merrily riding through the sun-dappled glades of the forest with my ladies. This was the first real relief I'd had from the tedium of court life, and I enjoyed it immensely.

Hardly any of the older ladies seemed pleased with this new entertainment, though they didn't dare to complain. My husband's younger brothers, Provence and Artois, decided they too wished to join my unusual retinue and included *their* friends, younger ones who quickly got into the spirit of fun. While the king and the dauphin amused themselves chasing after some poor beast in another part of the forest, our hunt was for the perfect place beneath the trees to stop for a picnic luncheon.

My newfound interest shocked nearly everyone. Madame de Noailles was particularly perturbed. "What if you should lose your seat?" she demanded, looking aghast.

"My seat?"

"Tumble from your mount, Madame la Dauphine," murmured the countess, as though she could scarcely bring herself to mention such a disgraceful possibility.

Her eyelids fluttered and her nostrils flared, as they did when she was shocked by something I had said or done—and that was often.

"I suppose, madame, that if I fell off my donkey, I would find myself seated on the ground," I said.

"But to the best of my knowledge there are no rules of etiquette governing what one must do in that circumstance," she said.

I could hardly keep from laughing. "Are you afraid I will be left sitting there?"

"I am afraid, Madame la Dauphine, that you do not take important matters seriously enough." She curtsied even more deeply than usual, and swept away.

There were occasional mishaps, to be sure. Sometimes, as Madame Etiquette feared, my little mount made a misstep and stumbled, and down I went into the soft mud, suffering no damage to myself though I returned to the chateau muddy and bedraggled.

It was only natural that, once I'd discovered the pleasure of riding, I wanted to be comfortable while doing so. I chose to wear informal gowns for my outings, but this brought up the matter of my stays and laces. I was expected to wear a garment called a *grand corps* under every gown—not just on special court occasions, but at all times, no matter how informal.

Beginning when I was old enough to walk, I had

worn stays, cloth stiffened with thin strips of wood and laced tightly up the back. As I got older, the flexible wood strips were replaced with pieces of wire or bone. Stays were necessary, according to my mother and my governesses, in order to keep a girl's skeleton in the proper position and to make sure her waist was under control. All ladies wore stays! But the stays of Versailles were much stiffer than the stays of Vienna, and the ones I was required to wear were made with rigid whalebone that didn't bend at all. The *grand corps* could stand up by itself. Once I was laced into it, I could hardly breathe or even move my arms, and I had come close to fainting the first few times I'd worn it. It was difficult to eat anything beyond a small morsel or two and impossible to ride in any sort of comfort.

I suffered with the *grand corps* through the hot summer, when I could not walk half a dozen steps without perspiring. Since I was quite thin and fit into my slim-waisted gowns with no trouble, I considered it senseless to keep wearing the *grand corps.* Other ladies wore it only when being presented at court—why should I be cursed with it every day of my life? It was just another of those stupid rules.

"I hate this thing," I complained to Madame de Noailles.

"Like it or not, as the highest-ranking woman in the French court you must wear it," the countess informed me haughtily, eyes half closed and nostrils flaring.

If she thought that was the end of it, she was wrong. I decided to ask Mesdames Tantes for advice. Their billowing black taffeta gowns covered them from their double chins to their toes, and I was certain that no *grand corps* lurked beneath.

"Why should you wear such a thing, my dear Antoinette?" Madame Adélaïde replied with a benign smile. "You are lovely enough without it."

That was all the encouragement I needed. Because it was impossible to get in or out of my stays without someone to do the laces, I bribed the maidservant who helped me dress for my riding expeditions. In return for a few pastries and other small gifts, the girl promised to hide the *grand corps* where the comtesse de Noailles would not see it. Now I could ride my little Fleur in comfort and joy.

This was my first real rebellion. How did I think I could get away with it? In no time at all Madame Etiquette had discovered my secret. She reported my rebellion to Count Mercy d'Argenteau, who wasted no time in telling Empress Maria Theresa. I soon received an alarmed warning and a harsh rebuke from Mama. *I know very well you are not taking care of your appearance. You have grown slovenly,* Mama wrote. *It is even said that you aren't cleaning your teeth!*

Now everyone knew I was not wearing a *grand corps,* and everyone was talking about it. There were suggestions that I was growing misshapen, my right shoulder noticeably higher than the left.

It has been said that your figure is becoming womanly, without in fact your being a wife, Mama lectured. She underlined that last part twice.

My mother's letters were my strongest tie with my home and family, but I had begun to dread them. I craved her approval, but Mama had always been better at dispensing criticism than giving praise. Now she hinted that I was falling out of favor in the French court, where I had once been so eagerly welcomed, because I didn't pay proper attention to court etiquette.

If this continues, she wrote ominously, *you might even find yourself put aside.*

By *put aside,* she meant "divorced." Divorced for refusing to wear their dreadful *grand corps*!

I really didn't know how to answer all this. Hadn't Mesdames Tantes encouraged me *not* to wear the *grand corps*?

One day while we were all at the hunting lodge at Compiègne, Count Mercy d'Argenteau managed to get a message through saying he needed to speak to me—alone. This was not easy to arrange, but Mama's ambassador seized his chance. As the court was preparing to return to Versailles, I took Mops for a little stroll before we climbed into my carriage.

Tall and thin, Count Mercy shortened his long stride to match mine. "Madame la Dauphine," he whispered urgently, "I must warn you: *beware of Mesdames Tantes.* I know you've grown fond of these ladies and spend a great deal of time with them, but you must be very careful."

"*C'est vrai, monsieur*—it's true that I'm required to pay

them three long visits each day, and sometimes four," I said as Mops tugged impatiently on his leash. "But I also believe that my husband's dear aunts are my best friends at this court."

"So you believe, but you are mistaken: Mesdames Tantes only pretend to be your friends. Unfortunately these ladies, like many others at court, do not wish to see you as their queen. They fear that you will have too much influence over the future king, to the advantage of Austria and the disadvantage of France."

I stared at the ambassador in confusion and disbelief. Mops sniffed Mercy's elegant calfskin shoes and had already lifted his leg when I reached down and scooped up my dog.

The ambassador appeared not to notice. "You are still too young, madame, too inexperienced, to understand that nothing—*nothing!*—would give many at this court more pleasure than to see you fail," he murmured close to my ear, "and to be sent home to Vienna in disgrace. You must exercise the greatest caution. Whatever advice Mesdames Tantes give you, I suggest you appear to agree but do exactly the opposite. And, *je vous en prie*—I beg you, madame—yield to the demands of etiquette and wear the *grand corps.*"

I wanted more explanation, more discussion of this, but at that moment I saw three stout figures in black advancing toward us. Count Mercy saw them too. He bowed low, kissed my hand, and strode quickly away, and

I prepared a bright smile for the three aunts who, I now realized, may have been my three greatest enemies.

Still, I was determined not to give in. For the next few weeks I ignored Count Mercy's well-meaning advice and shunned the *grand corps.* What could be lost? There was no truth to the ridiculous rumor that my shoulders were uneven or that my waist had begun to spread. *Let people gossip, if they have nothing better to do,* I decided. *Let them say whatever they like, for I know the truth, and so do they.*

No. 22: Do not show disregard for the manners of the court

IN THE MIDST of my silent rebellion I received some truly unwelcome news: my husband's brother the comte de Provence would soon marry Marie-Joséphine of Savoy. Even before the king made the official announcement, Mesdames Tantes began twittering about the wedding, which would take place in May.

"Oh, my dear child." Madame Adélaïde sighed, and pulled a long face, "how very unfortunate if Louis-Stanislas-Xavier's little Savoyard princess were to produce a son before you do!"

The aunts didn't need to remind me of this possibility. "But there is always the chance their first child will be a girl, is there not?" I asked.

Madame Adélaïde agreed that such a chance did exist.

To make matters worse, the loudmouthed Provence, so fat he waddled, would not stop boasting about the fantastic wedding night feats he expected to perform. "You may all anticipate a royal birth exactly nine months later!" he trumpeted. He did this just to humiliate my poor husband—the comte de Provence was plainly envious that Louis-Auguste was the dauphin, and he made a habit of taunting him. My loutish brother-in-law's boasts angered and embarrassed me, but I could say nothing.

Just days after learning of Provence's coming marriage, I received another letter from Mama.

As your loving mother, I beg you, do not neglect your appearance or show disregard for the manners of the court. It is a grievous mistake. It is up to you to set the example. I promise you this: if you do not heed my advice, you will soon come to regret it, but it will be too late.

Deeply wounded, I burst into tears as I read her letter. Eventually, though, I dried my tears and added this letter to the others I kept in a little locked chest, where I hoped they were safe from prying eyes. I'd already come to a decision: I would show these petty lords and ladies with their mean-spirited gossip that I could shine as the court's brightest star, and I would put them all to shame. And I would prove to my mother that I had not failed.

But I had to admit to myself that if wearing the awful *grand corps* was the way to earn the court's respect, then I must submit to imprisonment by inflexible stays. It seemed terribly unfair. Madame Etiquette took notice of my surrender, and her lips twitched in her version of a smile.

Word spread with amazing speed, as rumors did at Versailles, and I soon observed subtle changes in the way I was treated. There was less whispering behind jeweled fans and fewer knowing smirks—all because I was wearing stays.

In September the entire court moved to Fontainebleau, a long day's journey from Versailles, as it did each autumn for the stag-hunting season. The beautiful palace was reflected in the calm waters of the Loire and surrounded by splendid gardens. I soon discovered that my husband's apartments, which adjoined mine, were being redecorated. Until the work was finished, he was assigned apartments at the opposite end of the chateau. There was no way in the world he would ever make the long walk through public corridors to visit my bedchamber. After a few inquiries I learned from a talkative servant that the person charged with preparing our quarters had been bribed to keep us apart for as long as possible. My mother was constantly admonishing me to entice my husband into making love to me, and at least one member of the court was determined he would not!

The next day while exploring the grounds and trying to decide what to do to change the situation, I came upon the king at the enormous carp pool teeming with fish raised for the royal table. The king was amusing himself by tossing bits of bread to the shimmering fish.

"I trust you will enjoy your stay here, Madame Antoinette," he said, greeting me warmly. "While your husband and I are riding through the forest in pursuit of the stag, you may wish to follow the hunt in the little calèche I've got for you."

I hoped this didn't mean I was never to graduate from a donkey to a horse, but now was not the time to pursue it. "I am truly grateful, Grand-Père," I said, "but there is one thing more I must ask of you."

"Then ask, *ma chère.*" He handed me a crust of bread, and I tossed it, bit by bit, toward those greedy mouths breaking the surface of the dark waters.

"The dauphin's bedchamber is separated from mine by an entire palace," I said. "I don't wish to sleep so far from my dear husband." I didn't mention that I believed the situation was intentional and that someone had been bribed.

The king didn't hesitate. "That shall be remedied."

"*Merci beaucoup,* Grandpapa King."

The king kept his word, and within a week Louis-Auguste's apartments adjoined mine.

But nothing changed. I still slept alone.

Early each morning I joined the royal hunting party in my new calèche, an elegant two-wheeled carriage with a folding top. We began with a marvelous breakfast in the forest. My husband consumed his usual enormous quantities of meats and pastries and wine, and King Louis made it a point to pay me special attention, telling me things he thought I should know.

"The stag is the noblest of the wild beasts," he explained at the start of the first day, "and hunting him *par force* is the noblest way to kill him. Our *grand veneur*—the grand huntsman—has already found the direction in which our quarry is moving. When we've finished breakfast, the dauphin and I will decide on the best way to conduct the hunt. The dogs are already being placed along the path. We will mount our coursers and begin the chase, and how exciting it will be, my dear Madame Antoinette—the hounds in pursuit, running the beast until he can run no more and turns to defend himself with his great antlers. At that moment I shall decide who will make the final kill—your husband or I. Or perhaps I shall allow one of the princes of the blood to come forward with his sword to put an end to the life of the noble animal!"

I gazed at the king as he described the scene with such passion. I didn't particularly care to see the stag chased until he was exhausted. Later, when I caught up with the men on horseback, the poor creature was facing the baying greyhounds. Did he know in his heart he was about to die? The thought made me shudder. Even worse was the final event of the hunt, after the kill, when the carcass of the stag was cut up and thrown to the hounds to reward them for their efforts. Blood was everywhere, and it sickened me, but I took care not to let on.

If this was what my husband enjoyed, then I'd do it. But the pretty calèche was slow and clumsy; I'd be able to follow much more easily on horseback. After a month of trailing behind the hunt, on a day when I sensed that King Louis was in an exceptionally good mood—he'd brought down a great stag with a dozen tines on its antlers—I brought up the subject again.

"Grandpapa King," I began, "donkeys are fine for picnics in the park, and the calèche is really comfortable, but if one wishes to join the hunt, a horse is essential. *Je vous en prie,* I beg you, allow me to ride a horse so that I may share more of the pleasures of the hunt with my husband. And his dear *grand-père,*" I added for good measure.

He studied me, frowning, for such a long time that I was afraid he'd refuse. "Very well, *ma chère* Antoinette," he said at last, "I shall grant your wish. You will observe your fifteenth birthday in a week or two, am I correct? My gift to you will be a fine riding horse, chosen for you by my equerry, and you shall have a groom to lead it. Should that prove to your liking, you shall then have riding lessons as you wish."

"Oh, *merci, merci,* dear Grandpapa King!" I cried, and I seized his hand and kissed it.

On the day before my birthday, the king's equerry escorted me to the royal stables and presented me with a gentle little mare. The groom helped me mount and then led the mare along a pleasant woodland path at a stately pace, followed, as usual, by a carriage with several of my ladies. The groom was patient—more patient than I. He looked to be about my age.

After we'd ambled sedately for a while, I told him, "Allow me to have the reins."

The boy glanced up at me. "*Oui, madame, comme vous voulez*—as you wish." He showed me how to hold the reins, but he kept a firm grip on the halter.

"Let go of the halter," I commanded.

He shook his head. "I cannot, Madame la Dauphine," he said. "King's orders."

I summoned my most imperious look, a look I'd learned from my mother and refined by observing Madame de Noailles. "I order you to let go!"

The groom stared straight ahead as though he had not heard me and kept a tight hold. I leaned down, put my face close to his, and when he turned I bestowed on him my most winning smile. *"S'il vous plaît,"* I said sweetly.

"Very well, madame," he said, eyeing me uneasily and blushing furiously. "But I shall walk beside you."

That satisfied me, but only for a little while. Then I gave the mare a nudge, and off she trotted. The groom ran after us, but I urged the mare into a canter. How gloriously free I felt with the wind in my hair and the little mare moving smoothly beneath me. I glanced over my shoulder. The groom had given up the chase and stood bent over, hands on his knees, panting. I realized he might get into serious trouble for letting me go, and I didn't want that to happen. I turned the mare around and trotted back. "You may lead us to the stables," I said, handing him the reins. I waved gaily at the carriage full of wide-eyed ladies.

The next day I learned that the king had authorized a stable of hunting mounts to be entirely mine.

In that annoying way of the court, everyone was soon talking about me and my horses. I didn't care one bit what Madame Etiquette or Mesdames Tantes or anyone else thought. I was at last on horseback, and I adored it!

I was determined that by the end of the month I'd be riding by the side of the king and the dauphin, sharing the life my husband enjoyed most. How could he fail to love me then? And fail to make love to me? I was on my way to solving my biggest problem.

No. 23: You are not to spend too much time with one person

At the beginning of the new year the comtesse de Noailles gave a little dance in her suite. My husband and I finished the first dance. He hated it, and he danced so awkwardly that I was always relieved when this part of the evening was over. Having stayed just long enough to be polite, he said good night and left. I turned to a lady seated nearby, and we began to chat.

The lady was Marie-Thérèse, princesse de Lamballe. A few years older than I, and already a widow at twenty-one, she seemed sweet, melancholy, and much in need of someone to bring her a little cheer. The princess had been presented to me when I first arrived at court, and I had been struck by her fragile beauty—a graceful figure, eyes the color of amethyst, lovely golden hair, and a brilliant complexion on which the required circles of rouge seemed an insult. She'd sat at the end of the royal table at my wedding supper with her father-in-law, the king's grand huntsman. I'd noticed her on many occasions since then, but this was the first time I'd had a conversation with her.

"Monsieur le Dauphin is no doubt going to work in his forge," I said. "He does this every evening."

I should not have said anything so personal and intimate, but the princess merely smiled. "Perhaps it is the way of the French, Madame la Dauphine," she said softly. I realized that she spoke with an accent.

"You are not French-born?" I asked. I had already taken in the excellent quality of her gown and the fine jewels she wore.

"I was born in Turin. My father is Italian," she explained, "and my mother is German."

The princess knew what it was like to be a foreigner at the French court, and I felt immediately that this pleasant lady would become my dear friend. She was much different from the ladies in my court, who seemed to spend their days gossiping and plotting intrigues and making unkind observations about one another—and, I was sure, about me.

For the rest of the evening we were inseparable, though I saw Madame Etiquette giving me one of her disapproving looks. She had instructed me not to spend too much time with one person.

As we prepared to leave the countess's suite, I drew aside the heavy window drapery. Snow had been falling since early morning, and thick flakes still swirled around the lamps. Versailles had been completely transformed. Most times it looked rundown and neglected, but that night it seemed magical. Remembering how I had adored sleigh rides around Vienna, I was quick to seize the opportunity. "Let's have a sleighing party tomorrow," I said to my new friend. "Please join me, madame."

Marie-Thérèse de Lamballe curtsied, eyes modestly lowered. "It will be my pleasure, Madame la Dauphine."

King Louis kept half a dozen sleighs at the royal stables, each beautifully carved and painted, with seats for just two passengers and a coachman. Wrapped in sable and ermine, the princess and I set out in a sleigh shaped like a giant turtle surrounded by dolphins and gilded acacia leaves, and mounted on gracefully curved wooden runners. Each afternoon for the next three days my friend and I directed the coachman, seated high on his narrow bench behind us, to explore a different part of the vast park surrounding the chateau. On the first day we drove along the frozen grand canal. On the second we glided over snow-covered paths that wound through the park lying silent beneath its glistening winter blanket. At the end of our third outing we passed near the king's private palace, the Grand Trianon, where he often came to get away from the strict routine of the court.

As we continued along the path, the horse's hooves muffled by the thick snow, I pointed to a lovely little building not far away, surprised I hadn't noticed it before. "I wonder what that is," I said. "Do you know?" The princesse de Lamballe did not, and I called up to the coachman.

"That is the Petit Trianon," he told us. "A pleasure house built by the king. Madame Du Barry is said to enjoy it very much."

The princess and I looked at each other. "That woman," I grumbled darkly, "gets absolutely everything."

"And deserves absolutely nothing," said the princess, completing my thought.

Our friendship and our confidences grew, and we expressed our innermost thoughts with no one around to hear. "You often seem melancholy, Thérèse," I observed. In private we had begun to call each other by our given names. "It can't be easy to be a widow at such a young age. Do tell me about your late husband. Was the prince de Lamballe much older than you? Quite elderly?"

"Au contraire," she said with a deep sigh. "I was seventeen when we married, and Louis-Alexandre barely eighteen.

Such a dear boy he was, though a bit on the wild side. I believe his father thought I would help to tame him."

"And did you succeed?" I asked. I was curious, and I hoped I might learn something from a woman only a few years older than I.

She smiled and shook her head. "I'm afraid not, but at first I believed I could. He was of a romantic frame of mind. I had not met him before the wedding, of course, but the night before the ceremony a servant came to my apartments to deliver a bouquet of flowers. The next day, when the prince and I came face to face at the altar, I realized that I had, in fact, seen him before—he'd disguised himself as the servant with the flowers. 'I could not wait to see you,' he confessed later. And apparently I had pleased him. Our honeymoon was lovely, Antoinette! I fell in love with him at once, and I think he fell in love with me."

I felt a stab of envy as Thérèse described the early months of her marriage. If only Louis-Auguste felt the same way about me! But then my friend's story took an unhappy turn.

"At first all went well. I had a good influence on him, and his father—whom I like very much—was delighted. But then Alexandre returned to his wild ways. He ran up large gambling debts and took some of my jewels to settle them. When the deed was discovered, he left our home in Rambouillet. I had no idea where he had gone. His father found him, quite ill, the result of being with a certain type of woman—you know of what I'm speaking. He died a few months later. We'd been married less than a year."

"Oh, my poor dear!" I cried. My envy gave way to pity.

Thérèse turned her large, expressive eyes toward me. A few tears sparkled like tiny jewels on her long lashes. "*Oui,* it was very sad indeed. But my father-in-law, the duc de Panthièvre, has been so kind to me. I'd become like a real daughter to him, and he begged me to stay at Rambouillet. I did so, contentedly, until I was summoned to court when you arrived to marry the dauphin. And here I am!" she concluded, smiling and on a much more cheerful note.

"How happy I am that you're here, my dearest heart!" I exclaimed, seizing her small hand. "I know that we shall be fast friends forever!"

No. 24: Every person who has been presented at court must be treated with courtesy

THE WHOLE WORLD was awakening to the warmth of spring. The snow melted on the forest paths, leaves gently unfolded on the trees, and flowers bloomed in the chateau gardens. But one thing that did not awaken that spring was my husband's passion. Nevertheless, we were on very good terms. Louis-Auguste gave me permission to hold a ball in my apartments each week, and he always put in a brief appearance. He seemed to enjoy my company when we were alone, and he sometimes gave me a little kiss, or squeezed my hand in a friendly way. It was as though we were brother and sister. When Louis-Auguste visited my bedchamber, as he did fairly often, it was to have his back scratched. He made no further mention of living together in the "kind of intimacy our union requires." I didn't mention it either.

A year after my wedding to the dauphin, his brother the comte de Provence married Marie-Joséphine of Savoy with all the usual pomp of a royal wedding. Before I met the new *comtesse,* I feared she would turn out to be prettier and more charming than I was, and I would lose my privileged position with the king. I needn't have worried. Marie-Joséphine, poor thing, was homely as a toad—if a toad had a long nose and one eye that turned inward, as she did—and virtually unable to open her mouth to speak.

The day after their wedding, my husband and I had to suffer Provence's boasts of his amazing feats in the marriage bed. He bragged that he'd performed "the act" no fewer than four times. "My bride enjoyed her wedding night marvelously!" he crowed. Suppose my unattractive new sister-in-law produced a male heir as the result of all that nuptial activity?

As it turned out, though, Stanislas-Xavier was no more talented in the bedchamber than was his older brother. The gossip immediately circulating throughout the court was that Provence had done nothing at all.

I reported all of this to Mama, as she demanded, but she wasn't satisfied. My mother's list of criticisms seemed endless, and she continued to lecture, admonish, and threaten me in her long monthly letters. *I am most distressed that you have taken up riding* (I had neglected to mention that I had lessons with my master of the horse three or four times a week) *and I must warn you this activity will surely bring on a miscarriage.*

Mama seemed to have forgotten at least two things. First, she had been an enthusiastic horsewoman in her younger days, and that hadn't prevented her from giving birth to sixteen children. Second, I was still a virgin—a condition she insisted was entirely my fault: *if you were a good wife, your husband would by now have consummated your union many times over.*

Foolishly, I looked forward to her letters, always hoping for praise and encouragement. I never got it. I confided my feelings to my friend Thérèse de Lamballe. "I love my mother dearly, but I'm afraid of her! Even living far away from her, I dread telling her when things go wrong."

"Perhaps, then, you should not tell her quite so much," Thérèse suggested.

But that was advice I seemed completely unable to follow.

Another problem plagued me: the comtesse Du Barry, the king's favorite. How could I possibly acknowledge such a woman? Some people at court referred to Du Barry simply as "the new lady"; I was more in agreement with those who called her the harlot. I thought she was stupid and presumptuous, and it pained me that the king had such a weakness for her.

"You must refuse to acknowledge her, my dear," Adélaïde insisted.

"For our father's sake," said Sophie.

"For the sake of his immortal soul," Victoire added, nodding vigorously.

"I dare not repeat what she said about you," Adélaïde murmured, twisting her jeweled rings.

"About *me?*" I asked. "She's spoken about me?"

"Oh dear, oh dear." Adélaïde sighed. I urged her to continue. "She's been heard to say, more than once, I'm afraid, 'I see nothing attractive in *l'Autrichienne*'s red hair, thick lips, sandy complexion, and eyes without eyelashes.' But perhaps I've not quoted her accurately."

"*Mais non,* dear sister," Sophie broke in, "you've quoted her word for word."

"What an impertinent creature!" I exclaimed. "Now I know that I shall not speak to her."

Ignoring her was the only correct and virtuous thing to do—I was absolutely certain of it.

Count Mercy had warned me not to be guided by the aunts. "Mesdames Tantes love to involve themselves in little intrigues," he'd told me. Nevertheless, I sympathized completely with their feelings. The aunts believed that vulgar woman was leading their father to eternal damnation with her immoral behavior. Surely it would be wrong of me to acknowledge such a scandalous person!

But it became harder to snub this dreadful woman. I was truly shocked when I learned what had happened to the duc de Choiseul, the French foreign minister credited with arranging my marriage to the dauphin. Choiseul detested Du Barry and often mocked her. Angered by Choiseul's disrespect, King Louis dismissed the minister from his position and replaced him with one of his mistress's friends, the duc d'Aiguillon.

After her old enemy had been sent into exile and Du Barry had triumphed, the king moved her into a beautifully decorated suite at Versailles, her rooms connected to his by a secret stairway. Soon Du Barry's suite was where everybody who was anybody at court came to take care of business.

"She dresses like a queen," I heard my ladies say. They spoke loudly enough so that I could hear them, exactly as they had intended. "She sits on the arm of his chair while he's meeting with his councilors and speaks the most utter nonsense, which he seems to find endlessly amusing."

"Shameful!" the other ladies agreed, and so did I. As a matter of honor, I would not speak to this aging courtesan. Du Barry must have been at least twenty-eight!

On one of those damp, chilly days so common in late spring, Count Mercy d'Argenteau sent word requesting a private interview. Dark clouds had gathered, and rain seemed likely, but I suggested that the ambassador and I go riding in the park. He knew even better than I that spies lurked in every corner of the chateau and that every overheard conversation was embellished and repeated.

"We can take my carriage, Madame la Dauphine," he suggested.

"I mean on horseback, Monsieur Ambassadeur."

Mercy grimaced. "But shall you be comfortable enough, madame? You may get wet."

I didn't care if it rained, but the ladies who accompanied me wherever I went were not at all pleased. "You may follow in a carriage," I told them, "but I intend to get a little exercise."

"I shall be utterly frank with you, Madame la Dauphine," Count Mercy began as we set off together. "The king summoned me to Madame Du Barry's drawing room and spoke to me as politely but as directly as I am now speaking to you. King Louis finds you charming, but he will not put up with insults to Madame Du Barry. You have insulted her by refusing to acknowledge her. Every person who has been presented at court must be treated with courtesy. Madame Du Barry has been presented, and therefore—"

"She should never have been presented!" I interrupted. "It's outrageous!" I was ready to explain that ignoring her was the *virtuous* thing to do, but the ambassador cut me off.

"That is not for you to determine, madame!" I sensed Mercy's irritation, which he was plainly struggling to control. "Madame Du Barry has been presented, and therefore you owe her the courtesy of acknowledging her. A word and a nod will suffice."

I remained stubbornly silent as we rode on, splashing through deep puddles. I glanced over my shoulder and saw that the carriage following us had become stuck. The coachman was trying vainly to free it.

Thoroughly wet from a passing shower and spattered with mud from head to foot, we returned to the chateau. I found it very amusing, and though the ambassador probably did not, he said nothing. As we made our way to my apartments, we passed the comtesse de Noailles in the corridor. I saw the look of horror on her face as she took in my ruined gown. Next it was the mistress of the wardrobe who looked as though she might faint. I flung myself down, mud and all, on a silk-covered chaise longue.

Mercy d'Argenteau gazed around the drawing room, eyebrows raised and mouth downturned in disapproval. It was a mess. I could imagine what he would write to my mother about the disorder. I didn't care. Mostly it was the fault of the dogs—I'd had a second little pug sent from Vienna to keep Mops company. Sick of being forced to follow the most tedious rules of etiquette and continually corrected by Madame de Noailles, I had decided that my pets would have no rules at all, and I allowed them to do whatever they pleased. What they pleased, it seemed, was chewing on the carved wooden table legs, jumping up on the pale silk upholstery of the chairs with their dirty paws, and ripping the heavy satin draperies to shreds. Though there were servants to attend to almost every aspect of my life, no one had been assigned the duty of cleaning up after my dogs.

"Will you do it?" Count Mercy asked finally. "Speak to Madame Du Barry?"

At last I surrendered, but only because I didn't want to offend the king. "*Oui,* Monsieur Ambassadeur," I promised. "I shall speak to her."

He pressed me to name a time and place. I agreed to a particular Sunday evening in July.

On the specified evening I entered the hall where Madame Du Barry, King Louis, Count Mercy d'Argenteau, and everyone of importance in the royal court awaited this great moment. But when the moment arrived, I could not bring myself to keep my promise. I swept by Du Barry without speaking or even looking at her.

A hum like swarming bees spread through the hall, and I knew I would receive a scolding from the ambassador, my mother, and possibly even the king himself. But I was certain I was right and they were wrong. I had yielded on everything else, but on this matter I would not—could not—give in.

No. 25: You must not ride like a man dressed like a man

NEARLY EVERY day I spent an hour or more with the riding master. By late summer I'd become an experienced equestrienne. Nothing equaled the pleasure I felt when I was cantering through the park on one of my horses.

My usual riding costume was a jacket and waistcoat; a shirt with a high, lace-trimmed collar that concealed my stays; and a full skirt. But I quickly grew tired of the cumbersome skirts, which were too wide even without panniers. I liked to ride very fast, and the sidesaddle used by ladies didn't give me the purchase I needed when I urged my horse into a gallop, especially when my mount jumped over a log or a small stream. I had already tumbled off more than once, so far without any injury. How much better—

safer—it would be if I could ride astride, like a man. That was clearly impossible when I wore a skirt.

First, I tried wearing knitted culottes under the skirt, but the skirt was still in the way when I attempted to straddle the horse. And so I set my seamstresses to work making velvet breeches that fit tightly in the leg and matched my royal blue jacket and waistcoat. There was no skirt.

When the court moved to Fontainebleau in autumn, I joined the hunt astride a fine hunting steed and dressed in my new breeches, my jaunty tricorn hat topped with a flutter of white feathers. I knew this new costume would shock. I was determined to wear it anyway. Naturally, everyone stared, and the scandalized whispers began. If the court wanted something to gossip about, they certainly had it now. *The dauphine wearing breeches? Is the dauphine trying to act like a man? What does her husband have to say?*

In fact, it delighted my husband. The king and the dauphin both told me they were enchanted to see me in the uniform of the hunt, an elegant costume not so different from their own.

My mother soon heard about it—the ambassador must have dispatched his fastest courier to inform her. She was *not* delighted. I had not expected her to be.

Mama asked me to have a painting done in my court finery and absolutely forbade me to wear what she called "man's clothing." I was bold enough to ignore her orders but instructed the artist to portray me from the waist up in my blue velvet jacket and the tricorn with the white plume. Mama claimed to be pleased by the likeness and the happiness she saw in my smiling face, but she wrote, *If you are riding like a man, dressed as a man, I have to tell you that I find it dangerous as well as bad for bearing children. That is what you have been called upon to do and that will be the measure of your success.*

I decided to ignore her warning. I would dress however I wished, and if others disapproved, that was none of my concern.

No. 26: You must acknowledge Madame Du Barry

As the months passed, Du Barry continued to make a spectacle of herself. She flaunted her jewels and her bosom, draped her body on the arm of the king's chair, stroked his cheek, and talked utter nonsense. The king still seemed completely enamored with her. And I still refused to surrender to Count Mercy's lectures and my mother's stern letters: *You must acknowledge Madame Du Barry, no matter how you feel about her and how distasteful you may find it.*

King Louis had taken to appearing in my boudoir every morning, accompanied by a servant bearing a gilded tray with a porcelain pot and two delicate cups. For half an hour the two of us cozily drank coffee together. I had won the king's friendship, and it was vital that I keep it. On the advice of Count Mercy I saw less of Mesdames Tantes. As

I gradually escaped the aunts' powerful spell, I began to see that it might be all to the good if I recognized the king's mistress in some slight way. But how could I do that without actually giving Du Barry any real satisfaction? I decided to ask the princesse de Lamballe for her advice.

We had gone walking on a blustery day of early winter. The first snow had not yet fallen, but the wind was sharp, and we took shelter at the Potager du Roi, the large garden that supplied the royal table. In the glasshouse, ceramic stoves kept the moist air as warm as springtime, and peasants carefully cultivated beds of tender vegetables. As we walked among the rows of lettuce and asparagus, I brought up the subject of recognizing the king's mistress.

"What do you think, Thérèse?" I asked. "How can I accomplish this delicate task?"

She thought carefully and then offered this advice: "Acknowledge Du Barry when as many people as possible are present—on New Year's Day, perhaps, when the ladies of the court come to pay their respects. And make it as simple as possible."

"Good idea," I agreed. "But what shall I say?"

"Something truly banal, like 'What a crowd there is at Versailles today.'"

"That's all?"

"It's enough. Why not try it, Antoinette? You're not required to like her, or even to have any further conversation with her." Thérèse plucked a feathery green frond of asparagus and examined it. "Just imagine for the moment that I am Madame Du Barry, and you're about to speak to me for the first time."

I laughed. "You don't resemble her in the least!"

"No matter." She stuck the frond in her hair, and with exaggerated gestures that perfectly mimicked Du Barry's, the princess dropped to her knees on the dirt floor of the glasshouse.

"What a crowd there is at Versailles today," I intoned solemnly, and we both burst out laughing.

"Not so difficult, was it?" Thérèse asked mischievously.

I followed my friend's advice to the letter. On New Year's Day, 1772, the ladies of the court gathered to offer me formal greetings. When Madame Du Barry in her turn knelt before me, I looked straight at her and said, "What a crowd there is at Versailles today."

There—it was done. The king was satisfied with my gesture and sent me a jeweled fan as a gift. But Adélaïde, Victoire, and Sophie were angry. I had betrayed them.

No. 27: Unless you produce an heir to the throne, you will be sent away

After two years I'd become completely accustomed to the routines in *ce pays-ci*—"this country," as everyone called Versailles, recognizing that life at the chateau was completely different from everywhere else, with its own demanding and irritating set of rules. I began to spend more time reading books selected for me by my librarian, Monsieur Campan. I practiced on the harp a little every day and improved enough that I could sometimes entertain Louis-Auguste with my music. He at least pretended to enjoy it. And I went out riding every chance I had.

I'd made friends with some of the younger women at court, but Thérèse de Lamballe remained my dearest friend and confidante. The court was preparing to move to Compiègne to observe the dauphin's birthday—he would be eighteen—and Thérèse and I were watching several small boys playing noisily with the dogs while servants loaded our trunks onto wagons.

"I long for children," I remarked a bit sadly. "But I don't know that I shall ever have them. Will you remarry?" I asked her. "I can just imagine you surrounded by little ones."

Thérèse smiled in the sorrowful way I found so appealing. "I love children, and I'd surely like to have my own, but there are many to whom I can give affection. The cost to remarry would be very great. I'm a princess through my marriage to my late husband, and I would almost certainly lose my rank. I am content to remain a widow and a princess," she said, adding brightly, "but you, Antoinette, will one day be queen, and surely a mother as well."

"I am a wife without truly being a wife!" I burst out. This was hardly shocking news to my friend. Everyone at court knew about my unhappy situation—people had been gossiping about us for more than two years. I began to weep. I had shed many private tears over my situation, but this was the first time I had confessed my anguish to anyone else. Thérèse's melancholy air gave me courage to continue.

"The dauphin has not yet made me his wife," I lamented between sobs. "The empress, my mother, blames me for this sorry situation, and the ambassador Count Mercy has told me, in so many words, that until I provide the dauphin with a son, I'm in danger of being sent back to Austria in disgrace. I've no idea what to do!"

"My dear Antoinette," she said, taking my cold hand in both of her warm ones. "You must speak to the dauphin. Use your sweet smiles to coax him to reveal the cause of his . . . reluctance. Only when you discover the reason can you hope to find a solution."

How wise she was! I knew that many at court dismissed the princesse de Lamballe as lacking in intelligence. It was true that we didn't discuss great ideas, but I found her both sensitive and sensible.

The next time Louis-Auguste came to my bedchamber and asked me to scratch his back, I said, "I will scratch as much as you wish, my dear husband, but first we must talk openly. We care deeply about each other, but we have not yet come together in intimacy, as we must if we are to fulfill our obligation to our country and the people of France."

The dauphin buried his face in his hands. "It is entirely my fault," he murmured. Suddenly he dropped his hands and looked into my eyes, something he had done only rarely. "When I think about making love to you—and I do think of it, quite often—I experience great pain. I have spoken to my physician. There is a problem, he agrees, and the cure is an operation. But the operation he describes is very painful, and I haven't the courage to endure it."

"Oh, my poor husband! Is there no other solution?"

"The physician suggests—" He hesitated, blushing, took a breath, and continued. "The physician suggests that we experiment."

"Well, then we shall experiment!" I cried gaily, not having the least idea what I was talking about.

Our first attempts did not go well, but we did report to the king that we were "working on our problem." It was not until months later and further consultation with the physician that our efforts finally met with some success. What a triumph when I could finally write to my mother and announce that I was—at last!—a real wife and a real dauphine.

No. 28: It is your duty to be loved as well as respected by your subjects

I WAS EXCITED. I was to make my first formal entry into Paris as the future queen. For three years I had spent most of my time at Versailles, with frequent journeys to the royal country palaces—Fontainebleau, Compiègne, La Muette, Choisy—for the hunt. But I had not yet been to Paris.

I had given my approval to the seamstresses for my *grand habit de cour* and was deciding which jewels to wear when Count Mercy d'Argenteau called on me. Visits from the Austrian ambassador had a history of bringing news I didn't particularly want to hear. This one was no different. He'd come to warn me that my welcome in Paris might not be so cordial.

"The French people suffer greatly under a burden of

heavy taxes laid on their shoulders by the French nobility," he explained after I'd dismissed my attendants. "They have been deeply disappointed by the failure of King Louis to give them any relief, and they are not at all fond of Madame Du Barry—in fact, they find her appalling. But your marriage to the dauphin has given them new hope. They may greet you with open arms or they may turn their backs on you—there's no way to predict. You must be prepared."

I had no idea such problems existed in France, and there was nothing I could do to change it. But as my mother frequently reminded me, "It is your duty—the duty of all royalty—to be loved as well as respected by your subjects." That, I thought, should not be too hard. I would be as elegantly dressed as anyone the Parisians had ever seen. I would smile and open my heart to them. How could they fail to love and respect me?

On June 8, 1773, dressed in a shimmering white *grand habit de cour* that sparkled with gems, I rode into Paris at the side of the dauphin. The royal carriages rolled slowly through narrow city streets. Well-wishers had turned out by the thousands to pay homage to their future king and queen. Sometimes throngs halted the procession for as much as three-quarters of an hour while cannons boomed and trumpets blared and people sang at the top of their voices.

Louis-Auguste, who despised wearing court dress and appearing at public events, looked just as uncomfortable and awkward as he had the first time I saw him. He peered around shortsightedly—etiquette did not allow even the future king to wear his spectacles to see where he was going!

We heard Mass at the Cathedral of Notre-Dame and endured speeches at the university, and after several long hours we arrived at Tuileries Palace. I hoped this was the end of it, but jubilant crowds had gathered outside and clamored to see us.

Louis-Auguste groaned. "I'm tired," he complained. "I want to go to bed."

"Tired or not, we must greet our people," I told him firmly.

Grumbling, Louis-Auguste followed me as I stepped out on the balcony to acknowledge the cheers. *"Vive le dauphin!"* they shouted. *"Vive la dauphine! Vive la France!"*

With tears pouring down my cheeks, I waved and waved with first one arm, then the other. "They love us!" I cried. "Our people truly love us!"

Standing beside me, the mayor of Paris exulted. "Madame, without insulting Monsieur le Dauphin, you have before you today two hundred thousand lovers."

Three days later we returned to Versailles. Compared to Paris, the chateau seemed dreary indeed.

I was determined to enjoy myself, and Paris, obviously, was the place to do it. With good carriage horses I found

I could reach the city in little more than an hour. I began to escape there as often as possible to attend the Paris Opéra or to join my friends at masked balls and mingle with the crowds, my identity concealed. I always stayed one or two nights in a pretty little suite of rooms at Tuileries Palace and allowed myself time to stroll on the Champs Élysées, to picnic along the Seine with my friends, to see the sights, and—most important—*to be seen.* Wherever I went, the people of Paris gave me a joyful welcome, making it clear I was everything they wanted their dauphine to be.

Comte d'Artois, Louis's witty and high-spirited younger brother, often joined my party. I much preferred Artois to that fat braggart Provence. Sometimes Artois brought his new bride, but more often he allowed her to remain at home with her sister, Provence's wife. Also in our company was Louis's cousin the conceited duc de Chartres, the sweet Thérèse de Lamballe, and lots of other young, amusing people who'd become my friends. And that's where I was to welcome the New Year of 1774.

The hour of midnight had struck only minutes earlier when I found myself smiling into the dark eyes of a tall, slim young man in the uniform of a military officer. His handsome features were not entirely hidden by his half mask. We were instantly drawn to each other. The ball was at its height, the crowd large and good-humored but noisy. I had long ago lost sight of my companions, including Artois, with whom I had promised to dance, and I assumed my brother-in-law had met up with one of his mistresses. Assured that the elegant stranger had no idea who I was, I decided to spend as much time in his company as the night would allow, dancing a little but mostly talking. He spoke French with an accent I didn't recognize. The attraction I felt for him was something I had never experienced.

"Madame, you must tell me who you are," he said. The sound of his voice affected me to the tips of my fingers. I blamed that on his lilting accent.

"Antonia," I answered, using my childhood name.

"Antonia? And your family name?"

I shook my head. "Why wear a mask if I tell you my name?"

"Because you are the most beautiful woman here," he said, daring to take my hand—and I dared to allow it. "I must know who you are."

"You will learn that soon enough," I assured him. I pulled away; what if Artois or someone else in my party saw me? "And you haven't introduced yourself properly, you know."

"Forgive me, Madame Antonia—I am Count Axel von Fersen, in the service of His Majesty King Gustavus the Third of Sweden. I'm visiting friends in Paris, and in a week I leave for England. But I cannot go until I know who you are."

I smiled and shook my head. "Not yet," I said, and asked Count von Fersen about his life in Sweden. I learned that he was eighteen, just two months older than I. I replied to *his* questions with vague answers. I lived in the country, I said, but enjoyed spending time in Paris. The German accent? I was born in Vienna. My favorite pastimes? That was easy: "I love to ride horses."

The time flew by as we talked, the hours unaccounted for. At about three o'clock in the morning I realized that I had promised to meet my companions in the royal box. People were beginning to put on their cloaks and furs. I excused myself. "Please don't follow me," I told him, though I knew he was unlikely to obey such a request. And I rushed away.

As I entered the box, the crowd realized who I was and began to cheer. I saw my new admirer standing off to the side. He had lifted his mask and gazed up at me with a bemused expression. *My God, how handsome he is!* I thought. I smiled and raised my hand just slightly. He bowed, just slightly. I turned then to respond to something the duc de Chartres had said—nothing about the Swedish officer, fortunately—and when I looked again, Count von Fersen had disappeared.

I attended a great many balls that winter, and at every one I looked for a particular man in a Swedish uniform and was disappointed when I did not see him. *He's surely gone to England by now,* I thought. *I'll never see him again.*

No. 29: It is not the custom to applaud

LOUIS-AUGUSTE did not share my enthusiasm for Paris, but on one of our rare visits together that spring, I persuaded my husband to attend the Paris Opéra to hear Gluck's *Iphigénie en Aulide.* When I was a child, my music tutor was Chevalier de Gluck, who had been given the title *chevalier*—knight—by the pope. I had not seen Gluck in a long time, but when I learned that he had moved from Vienna to Paris and made a name for himself as a composer of operas, I decided to use whatever influence I had to assure his success. I became even more determined when I learned that Madame Du Barry was promoting *her* favorite composer, an Italian, at the expense of *my* favorite.

Iphigénie en Aulide was absolutely splendid, and when it

ended I sprang to my feet and applauded. Heads swiveled, and everyone in the audience stared at me.

"Why are they staring?" I whispered to the princesse de Lamballe, who was seated beside me.

"It is not the custom to applaud," she murmured. "Usually the ushers stop anyone who is bold enough to clap."

"What nonsense!" I cried, and clapped all the harder. Louis-Auguste rose slowly and joined me, smiling slightly, and so did Thérèse and the princes of the blood, until everyone in the royal box was clapping. The audience in the parterre below us also began to applaud. The performance was a great success for Chevalier de Gluck, and, I thought, a telling defeat for Madame Du Barry and her Italian composer.

No. 30: It is a grievous offense to laugh aloud when one is in mourning

King Louis had fallen ill while hunting near the Grand Trianon. He was taken to the chateau, where his physicians diagnosed smallpox. Surgeons bled him and apothecaries administered purges, but he did not improve. Concerned for our safety, the physicians would not allow us to visit him, and we depended on official reports from the chamberlain and the gossip of servants.

During the last dark days of his illness, the king sent for a priest to hear his final confession. Louis-Auguste was distraught, understanding that his grandfather's death was near. "He has not made a confession in forty years," my husband told me. "He truly fears for his immortal soul."

As Louis-Auguste and I waited in my drawing room for news, an extraordinary scene was unfolding in the king's bedchamber. After the king made his confession and his sins were forgiven, he called for Madame Du Barry. "With tears in his eyes," witnesses told us later, "the king bade a fond farewell to his favorite and told her that she must now leave her apartments at Versailles." She took refuge that very day with the duc d'Aiguillon, her friend who had replaced Choiseul as foreign minister. Madame Du Barry and her supporters may have hoped for the king's recovery and her restoration to favor, but it didn't happen that way.

A candle was placed on the sill of a window in the king's bedchamber, its wavering flame a signal to the courtiers that the king still breathed. Louis-Auguste and I joined other members of the royal family gathered in the antechamber known as the Oeil-de-Boeuf, the Ox-Eye, for its large round window at the entrance to the king's apartments. In the early afternoon of May 10, 1774, the flame flickered and died, and we heard a sound like distant thunder or rushing wind. Dozens of courtiers crowded into the Oeil-de-Boeuf as the door opened and the grim-faced grand chamberlain appeared and proclaimed in a loud voice, *"Le roi est mort. Vive le roi!"* The king is dead. Long live the king.

My husband grasped my hand. Together we knelt and prayed. "Dear God in heaven, we ask you to guide and protect us." Louis-Auguste added in an anguished sob, "We are too young to reign!"

Louis-Auguste rose unsteadily and faced the crowd

that had dropped to its knees before their new king. He gazed at them shortsightedly without saying a word. As we left the chamber together he murmured, "I wish to be known as King Louis the Sixteenth."

He had always hated being called Louis-Auguste.

Three days later the body, sealed in a lead coffin, was taken in a large carriage draped in black velvet to the Basilica of Saint-Denis, north of Paris. Nearly all the kings of France since Clovis had been interred there. The cortege that followed the coffin was starkly simple, according to the old king's wishes, and after a few solemn prayers the body of King Louis XV was laid to rest. My husband and I weren't present. We had left Versailles for our palace in Choisy, outside of Paris, thought to be safe from infection.

The death of our grandfather came as a shock to us both. My husband was not yet twenty; I was still six months from my nineteenth birthday. Neither of us had given much thought to what it meant to be the absolute ruler of France. Now I found myself waking up in the middle of the night and thinking, *I'm the queen! I'm the queen of France!* It was both exciting and alarming.

Louis—I had to remember not to call him Louis-Auguste—was surely frightened of the awesome responsibilities he faced. How could he not be? As far as I knew, his grandfather had not spent so much as an hour discussing with him his future duties. All they ever talked about within my hearing was hunting. I wondered what my husband would do now. He had never liked the public part of being dauphin—how would he endure being king? I was prepared to help him in any way I could. We were, after all, good friends.

I was delighted when one of the first things Louis did after his accession to the throne was banish Madame Du Barry to a convent. No more lavish suite at Versailles, no more chateau at Louveciennes, no more Petit Trianon as an indecently sumptuous pleasure house—and all of her jewels and expensive gowns and furniture and golden dinner services must be returned. I had triumphed over that brazen creature once and for all.

All of Europe went into deep mourning. Owing to the infectious nature of Grandfather's final illness, Louis delayed for a month the formal services in praise of his memory. I dressed in the heavy black silk gowns and crepe veils that I was expected to wear throughout the mourning period; they would eventually give way to gray and then to violet. At least during the mourning I didn't have to wear a thick plastering of rouge!

Immediately after my husband's accession, it was my duty as the new queen to receive every lady of the court, who was now bound to acknowledge me as her sovereign. For this important occasion I dressed in an elegant black gown with a few of my diamonds and called for the new friseur, Monsieur Léonard, who had just introduced a dramatic hairstyle he called the pouf. Monsieur Léonard erected a large structure on my head, beginning with a foundation of wire and gauze and horsehair, and then arranged my own hair to cover this edifice. After powdering my curls with white flour, he draped a filmy black veil over the coiffure, wound it with black mourning ribbons, and set a silvery crescent at the very top. When the friseur presented me with a mirror, I could not stop gazing at myself. I thought the pouf was the most marvelous coiffure I had ever seen.

The ladies came by the dozen, by the hundred, an endless procession of austere gowns and heavy veils, everything black down to the stockings and fans. Some of those ancient duchesses must have been saving their fusty, old-fashioned mourning gowns since the death of my husband's mother seven years earlier.

I wasn't in the least surprised at the stares my coiffure attracted, and I enjoyed watching their startled glances and the scant efforts to conceal their dismay. Disapproval darted from their eyes. It was a big relief when a few of my young friends appeared in the crowd and curtsied with wide smiles. Then it was the turn of the princesse de Lamballe. Whether it was owing to nervousness or weariness or some wildly irreverent impulse, I leaned forward and whispered a little too loudly, "Have you ever seen such a lot of dreary old crows, Thérèse? It's beyond understanding that anyone past thirty would even think of appearing at court."

Thérèse gave me a tiny shake of her head as a warning, but I couldn't manage to suppress a burst of laughter that offended a whole flock of ladies. The comtesse de Noailles turned pale and shuddered. I knew that Madame Etiquette would not forgive my latest infraction of the rules, my laughing aloud while in mourning. Within days I held in my hand her letter begging my pardon but expressing her desire to retire from my service as mistress of the household.

The years have begun to weigh heavily upon me, she wrote.

I accepted her resignation "with great reluctance," I assured her. That was a lie. I was delighted to see her go, and I'm sure she knew it. There was an obvious reason she might have chosen that moment to resign. I had appointed the princesse de Lamballe as superintendent of the household, outranking her.

Adieu, Madame Etiquette!

I was now the queen of France, and I intended to set my own rules.

Part II

Rules for the Queen
1774

No. 31: The Queen is requested to stay within her allowance

FOR MONTHS AFTER the death of Louis XV, I dressed in mourning. As queen, I chose fashionable black gowns and continued to have my friseur arrange my hair in extravagant poufs. A few of my fashion-conscious ladies had begun to adopt the style as well, and soon nearly everyone was wearing a pouf—and complaining about how hard they were to manage.

"I have to kneel on the floor of my carriage," said one lady. "There's not enough room for me and my pouf." Another showed off the little ivory-tipped sticks she used to relieve her itching scalp under the mass of hair, both real and false. In no time at all we were all carrying precious head scratchers.

By the time of Louis's twentieth birthday, in late

August, when the court traditionally moved to Compiègne for the hunting season, the official mourning period was declared at an end. I banished my black gowns, and my poufs grew ever higher and more spectacular. When Louis had an inoculation to protect himself against smallpox and urged others in the court to do the same, Monsieur Léonard created a pouf featuring a serpent coiled around an olive tree and topped with a rising sun. "To commemorate this great event," I explained to anyone who asked.

The people of Paris loved me—I went there as often as I reasonably could—but I knew that many at court resented me. They still whispered *l'Autrichienne* behind my back, putting the emphasis on *chienne:* bitch. Austria and France had not had warm relations for a very long time. My mother had hoped that the marriage of the Hapsburg archduchess to the Bourbon dauphin would change that, but so far it had not. It was common knowledge that I failed to inspire passion in my husband. He did visit my bedchamber, and he did occasionally manage to perform "the act" with clenched teeth and a complete lack of pleasure. He did it not from desire but because he knew that he must.

Still, Louis wished to please me, perhaps because he felt guilty that he did not treat me as a real wife. When I told him that I wanted to start giving parties at Versailles—lots of parties, a masked ball every Monday night, and then another less elaborate party later in the week—he didn't refuse.

The first masked ball was held just after a snowstorm at the beginning of 1775, and I declared that snowy northern lands would be the theme. Guests arrived costumed in white and smothered in their most expensive furs, declaring themselves Swedes and Norwegians for the night. (The one Swede who would have made the ball authentic was, of course, not present, nor had I heard any word of Count Axel von Fersen. But the truth was that I had thought of him often during the past year.) The ball went on until daybreak, and everyone pronounced it a triumph.

After that success, it was a challenge to introduce a new and different theme each week that would excite my guests. On one occasion I issued orders for the ladies to wear white taffeta and the men to dress in blue velvet. Another time everyone was required to dress in the manner of the sixteenth century; at the next ball they were told to wear Tyrolean attire. Oh, it was great fun! I even succeeded in convincing my husband to don a costume and attend some of my parties.

The only one who made any objection to the extravagant balls was the steward in charge of the budget. He was a short man with a potbelly, and he was somewhat embarrassed by his stature, which may have caused his nervous stammer. "M-m-m-madame," he began, shuffling a stack of papers, "I m-m-must point out to you that in one month you have spent more than is in the king's budget for an entire year of balls. P-p-perhaps Your Majesty wishes to c-c-curtail her expenses for entertainment in future?"

"Non, monsieur," I replied. "I have no such wish. The king has given permission for these entertainments, and the expenses involved are not my concern." I dismissed him with a wave.

Before the beginning of Lent and the temporary end to entertainments until after Easter, I proposed a ball with a Renaissance theme. Louis agreed to dress in trunk hose and a jerkin stitched all over with jewels (unfortunately, the trunk hose were not at all flattering to my husband's rotund figure). But it was my costume that brought gasps from everyone: a stomacher and girdle that glittered with diamonds, a white skirt trimmed with silver stars and gold fringe, and a white-plumed hat studded with four large diamonds and a string of precious gems. It was spectacular!

And so, complained the steward, was the bill. This time he sent a servant to deliver the bundle of receipts for my gowns to my mistress of the wardrobe, and she passed along the steward's note: *The Queen is requested to stay within her allowance.*

I paid no attention to the steward's complaints. King Louis XV had showered his vulgar mistress with a vast fortune in jewels and gold plate and furniture. Why then should King Louis XVI do any less for his lawful wedded wife and queen? Surely, I deserved it!

No. 32: By following such a path, you are hurtling toward an abyss

THE CORONATION of King Louis XVI would take place in mid-June, and nearly everything about the great event produced an argument. Should it be held in Paris or in the Cathedral of Rheims, two days' journey to the northeast, where all the kings of France had been crowned? Was I to be crowned queen or was I merely to accompany my husband as his consort? Monsieur Turgot, controller general of finance, maintained that the expense of a double coronation would be too great.

I had disliked Turgot on sight. Money, money, money—that was all the controller general talked about, constantly harping that the country was in dire financial straits, recent harvests had been poor, the peasants were complaining, people were hungry, royal expenditures had to be trimmed. *What a nuisance,* I thought. King Louis XV hadn't spared any expense. Why should the new king worry about royal expenditures? Why should *I?*

Turgot's appointment to the important post of controller general was not the only one my husband made without consulting me. He named the ancient comte de Maurepas as his closest personal advisor. When Louis moved into the king's apartments, as was expected, Maurepas immediately claimed the rooms below, rooms that had once belonged to Madame Du Barry and were connected to the king's apartments by a secret stairway.

"Maurepas, of all people!" I remarked to Louis when I found out. "The man despises me! He's the uncle of the contemptible Aiguillon, who, you know as well as I, is one of Madame Du Barry's 'greatest friends.'" I was hinting that Aiguillon was one of her lovers, of which she had several. "And he's also a close friend of the loathsome La Vauguyon."

La Vauguyon, Louis's former tutor, whom we'd caught spying on us from behind a door, had always disliked me, mostly because I was Austrian. I understood perfectly that La Vauguyon feared I would have too much influence over the new king. Maurepas no doubt agreed.

Louis looked uncomfortable. "Maurepas was Tante Adélaïde's suggestion," he muttered. "She persuaded me that he's best suited."

I stared at Louis. I was not easily roused to anger, and in fact this was the first time I had become truly angry with my husband. Why would he appoint someone to such an important position who was so obviously opposed to anything and anyone Austrian, especially me? Why would Adélaïde suggest such a person? I managed to conceal just how furious I was and said calmly, "Perhaps in the future, monsieur, you and I might discuss some of your appointments."

It was Louis's turn to stare. "I had not considered that as a possibility, madame."

Not a possibility? I could imagine very well with whom it *was* a possibility to discuss appointments: Mesdames Tantes. I turned on my heel and stalked out of the king's chamber without another word.

When I learned that the king's personal advisor and the controller general had deemed a double coronation unnecessary and that Louis had not disagreed, I pretended not to care. But I vowed to accompany my husband to his coronation dressed in a gown never equaled in magnificence. The whole world would have to acknowledge that I, Marie-Antoinette, was worthy to be queen of France.

I summoned Rose Bertin, a young couturière who had become all the rage among the most fashionable ladies in Paris. Madame Bertin had been presented to me by the duchesse de Chartres, unhappy wife of Louis's cousin. Madame Bertin's shop near the Paris Opéra specialized in the most outrageously luxurious fashions. I often visited her shop when I was in Paris, but it was more convenient to have her come to Versailles when I needed something truly brilliant.

Madame Bertin created a *grand habit de cour* of lustrous ivory silk as thick and smooth as cream, embroidered all over with gold thread in fanciful designs, with sapphires the exact color of my eyes scattered like stars in the heavens. It was a dazzling work of art that owed nothing to tradition but everything to a modern fashion sense. "Gorgeous," I said. "Perfect."

The gown was so heavy that Madame Bertin insisted it be carried to Rheims on its own special litter. While the practicality of this was being debated, my mother learned about my fabulous gown from Count Mercy d'Argenteau, who seemed to derive a peculiar pleasure in reporting to Mama on my little extravagances. Only nine days before the coronation I received her stern reproof. My breathtaking fashions, beginning with my spectacular poufs—which, I admit, did sometimes rise as much as three feet above my brow—were a terrible mistake.

By following such a path, she wrote (and I could almost hear the angry scratching of her pen), *you are hurtling toward an abyss.*

I chose to ignore her dire warning, for I was now dealing with a threat that had nothing to do with fashion: my new sister-in-law, the comtesse d'Artois, was pregnant. I had long ago stopped worrying about the other sister-in-law producing an heir before I did. Despite his boasts, the comte de Provence was as ineffectual in bed as my own husband. But Artois and his wife, Madame Artois, who was nearly as homely as her sister, Madame Provence, were a completely different matter. If Madame Artois produced a son and I did not, that boy could someday become the dauphin and, in time, the next king. I had failed to provide the heir to the throne, and my reputation would surely suffer from that—and not from my gowns and coiffures.

Early in June our procession set out for Rheims. Members of the royal entourage turned out for the coronation in costumes made of cloth of silver and cloth of gold trimmed with ermine, but they merely provided a backdrop for my spectacular gown, which gleamed in the candlelight, and my sky-high pouf topped with plumes of white ostrich feathers.

The ceremony was everything one could desire. When the gold crown studded with huge precious stones was lowered over the head of my kneeling husband and placed on his brow, I felt so moved by the solemnity of the moment that I could not hold back my tears. I knew that even if I lived to be a hundred years old, I would never forget this day. But as King Louis XVI rose to acknowledge the exuberant applause of the crowd, I was close enough to hear him complain, "This crown is too heavy. It's hurting me!"

The celebrations continued for days, and for each event I wore an elaborate new gown. I wouldn't have minded if the balls and feasts had lasted even longer. I dreaded the return to Versailles, the birth of Madame Artois's baby, and my entrapment in the suffocating web of court etiquette that I knew would be difficult to change. All of this was on my mind during the long journey back.

Droves of country people turned out along our route to stare at our glittering procession, to cheer their king and queen, and to hold up their little children who could someday say they had once seen their sovereigns.

"It should be plain to anyone that the lives of the poor are so hard we are completely unable to imagine their suffering," I said to the comtesse de Provence, who was riding in my carriage. "Yet they treat us as well as they can, despite their own misfortune."

"Most of them have surely brought their suffering on themselves," sniffed the countess. "Don't you agree, madame, that God intends them to be poor and to labor for their bread?"

"If God intends the poor to be poor, then surely He also obliges us to work as hard as we can for their happiness," I cried.

The homely countess regarded me pityingly. "Such a tenderhearted person you are, madame!"

"My husband feels as I do," I told her sharply. And then I felt rather tenderhearted toward her as well, because both of us now had to endure the birth of a royal child not our own.

What a humiliation it was for me to be present through the hours of the comtesse d'Artois's labor and delivery! Etiquette required my attendance at the accouchement of a royal princess, and so I was there when the little bundle made its entry into the world and was declared a male. "My God, how happy I am!" rejoiced Madame Artois, and I forced myself to step forward to embrace her, to heartily congratulate my brother-in-law, and to murmur admiring words over the tiny boy, named Louis-Antoine by his parents, and by the king's order given the title duc d'Angoulême.

Summoning all of my dignity and showing nothing of how I felt, I hurried back to my apartments. I flung myself on my bed and cried until I was left with only the bitter taste of deep private disappointment and public mortification. I couldn't bear the way the courtiers looked at me and laughed behind my back and Louis's. They speculated when I might take a lover, if I hadn't already, and who it was likely to be, and, once that vital fact was known, how this would give certain factions in the court power over me. But most of all I could not bear the fact that I did not have a child.

And then I had to gather my strength to celebrate the marriage of Louis's sister Clothilde—referred to as Gros-Madame because she had grown so fat—to Charles Emmanuel IV of Sardinia, brother of Madame Artois and Madame Provence. I was surrounded by one big happy, and homely, family.

Louis said nothing about the birth of little Louis-Antoine, nor did he wish to discuss "our problem"—*his* problem, really, for his physician had again suggested a simple but painful operation on his most private area. The doctor claimed the surgery would improve the possibility of my becoming pregnant. But when my husband saw the sharp instruments the physician intended to use, he fainted dead away. The subject had not been mentioned since.

I behaved solicitously toward Madame Artois, though I did think she was more than a bit stupid, and I found ways to distract myself from a situation I could not change. I had already given up horseback riding, which I had taken up in the vain hope that my husband might yet kindle some passion for me and make me pregnant, and I replaced that enthusiasm with a keenness for gambling and for spending enormous sums of money on gowns, shoes, and monumental poufs.

Gowns were my weakness, there is no denying that. Each season—summer, winter, spring, and fall—I ordered a new wardrobe, a dozen of each kind of *grand habit de cour* and *robe à la française* for the formal occasions and balls, and lace-trimmed petticoats for my little supper parties in addition to all the dresses needed for visiting and receiving guests. Henriette Campan, the first lady of the bedchamber, was in charge of a dozen women who cared for my gowns.

Madame Campan, daughter-in-law of my librarian, had been a reader to Mesdames Tantes. Now she had come to serve me. A few years older than I was, she became a trusted confidante. Every morning soon after I awoke, Madame Campan appeared at my bedside with my wardrobe book and a pincushion. Each page showed a drawing of a gown with a swatch of fabric and tiny samples of the lace and other trimmings. When I was the dauphine, the decision was made for me. But as queen, my first duty of the day was to mark with a pinprick the gowns I wanted to wear. The book was a guide for an army of women to gather up the gowns and, at the proper time, deliver the costumes. And so my day began: thinking about clothes and not, as my mother had predicted so gloomily, imagining that I was hurtling toward an abyss.

No. 33: The work must be completed quickly

As Louis neared his twenty-first birthday, he brought me a gift, an intricately wrought golden key studded with hundreds of tiny diamonds.

"It's the key to the Petit Trianon," he explained. "I know that you have long wanted a little country retreat of your own. It's now yours. These beautiful houses have always been the pleasure palaces of the king's favorites." He smiled shyly. "And you, madame, have always been and shall always be the favorite of this king. You adore flowers, and with this key I give you a whole bouquet." He rose, bowed, and left my chamber before I could even thank him properly.

The Petit Trianon! I wanted to visit it at once, that very hour. I had not passed by the lovely little chateau since that brightly cold afternoon with Thérèse de Lamballe when the driver of our sleigh had informed us that it was the pleasure palace of Madame Du Barry. I had not wanted then to be near anything belonging to that horrid creature. But now Du Barry was shut up in a convent, and the Petit Trianon was mine!

Thérèse was busy overseeing the tiresome details of the annual move to Compiègne. Impatient, I called for one of my new friends instead, Comtesse Yolande de Polignac.

Yolande was cheerfully ready to go anywhere I suggested, and we set off in a calèche. I was trembling as I fit the ornate key into a lock and the door swung open. The concierge, surprised to see us, ushered us into the entry hall on the ground floor; from there, a graceful stairway rose to the main floor.

Madame Polignac shared my excitement. We crept up the stairs, giddy as children. Sunlight poured through the tall windows. Doors opened to a receiving room and a small dining room with a larger dining room beyond. We explored the *salon de compagnie,* for entertaining guests. On the top floor we found several suites of bedrooms, each with a view of the carefully cultivated gardens. I ran from room to room, delighted with each new discovery. Yolande helped me throw open the windows to let in fresh autumn breezes. Compared to the immensity and somewhat shabby grandeur of the chateau of Versailles, this was a precious jewel box. It was the perfect place to bring my friends, far enough from the suffocating layers of court etiquette to be free from prying, spying eyes.

"It's beautiful." Yolande sighed rapturously at almost every turn.

"And I can't wait to start changing everything!" I declared.

I would begin with the monograms on the wrought-iron railing of the stairway. It must be my monogram—*MA*—not the king's.

The furnishings, though sumptuous, were definitely not to my taste. Huge paintings in the grand dining room depicted scenes of fishing, hunting, and harvesting grains and grapes, and all of them featured a great many nude bosoms and buttocks. They might have suited Madame Du Barry, and probably Grandfather King as well, but they didn't suit me. They would have to go. And I imagined gardens in the English style, charmingly wild and uncultivated, very free and romantic, not the rigidly geometric gardens that now surrounded the chateau.

The next day I sent for the royal architect Richard Mique—a distinguished-looking man with a broad forehead and fine, aristocratic features—and described the changes I wanted. First, he was to get rid of the old king's botanical gardens, row upon row of vegetables and flowers—more than four thousand specimens.

"I want them replaced with informal arrangements of flowering bushes and trees, with little pavilions and rocks and pools to delight the eye no matter which way one looks," I told Monsieur Mique. "Perhaps even a mysterious grotto with a waterfall. Everything must be as unlike Versailles as possible. How soon can this be accomplished?" I asked when I had finished.

"In perhaps two to three years, Your Majesty," he replied.

"Two to three years!" I cried. "That's ridiculous! Can't you dig up the old gardens this winter, plant the new ones in the spring, and have everything blooming by next summer?"

Monsieur Mique shook his head. "Even at the order of the queen of France, the plants do not grow any faster," he said with a faint smile. "Patience is required, madame."

"I am not a gardener," I told him firmly. "I am the queen, and I merely ask that my orders be carried out. The work must be completed quickly."

"Of course, Your Majesty. As quickly as possible." He bowed and left.

There was no point in fuming. I would work on the interior in the meantime. I had the bosom-and-buttocks paintings taken down and wrote to Mama, asking her to send me the painting of my brothers and me dancing at Joseph's wedding. I'd always loved that picture. It reminded me of my family and my Viennese childhood.

I wanted everything at the Petit Trianon to be very simple. The carved panels of the walls would be finished in pale green. Chair and table legs would be delicately carved, as though made of bundles of reeds, and painted white—no more gilding—and the upholstery would be flowery silk or embroidered linen. I wanted flowers everywhere, and candles in glass lanterns so that the windows could be left open on summer days without breezes blowing out the flames. I wanted mirrors in my boudoir that could be raised like shutters over the windows for privacy, and I hired an engineer to figure out how to do that. I had so many ideas, and—it's true—I was impatient to have it all done at once. I never gave a thought to the cost.

No. 34: Behave, or you shall be sent back

I NOW SPENT MOST of my time thinking about what I wanted done to transform Petit Trianon. I talked and Yolande listened, sometimes adding her own suggestions. We had become much closer friends, partly because I had grown fond of her young son and daughter and she understood how deeply I yearned for children of my own. I confided to her my newfound desire to take in one of the servants' children and to bring it up myself and care for it as though it were my own. Yolande said that this might indeed be possible, if a proper child could be found and the parents were agreeable.

But then God blessed me in an amazing way. One day in late autumn Yolande and I had gone out for a drive through a nearby village when a little boy ran eagerly into the road to stare at my carriage. He fell down and was nearly run over. The coachman immediately stopped the carriage, and the postilion gathered up the child and set him on his feet. The boy commenced howling.

I leaped from the carriage, crying, "Oh, dear God, is he hurt? Let me see to him!"

The postilion assured me that the child was uninjured. "He cries more in fright than in pain," he said. An old woman in a mobcap rushed from a nearby cottage and, saying she was the boy's grandmother, reached out to take him. But I was already kneeling beside the little one and covering his dirty face with kisses. He was a sturdy fellow, fair-haired and blue-eyed and, despite the grime, quite handsome.

"Oh, let this child be mine!" I cried. "I believe with all my heart that God has sent him to console me for having none of my own. Has he a mother?"

The old dame twisted her apron, and tears dribbled down her weathered cheeks. "No, madame, my daughter was taken from us last winter, and now I have five small children to care for."

"Then let me take this one!" I implored. "With your consent I'll provide for the others as well."

The woman dropped to her knees, clasping her hands in gratitude. "Madame, you are most generous to us, but our Jacques-Armand is not a well-behaved boy. I pray that he will stay with you!" The child had thrown his arms around his grandmother's neck and clung to her, refusing to let go.

"He will get used to me, I'm sure," I said.

I instructed the postilion to detach the boy from his grandmother and hand him to me, and then to drive on as quickly as possible. The boy screamed and kicked like a wild animal, so violently that I was forced to give him over to Yolande, who had experience with her own children.

"Take us back to the chateau with all speed!" I ordered the coachman, and we made a dash for Versailles while the child shrieked as though he were being murdered.

"What do you think the king will say?" Yolande called out above the noise.

"I'm sure he'll come to love him too," I said, though I wasn't entirely certain about that.

Our arrival in my apartments at the chateau was met with undisguised astonishment as I led in the somewhat more docile child, clad in his rustic costume of red smock, wooden sabots, and knitted cap. But his calm was only momentary, and he started screaming again, calling out for his brothers and sisters. My attempts to soothe him were futile. "Behave, or you shall be sent away!" I warned him, to no avail.

Finally, exhausted by the effort, I handed him over to one of my servants, Mistress Claire, a motherly woman who spoke to him in the accents of his *grand-mère* and dragged him away, ignoring his protests. I could hear his heart-rending cries even after the doors closed behind him.

"What are you going to do now, madame?" Yolande asked, her eyebrows raised.

"Lie down and rest," I said.

Two days later Mistress Claire brought him back to my apartments. Jacques-Armand seemed a different child. He had been bathed; his fine light hair had been cut; and he was dressed in a white lace-trimmed silk suit, a rose-colored sash, leather slippers, and a cap adorned with feathers.

"How beautiful you look, my child!" I exclaimed, charmed by his appearance and his sweet demeanor. He grinned and made a polite little bow. I cannot guess how Mistress Claire had accomplished this transformation.

This adorable little boy was so enchanting that I gave orders to have him brought to me each morning at nine o'clock, unless I was still asleep or had stayed for the night in Paris. We breakfasted together—he was especially fond of hot chocolate—and then he went off to his lessons, where, his tutor told me, he was quick to learn. After a few agreeable days I felt the time had come to present him to the king. Knowing the speed with which any sort of rumor made its way around the palace, I was sure Louis had already heard about my little Jacques-Armand.

The child delighted me and pleased my husband by

making a perfect bow and speaking to him beautifully. The king responded by inviting the boy to join us for the *grand couvert.* I had no idea if Mistress Claire had had time to teach him any sort of proper table etiquette, but he did well enough and was, naturally, the center of all eyes. And I was happy to have him in my life, for I had just learned that my sister-in-law the comtesse d'Artois was pregnant again.

No. 35: No serious discussions are permitted here

THE PETIT TRIANON had to be closed during the harshest months of winter, but when it was opened again, in the spring, work was already in progress on the gardens, and new furniture was in place. I began to invite my friends to visit my little pleasure palace, explaining that it was entirely different from the chateau and that court etiquette could be suspended. Life there was to be informal. In this place, I and no one else would make the rules.

"Here, I am myself," I told my friends. "When I enter the room, I want every one of you to go on doing whatever it is you've been doing—reading, or playing cards or backgammon, or making music, or simply talking. You are absolutely forbidden to rise to greet me."

Guests were by my invitation only—not at all like the

chateau, where people came and went as they pleased, depending on their rank and their rights of entry. Among those *not* invited were the old ladies who made such a fuss over who was to hand me my chemise or a glass of water. I wasn't surprised that a lot of the members of the court felt insulted by this. I didn't care.

Even my husband abided by my rules. I always invited Louis to my little dinners and musical evenings, and he often came—when he wasn't engaged with his locks and his clocks and his studies of geography or whatever it was he preferred doing. He didn't stay long, always leaving by eleven (I once caught Artois moving the hands of the clock forward to fool Louis into leaving earlier).

Then one hot July evening so still that not a candle flame flickered and every lady's fan fluttered at top speed, Louis surprised us all.

We were in the small dining room, nibbling at a cold collation of meats and fruits. The others were drinking champagne, though I drank only lemonade, as usual, when the king took the liberty of removing his coat and, in his shirtsleeves, rose and proposed a toast. "Let us drink to the British colonies in America," he said. "They have declared their independence from England."

"You want to toast colonies who are breaking with their king?" Provence asked, his lip curled in disdain. "Doesn't it make more sense to deplore what they're doing? That's a revolution! I daresay your opinion would be otherwise if such a thing happened in France!"

"Au contraire!" said Artois. "Serves England right! It will be pleasant to watch our old enemy squirm a little."

"England may not be the only one to squirm," drawled their cousin the duc de Chartres, waving a languorous hand. His eyelids drooped, giving him the look of a sleepy lizard. "If you were paying attention, you'd see that the mood could turn ugly here. The people complain about the scarcity of bread. They say there's no flour. They say their children are hungry."

My husband disliked discussing politics, and he surely regretted bringing up the subject. "No serious discussions are permitted here!" he said in a loud voice, and he turned to me. "Is that not so, madame?"

"Indeed it is!" I cried merrily. "I beg all of you to join me in the *salon de compagnie.* Perhaps we can persuade Madame Provence to sing for us."

The woman had a voice like a crow, though she flattered herself that she sounded like a nightingale. But we all left the dining room, and the subject of revolution was dropped.

As the months passed, no more was said within my hearing about the British colonies' desire for independence. Then in December of 1776, the ambassador from America arrived at Versailles. King Louis and I welcomed Benjamin Franklin, the most plainly dressed—and plainspoken—ambassador I'd ever met. No wig, no powdered hair, no elaborate court dress, no high-heeled shoes, no ceremonial sword, no royal title. And he wore spectacles, even to official functions, which shocked everyone. Though lowborn—he had been a printer by trade, I believe—Monsieur Franklin was no rustic but well-read and highly intelligent.

My husband spoke English well and enjoyed the company of this elderly gentleman. "We're interested in many of the same things," Louis told me. "He's an inventor, and he has expressed much admiration for my clocks and locks."

As our American visitor's French improved, I found him amiable and witty. When he learned of my interest in music, he offered to teach me to play the glass armonica, one of his several inventions. With his great charm Franklin soon persuaded the king and many of the court ministers to support the American cause. Among the strongest sympathizers was Louis's new foreign minister, the comte de Vergennes, who saw the revolt against England as good for France. Monsieur Franklin soon settled in a house on the outskirts of Paris. We would be seeing more of the new ambassador and hearing more of this American Revolution.

No. 36: You must stop your imprudent spending

In the early months of 1777 we prepared to receive another important visitor: my brother Emperor Joseph II. I looked forward to seeing him, but I wondered if my mother was sending him to scold me. Lately I had taken to ignoring Mama's lectures. Then when Joseph began to send me admonishing messages, I became more determined than ever to do things my own way. I was the queen of France, and I did not need to listen to my mother criticize me at every turn.

Nevertheless, I was pleased that my brother was coming. Joseph had always been fond of me, as I was of him, and he was arriving just at the time I most needed his support. The comtesse d'Artois was expecting her second child, and I could scarcely remember the last time my husband had visited my bed, even to have his back scratched.

I wondered what Joseph would have to say about the rules of etiquette at Versailles. When I left Vienna, he had been trying to simplify the customs in our Austrian court. He detested the wide panniers the women loved to wear under their skirts and had forbidden such extremes. After seven years I scarcely thought about the morning *lever* and evening *coucher* and the tedious daily toilette. But there was no telling how he would react to our rules, which I was powerless to change. The French courtiers believed all Germans were barbarians, and they resented what they called my Austrian heart. I prayed that Joseph wouldn't make matters worse.

Count Mercy d'Argenteau planned to greet Emperor Joseph in Paris and escort him with suitable pomp and ceremony to Versailles. But the emperor chose to travel incognito under the name Count Falkenstein and arrived in Paris without an escort. It was raining hard, and the "count" was riding in an open carriage. The ambassador was indisposed and couldn't come to meet him. None of this seemed to bother my brother. He traveled on to Versailles and refused to stay at the chateau, insisting on taking a room at an ordinary inn in the village. The next morning he was up and out sightseeing before I had even opened my eyes.

Joseph appeared at the chateau in time for my toilette, and his rank gave him right of entry. I soon wished he had delayed his arrival for another hour or two—maybe until after the *grand couvert.* I had long forgotten my shock the first time the comtesse de Noailles had advanced on me with her rouge pot and painted big red circles on my cheeks. Now I relived my own shock in my brother's look of total disgust.

"Can't you manage to smear on a little more?" he bugled, startling the first lady of the bedchamber. "Surely you can get some more under her eyes, and why not paint right over her nose? Here, madame, give me the rouge pot and let me help you try!" Madame Campan dropped her brush and fled.

My brother mocked my pouf and made clear his disdain for some of my friends. "Are they all as silly and empty-headed as the princesse de Lamballe?"

"She's highly intelligent!" I protested, rushing to the defense of my superintendent of the household, though I too had begun to find her a little tiring. My affections had cooled toward Thérèse and now centered mostly on Madame Polignac, who was more beautiful and certainly much wittier, but I still had to put up with Thérèse de Lamballe, who had begun to claim she was so delicate, even the scent of a bunch of violets caused her to swoon. Unfortunately, by tradition, once appointed to the post, the superintendent could not be removed. Thérèse drifted like a ghost through the chambers and corridors of Versailles.

"And what about that fop Artois?" Joseph demanded. "He seems inordinately fond of you, my dear. No scandal there, I hope?"

I shrugged. "One does not choose one's in-laws," I pointed out. "Though I admit my brother-in-law does have a great fondness for lace and ribbon on his clothes."

"And perfume," Joseph added with a grimace.

"He also has high spirits and a wonderful wit," I pointed out. "Artois amuses me and makes me laugh. But no, I'm not involved with him in any way. He has mistresses in every quarter of Paris and several more in the countryside, I'm told. And his wife is about to produce another child."

Joseph's rough-edged remarks and crude humor sometimes brought me to the brink of tears, but I sensed that he loved me deeply. For six weeks he stayed with us, and he had plenty of opportunity to see what my life was like. We often dined alone at the Petit Trianon, and the time I spent with my brother meant a great deal to me. I was his little sister—he was fifteen years older—and sometimes he played the father role, sometimes the teasing brother.

It didn't take him long to target those items that had prompted our mother to write me scolding letters. I suppose Count Mercy had told her about the gambling parties that had become one of my main diversions. I loved the excitement of risking a large amount of money and the triumph of winning, especially at the expense of someone like Artois. But my losses were often large—*very* large—and I had to ask my husband for money to cover them.

"What can you be thinking, dear sister?" Joseph asked. "You must stop this imprudent spending. It's well known that France is in deep financial trouble, and yet you throw *livres* around as if they had no more value than feathers from a pillow."

"And what else would you have me do, dear brother?" I replied. "My husband doesn't want me to be involved in governing. I have no real duties, except making the required formal court appearances. I've tried to do away with the most ridiculous rules of court etiquette, which are as unyielding as marble. So far I've been completely unsuccessful, though I've not given up."

I grew more heated as I tried to describe my empty life. "Besides," I insisted, "if I spent less on gowns and all the rest of it, at least two hundred places of business that cater to the trade would be forced to shut their doors."

The rain that had fallen steadily through the first weeks of my brother's visit gave way at last to gentle May sunshine. I took pleasure in showing him around the gardens at Petit Trianon, by then in various stages of disruption and rebuilding. He seemed greatly interested in my plans and ideas, which were slowly—much too slowly, I complained—coming into existence. I was eager to demonstrate for him the *jeu de bague,* a merry-go-round, in my newly finished Chinese garden and persuaded him to sit in one of the seats carved in the shape of a dragon.

"Another of your expensive notions, I suppose?" Joseph asked wryly.

Ignoring his question, I sat down beside him. "Shall I call for a servant to turn the crank?" I asked. There was a mechanism in the pit beneath the *jeu de bague* that set it in motion.

"No, please don't, Antoine. We need to have a talk about another serious matter, and I don't want to be going in circles when we do." He looked hard at me, and I forced myself to meet his gaze directly. "I have come here to discuss two important subjects. You know that Count Mercy keeps the empress well informed—"

"Too well informed," I interrupted sourly.

"Perhaps so, from your point of view. But the ambassador is loyal to the empress, and that's his responsibility. He's deeply concerned about your excessive spending. It's receiving a great deal of criticism."

"We've already discussed that," I snapped. "And I believe I've explained myself."

Exasperated, Joseph lifted his hands and let them fall again into his lap. "Then you will have no objection if I continue to the second matter of importance?"

"Please do," I said. I could guess what was coming.

"Why have you not yet provided France with an heir to the throne?"

There followed a conversation—Joseph's blunt questions, my blushing answers—about my marital relations with Louis. My brother stared at me, shaking his head in disbelief. "What sort of husband do you have here?" he demanded. "Neither one of you seems to have the least idea of what is expected of you!" When I said nothing, nervously twisting the rings on my fingers, he added, "I shall speak to him myself."

I have no idea what my brother said to Louis later in the day, but I gather that he didn't mince words. Apparently what we had been doing on my husband's brief and infrequent visits to my bed were not sufficient to result in a pregnancy. Surgery was not necessary, Joseph assured us.

"You know your duty! Just do it!" the emperor ordered, and soon after issuing that command to us both, Joseph left Versailles.

My brother's frankness shocked my husband and me. Nevertheless, a few nights later Louis came to my bedchamber after my *coucher.* My gown and stays had been removed, and I wore only my sleeping shift. He dropped awkwardly to his knees and took my hand in both of his.

"My dear Antoinette," he said, "I most humbly apologize to you for my failure to be a proper husband. I ask your forgiveness, and here, on my knees before you, I do promise from this day forward to do all that's required of me, out of my love for you and for France."

Deeply moved, I knelt beside him. "Dear Louis," I

said, "I have only the warmest affection for you in my heart, a love that increases daily."

He reached out tentatively and began to caress me. *Did Joseph tell him to do this?* I wondered as my body responded to his tender touch and his did to mine. Then—just as Madame Lulu had promised long, long ago—our two beloved bodies became one, at last!

No. 37: Pursue a simple life

JOSEPH HAD LEFT a detailed list of exactly how I was supposed to improve my life.

There are to be no more masked balls in Paris, no long nights of gambling, he wrote. *You must rein in your spending, pay more attention to your husband, and pursue a simple life at the Petit Trianon, with just two or three of your most honorable ladies for companionship.*

My brother also prescribed at least an hour and a half daily of serious reading. I'd told him that I had been earnestly studying Hume's *History of England,* leaving out the fact that I had been engaged in this earnest study for more than four years and was not even halfway through the book.

I did not tell him I was caught up in *Julie,* a novel by the writer and philosopher Jean-Jacques Rousseau. In the story, the daughter of a nobleman falls in love with her tutor, Saint-Preux. Naturally, Julie's father opposes the marriage. When her lover goes off on a ten-year voyage around the world, Julie yields to her father's wishes and marries Wolmar, an older man by whom she has two children, and tries to forget Saint-Preux. She has done the virtuous thing, but she is sunk in profound discontent. Saint-Preux returns, becomes a tutor to Julie's children, and prepares to marry Julie's best friend, Claire. But Julie still loves Saint-Preux; her virtue has not saved her from her deep love for him. When she falls ill and is about to die, she welcomes death in the hope that she will someday be united with her lover in heaven.

All my ladies were reading the novel, weeping over the sad fate of the characters and discussing what Julie should have done differently. No one thought she should have disobeyed her father's wishes and married the penniless Saint-Preux, but several felt she should have simply become his mistress. Perhaps the deceived husband could have been persuaded to have an affair with Claire. We could not agree on what was better: to have the lover come back and be a tiny part of Julie's life, or to have him never come back at all.

"What do *you* think, Madame Thérèse?" Yolande de Polignac asked the princess, whose reputation for purity was spotless. If Thérèse had had a lover since her husband's death, she'd guarded the secret well.

"Julie did the only possible thing," Thérèse replied

primly. "Virtue is seldom rewarded in our earthly life. I'm sure her reward will come to her in heaven."

"And she and Saint-Preux will be lovers in eternity?" Yolande pressed.

"I didn't say that," the princess protested, her pale skin showing a faint blush. "A heavenly reward doesn't necessarily mean a lover."

Yolande glanced at me and winked. "And you, Madame Antoinette? Do you agree?"

"I feel a little sorry for Wolmar," I said. Secretly, though, I hoped Julie and Saint-Preux would be eternal lovers and that maybe poor old Wolmar would find his reward too.

After Joseph left, I truly did try to follow his guide. But life once again became unbearably dull. I stopped the required reading completely—Hume stayed on the shelf. My next step away from my brother's rules was to allow myself to play at faro, my favorite gambling game, but only in my own apartments. *Nothing could be wrong with that,* I reasoned. But only three months after my brother's departure I was again deeply involved in entire nights of gambling that got completely out of hand. I always lost more than I won—a *lot* more. I thought things might be kept under better control if I played in the apartments of my friend Princesse Marie-Louise de Guéméné, but that proved to be no solution.

Then there were the diamond earrings I bought although I had no money left in my allowance to pay for them. I had to ask my husband to advance me the additional funds.

I also broke Joseph's rule of having only simple entertainments at the Petit Trianon. To celebrate the completion of a charming little pavilion built on an island in the middle of a small artificial lake and named the Temple of Love, I ordered a mock village square to be created, surrounded by quaint little booths where food would be served. Wearing a costume with a pretty ruffled apron designed by my couturière Rose Bertin, I played the part of a maid and poured lemonade for my guests. Inspired by one of my favorite artists, Watteau, known for his scenes of people enjoying themselves outdoors, I arranged for more than two thousand colored lanterns to be placed throughout the gardens and lit as darkness fell while a band played music for dancing. The evening was pronounced delightful by those invited to attend and a disgraceful waste of money by those who were not.

All of this was duly reported to my brother by Count Mercy d'Argenteau. The results were predictable. Joseph began to bully me. In short order I received six letters from him, each harsher than the last, all lecturing me on the evils of gambling and unwarranted extravagance. I didn't even bother to answer his letters. I tore them up and threw them into the fire.

My brother should have known that bullying had

never been the way to persuade me to change my behavior. The one thing that I felt sure would put an end to my frivolous ways was giving birth to a child. I explained tearfully to Count Mercy, "Do you think for a moment I would have fallen into such dissipation if a gracious God had granted me my most ardent desire, to become a mother? Meanwhile the comtesse d'Artois already imagines her son on the throne of France!"

If I couldn't get pregnant, then I simply wanted to enjoy myself. And that always seemed to involve spending lots and lots of money.

No. 38: Allow nothing to go wrong

SPRING WAS MAKING its first tentative appearance when we learned that our friend from America, Monsieur Benjamin Franklin, was coming back to Versailles. In February of 1778, Louis had signed a treaty pledging France's help to the American colonies in gaining their independence from England. Now, a month later, the king and I prepared an official reception at court for Ambassador Franklin. Our previous meetings with him had been private and informal, but a large crowd had gathered for this reception—diplomats, princes and princesses of the blood, courtiers of all ranks, and anyone else who wanted to attend in full court apparel.

The American arrived dressed in what must have been the same brown wool suit and low-heeled shoes he'd worn when he visited us months earlier, and still without a wig or powder in his hair. Every Frenchman present that chilly spring day tripped along in high-heeled shoes carrying a gleaming ceremonial sword on his belt. Franklin wore his steel-framed spectacles. To the roll of drums, the ambassador climbed the grand staircase of the chateau in the company of the foreign minister, Comte de Vergennes. The French guards presented arms, and both doors of the king's apartments swung open wide—an unusual honor, for normally only one door was opened, except for princes of the blood, who were entitled to two. The sergeant major proclaimed in a loud voice, "The ambassador of the Thirteen United States!"

Once the formal greetings and polite exchanges were done, Vergennes escorted the American to his palace for a sumptuous dinner and afterward brought him to my apartments. We were playing baccarat. I expressed my pleasure at seeing the ambassador and invited him to join the card game. He acknowledged my greetings but declined to play.

"Madame, I look forward to seeing more of you in the months to come, now that our countries are bound by such a happy allegiance," he said in decent French, and bowed and kissed my hand. I thought him a thoroughly agreeable gentleman, despite his friendship with testy old Vergennes.

Later that night at an hour when Louis was usually in bed and asleep, my husband came to my bedchamber. I was afraid he'd heard about my sizable losses at cards and intended to rebuke me, but he was in an excellent mood and wanted to talk about our interesting American friend.

"A true philosopher," Louis said. "A genius. And very persuasive."

We talked until the candles burned down. For some reason—I don't know what caused it—my husband, who was usually motivated more by duty than by passion, took me in his arms and demonstrated his love for me in surprising new ways. He was twenty-two, and I took this as a sign that he was awakening to the pleasures of love.

Général Krottendorf had not made his monthly appearance by the end of April. Sometimes the *général* arrived a little early or a little late, but never *this* late. For nearly eight years I had been forced to send the same disappointing report in letter after letter to my mother. But since my brother's visit the previous summer and whatever blunt advice he'd given my husband, Louis had become more attentive, though not exactly amorous until his surprising visit in March. Now I dared hope that I might really be pregnant, but I was reluctant to send Mama the wonderful news, in case it proved false.

Was I, or was I not? I waited, nearly ill with anxiety. A week passed, and then another, and still no sign of Général Krottendorf. I nervously consulted my physician, afraid even to hope. But the good doctor confirmed my greatest desire: *I was pregnant at last!* Louis wept when I told him the news. I sent a joyful letter to my mother by fastest courier. Her swift reply was filled with advice: *You must do everything absolutely correctly, so there can be no possibility of anything going wrong.*

For once I welcomed her advice and did my best to follow it. I drank milk and got plenty of rest. I took pleasant walks with my ladies and spent quiet days at the Petit Trianon, watching over the progress on my English garden. I read the works of Jean-Jacques Rousseau, determined that my child would be brought up in the simplicity and naturalness that Rousseau recommended. I continued to entertain my friends at the Petit Trianon, holding salons on Sunday afternoons with card games (but no gambling—I'd forced myself to give it up) and music and conversation, followed by light suppers of healthful foods.

By the end of August I had grown quite large, and I ordered Madame Bertin to design cool, loosely cut dresses in soft shades of yellow and blue and rose.

One day I was pleasantly surprised to notice a handsome face among the guests to be formally presented at Versailles, the good-looking Swedish officer I had met several years earlier. His snug white breeches and tight-fitting dark blue doublet showed off a tall, lean body to perfection. I thought he'd grown even handsomer. "Ah, it's an old acquaintance!" I said. "Count von Fersen."

"Your Majesty flatters me to remember," he said with a gallant bow.

"I'm delighted to see you again. You've been in England, I believe?"

"Only briefly," he explained. "Then I returned to Sweden. But I am pleased now to be back in France."

"Then you must come to visit me at the Petit Trianon, my little country place. Shall I expect you on Sunday afternoon?"

"With pleasure, Your Majesty." Another bow. Another smile.

From that day on, Axel von Fersen entered my circle of friends and became immensely popular. Yolande de Polignac immediately set to work to discover as much as she could about the good-looking Swede who invariably turned heads at the Petit Trianon in his dazzling uniform.

"The purpose of his journey to England was to persuade a certain young lady to marry him," Yolande reported breathlessly, "but she refused him—why, I cannot imagine! Have you ever seen anyone more charming, more intelligent, more delightful, more well made than our friend Fersen?" Yolande flicked her jeweled fan open and closed, open and closed. "There are no doubt a dozen women in love with him—and who can blame them? He's always the most attractive man in the room!"

"But is he in love with any of *them?*" I couldn't resist asking.

"I've heard that he can pretend to be in love most convincingly for a few hours, or even for a whole night."

"Ah," I said. I wanted to hear no more.

No. 39: The child must be named in my honor

THE AUTUMN OF 1778 passed quietly. There were no more outrageously expensive parties, just simple gatherings at the Petit Trianon, the kind my brother would have approved of. My thoughts were continually on the child I was carrying. It was assumed by those close to me that the baby would be a boy. My mother, invited to be the godmother, fretted that the child might turn out to be a girl after all, despite all her prayers to the Virgin. A girl held no value; according to French law, she could not inherit the throne, a privilege that then might still go to Madame Artois's son.

I went into labor on December 19. Everyone in the world seemed intent on crowding into the birthing room to watch. It was horrible, all those people, chattering as though it were just another morning toilette. I thought I was going to suffocate. Then in a blinding rush of pain, the baby was born. The chatter stopped. I heard no great cheers.

"Madame, you have given us a fine dauphine!" said my husband, who had stayed by my side.

I turned my head away. So it was a girl after all. I knew that everyone was disappointed, especially Louis. But I was not. A son would have belonged to France; he'd have been taken away from me immediately to be raised in the traditional manner. But a daughter—a daughter was different. I could bring her up as I liked, in a completely natural way.

When the newborn infant was swaddled and laid in my arms, I whispered fervently into her tiny pink ear, "My poor little girl, you are certainly not what was so much wanted, but you are no less precious to me because of it. You shall be mine, and you shall have the best care I can offer you. I will feed you the milk of my own breasts. You will share my every happiness and help me to bear every pain." And then I kissed her downy little head and allowed her to be carried away by Marie-Louise de Guéméné, once my partner in gambling but now appointed the lofty governess to the Children of France.

We named our daughter Marie-Thérèse-Charlotte, on Mama's orders. *The first girl born to each of my children must be named in my honor,* she wrote.

Now all I had to do was get my strength back and get

pregnant again as soon as possible. The next child would surely be the right kind—a boy, a dauphin.

Marie-Thérèse was a strong and healthy infant with a loud, insistent cry. When she was three months old, her father decided the time had come to formally celebrate her birth at Notre-Dame in Paris. I thought it a fine idea, remembering the outpouring of joyous enthusiasm with which the people of Paris had welcomed me a few years earlier, how the procession of royal carriages had been slowed and often halted by the exuberant crowds, how the cheers had gone on and on when we stepped out onto the balcony of the Tuileries Palace, the mayor of Paris saying, "Madame, you have before you today two hundred thousand lovers."

I expected no less of a welcome for my child. I was wrong.

The crowds gathered as twenty-eight gilded carriages entered Paris; the narrow streets were lined with people who had turned out to see their sovereigns and the newest member of the royal family. But instead of cheers, we received only silent stares. Their sullen silence unnerved me.

"What's wrong?" I whispered to Madame Guéméné who rode beside me with Marie-Thérèse in her arms. She was ready to hold the infant up for the crowds to smile at and point at and applaud. But some in the unfriendly crowd had actually turned their backs.

"I don't know," the governess murmured. "I can't explain it."

Later, after we'd attended Mass at the cathedral, after we'd made our way to Tuileries, what I heard was not surprising: the infant was, after all, a girl, and could not be her father's successor. There was also the rumor—and this sickened me—that she was not my husband's child at all, that I had been sleeping with Artois—Artois, of all people! My husband's brother was high-spirited and amusing, but I would have had to be insane to have an affair with him. If not Artois, whispered the vicious gossips, then perhaps the father was one of the other young men who attended my salons and card parties and musical evenings. The duc de Chartres, for instance—Louis's imperious cousin.

Such talk sent a chill through me. Others at court had their flirtations, certainly, and many had their affairs—my dear friend Yolande often hinted that she herself had a lover. I'll admit that I did enjoy the flattering attentions paid me by some of the older men at court as long as they weren't foolish enough to step over the line. But I would never, ever betray my husband.

Whatever the reason for the coldness of the people that day in Paris, I could not forget their terrible silence.

No. 40: You must not wear fashions that bring dishonor to the court

EXCEPT WHEN I had to attend some official function, I spent most of my time at the Petit Trianon. Work was proceeding on the eight-sided belvedere on a hill with a view of the lake. The secret grotto would soon be finished, with its newly created rock and waterfall. I had always returned to the chateau for the night, but with the coming of warm weather, I found that sleeping in my pretty little bedroom in my country house was much more pleasant.

That summer I convinced the king that the world would not end if court ladies were allowed to wear smaller panniers under their skirts, and shorter, more manageable trains on the *grands habits de cour.* I loved the beautiful new *robe à la polonaise;* its skirts were designed to loop up in swags over petticoats ending above the ankle, so that I could walk easily about the gardens. The old ladies of the court reacted with horror to the exposed ankles and the clever little bustle in the back. As I expected, Mesdames Tantes were scandalized. "You must not wear fashions that bring dishonor to the court!" they cried.

But my friends followed my fashion lead. When Madame Bertin and I introduced a new color, a kind of pinkish brown that my husband described as *puce*—meaning "flea"—every fashionable young woman at Versailles simply had to have a gown made up in puce. Now they all wanted swags and bustles.

Next I began to wear loose-fitting gowns with a lacy fichu at the neck and a little silk scarf or a length of pretty ribbon tied around the waist. No more tight sleeves and half-exposed bosom as in traditional gowns! Soft bonnets and straw hats were now in vogue. We wore our hair loose and unpowdered and used far less rouge, a change that would have pleased Emperor Joseph.

Men's fashions were changing too. King Louis frowned on the open coats and vests and forbade men to wear them at court, but rebellious Artois adopted the new style immediately and sported it whenever he visited the Petit Trianon, where *I* and no one else set the rules.

I had created a lovely world for myself and my friends. I believed now that my life was in perfect balance, just as the gardens of the Petit Trianon were achieving a balance of the classical and the romantic. And if those who were excluded were angered and spread stupid lies about me all over Paris—it was hinted that I had not only male lovers but female lovers as well—I chose to ignore the ugly rumors. I took pleasure in my life with my little daughter, who was my greatest delight, and my friends, who were as devoted to me as I was to them. Louis and I enjoyed a deep bond of affection and respect, and though my husband's visits to my bed were infrequent, I still hoped to become pregnant again soon.

By the winter of 1780 the involvement of France in the Americans' revolution against England had gone beyond the financial support promised by the king and now included French troops. The comte de Rochambeau was made a lieutenant general with five thousand in his command. My friend Axel von Fersen joined the French regiment as Rochambeau's aide-de-camp.

"Our regiment leaves soon for America," Fersen announced one snowy evening when my friends were gathered in my apartments at the chateau. "I'm to be General Rochambeau's liaison with General Washington. It should be a very interesting experience."

He made the announcement to the whole group, but the sharp pang I felt was personal. Of all the men in my circle of friends, Axel von Fersen was the one I found most amiable, most attractive, most interesting. Conversation was always easy between us. I sensed that we had much in common. He understood completely my yearning for a simple life—simple, that is, in comparison to life at the court of Versailles. It had not occurred to me that he might someday leave our intimate circle, and I realized then how deeply his absence would affect me.

"You will not be here for the inauguration of my little theater," I said, hoping my voice didn't betray the feelings churning beneath my calm surface. My theater, built close by the Petit Trianon, was designed to be an intimate space, just large enough to hold my invited guests but equipped with the most advanced machinery for staging full-scale productions. Because I'd spent so much money on the gardens and pavilions at the Petit Trianon, I thought it would be amusing to have the theater decorated with gilded papier-mâché and wood painted to look like marble. Even with such economies, there were the usual outcries against my extravagance. "I expect it will be finished in June," I continued. "The best theatrical companies in Paris are coming here to perform, and we'll put on some little entertainments ourselves. I'd hoped you would join us."

"It would have been my great pleasure, madame," he said. "And it will be my even greater pleasure when I return."

Each week that he appeared at Versailles I thought would surely be the last. I was always happy to see him again but braced myself for the day he would not be there. Then, late in March, he kissed my hand and said, "I've come to bid you farewell, madame. My regiment leaves in two days."

"You will be sorely missed," I said, not saying by whom exactly. "And welcomed back most heartily."

"I beg you, Antoinette, do not forget me." It was the first time he'd called me by my name.

I swallowed hard and found that I could scarcely speak. Finally I managed a thin smile and a nod. "Never, Axel, never," I said, blinking back tears.

This is insane, I thought later, after the *coucher,* as I lay sleepless in my bed. *I'm afraid I've fallen in love.*

No. 41: You must hand over your child to a wet nurse

SHORTLY AFTER my twenty-fourth birthday, in November, Abbé de Vermond gently broke the devastating news that my mother, Empress Maria Theresa, had died. I knew that her health had been declining, and so the news was not completely unexpected. I burst into tears. She had died still believing I was a failure. She had sent me to France to cement an alliance between the two countries and to provide an heir for the French throne. I had been her greatest hope, and I became her greatest disappointment. I was overwhelmed with grief.

Later, when I was calmer, I spoke to the *abbé* of my feelings. "I've always been afraid of my mother," I confessed. "I loved her, but I feared her more. I never lived up to her expectations of me."

The *abbé* tried to comfort me. "Your mother cared deeply for you."

"Oui, je le sais." I sighed. "I know. But caring deeply is not the same as loving me with her whole heart, no matter what." I was thinking of my sister Mimi, who could do no wrong; Mimi, whom Mama had loved above all.

The courts of Europe went into mourning at the death of the empress. Mourning clothes had to be ordered for everyone, including the servants. I thought about my mother with profound sadness. The tiny gold watch she'd given me when I left home—and that I had managed to hide during the ceremony of the *remise*—was my most treasured keepsake. I would never again receive one of her stern lectures, expressions of her relentless disapproval. In an odd way I would miss them.

Mama would have been the first person I informed a few months later, soon after the mourning period ended, when I discovered that I was pregnant again.

This news made everyone happy—with certain exceptions. My sister-in-law Madame Artois seemed more pinch-mouthed than usual at the renewed possibility that another heir to the throne might yet displace her two sons. Louis was delighted, naturally, and my brother Joseph wrote that the news gave him the greatest pleasure and that he had, in fact, decided to make a second trip to Versailles to visit me. He would again travel incognito as Count Falkenstein, and he would stay at the same village inn as before. Even as holder of the title Holy Roman Emperor, he disdained any sort of luxury.

To entertain him I arranged a nighttime spectacle at the Petit Trianon. Torches glowed in earthenware pots hidden throughout the English gardens, and fires blazed in trenches, illuminating the pavilions and giving the belvedere on the hill and the rock above the grotto a magical glow. Joseph seemed pleased by the effect, but he didn't miss the chance to lecture me one more time about my spending. "Put an end to this extravagance!"

I pretended to listen and shrugged it off.

"King Louis and I would be honored if you'd be the godfather of our child," I told my brother. That gave him the privilege of choosing the proxies for the baptism immediately after the infant's birth. He picked Artois and Provence. And then he kissed me, gave me his blessing, and after a visit of only one week, he left.

There were no crowds in my bedchamber when I went into labor—only about half a dozen people besides my husband, including Artois, Provence, Mesdames Tantes (whom I could easily have done without but who could not be turned away), and a few others. The baby was born shortly after midnight on October 23, 1781. I heard its cries, but I had to endure several minutes of not knowing its sex.

Then Louis bent over me and, grasping my hand, said tenderly, "Madame, you have fulfilled our wishes and those of France. You are the mother of a dauphin." I felt his tears drop onto my cheeks and mingle with mine.

I have done it! I exulted. *After eleven and a half years, I have done it at last!*

As my son was bundled off in the arms of Madame Guéméné, the royal governess, I heard the applause, the shouts, the cheers that spread through the chateau, the news to be taken to Paris and to all the great capital cities of Europe. And then, exhausted, I slept.

Within an hour of his birth the dauphin was christened Louis-Joseph-Xavier-François. I wanted to nurse my son, but Mesdames Tantes raised a great fuss. "It is unthinkable that the queen would nurse her child!" they cried.

After many tears I relinquished the honor to a wet nurse, a buxom woman whom we nicknamed Madame Poitrine, "Madame Chest." From then on I would see precious little of my infant. Madame Guéméné devoted herself to his care. Her only other interest in life was her collection of little dogs, through which she claimed to communicate with the world of spirits.

When Louis-Joseph was three months old, we took him to Paris for his formal presentation. Remembering the coldness and the hostility of the crowds three years earlier, at the presentation of his sister, I feared for our safety.

In the end I let myself be convinced that all would be well. Food and wine, fireworks and masked balls were offered throughout the city and seemed to keep the people content. But I could not help noticing that the king's carriage was cheered loudly as our cortege made its way through the narrow streets, while mine was practically ignored.

That evening we held a festive banquet at the Hôtel de Ville. Among our guests was the marquis de La Fayette. Using his vast family fortune to fit out his own ship, La Fayette had sailed to America in 1777 and volunteered his services in the Americans' fight for independence. He had just returned to Paris that day.

"All has gone well for the Thirteen States," the marquis told me as we sat by the window watching the display of fireworks. "Rochambeau and his regiment were of great help to General Washington at the battle of Yorktown. Our French soldiers acquitted themselves heroically in bringing about the defeat of General Cornwallis."

At the mention of Washington and Rochambeau, my thoughts flew at once to Axel von Fersen. "Do you expect Rochambeau and his regiment to return soon to France?" I asked carefully.

"Oh, I should think so. The fighting can't go on much longer. Clearly the English are tiring of it all."

While he spoke, a rocket burst over Paris and a dazzling shower of blue, white, and red sparks spilled across the sky like stars, mimicking the sudden flutter of my heart.

No. 42: You must control your spending

COURT LIFE AT Versailles wearied me half to death. There was talk of financial problems, not only for France as a whole but for individuals whose wealth had never before been questioned. The most shocking was the Guéméné scandal: the prince de Guéméné, husband of the royal governess, was forced to declare bankruptcy. Deeply in debt to thousands of creditors who would never see a single *sou,* the prince and princess quietly resigned their posts and retired to the countryside with Marie-Louise's horde of little dogs. I chose the duchesse de Polignac to assume the post of governess to the Children of France.

Everyone at court owed huge sums of money to everyone else. I confess that I was among those who owed, though the king always generously covered my gambling debts and paid for my gowns and jewels and my parties and entertainments at the Petit Trianon. Money always seemed to come from somewhere, and I saw no reason to worry.

Perhaps I should have been content to escape whenever possible to the Petit Trianon, but I had a wonderful new inspiration, a vision that gave purpose to my life and took me far away from the problems that plagued the court. I'd been reading the works of Jean-Jacques Rousseau on the education of children, and I summoned the court architect who had created the decorative little pavilions in my English garden. "I want a special place where my children and I can live a truly simple life, among cows and sheep and a little garden to provide our food," I told Monsieur Mique.

"A farm, madame?" Mique asked with a puzzled look.

"A hamlet, an entire rustic village," I explained. "Everything must be simple, like a real peasant village." I had always enjoyed the comedies and light operas in which I played an impertinent servant or a clever peasant girl in my little theater. I loved the costumes that went with my roles, with lots of flounces and ribbons on a saucy little apron for the servant and perhaps a jaunty bonnet for the peasant. This hamlet would allow me to experience an even more authentic peasant life.

I described to the architect a mill with a waterwheel,

like those I'd seen on my drives through the countryside. "In the center of my hamlet will be the queen's house, designed to look old, as though it's been there for centuries, not just built for the whim of a silly queen," I added with a smile. "I want thatched roofs on the cottages, and the outside walls must be painted so that everything looks weathered, almost decrepit, but the interiors must be unfussy and luxurious, in the best possible taste and comfortable as well."

"Of course, madame," said Monsieur Mique agreeably, as I expected he would. "Your vision is idyllic, and it will be my pleasure, as always, to be of service to Your Majesty."

"Done as quickly as possible," I added.

It was his turn to smile. "As quickly as possible—as always."

I dismissed him with my thanks. As he was about to leave, he stopped and regarded me with a serious expression. "The hamlet will be charming and beautiful, but it will also be very expensive," he said. "What you have described will cost much more than anything I have undertaken for you thus far."

I frowned, annoyed. "I'm quite aware of that, Monsieur Mique. But it's what I want."

"I mention it only because—" He hesitated, searching for the right words. The man was an architect, not given to elaborate speeches.

"Because I have been criticized for my extravagance in certain circles?" I asked, completing his sentence. "I care nothing for what my enemies say. It's only what my friends say that is important to me."

"As you wish, Your Majesty," the architect murmured, bowing.

Over the next two or three months Monsieur Mique returned once a week to report on the progress of Le Hameau, the hamlet. He often brought with him the painter responsible for the artistic arrangement of the buildings, a second artist to present sketches of the buildings I envisioned, and a model maker to build miniatures of these buildings. It was like watching a dream slowly unfold. But construction of the actual buildings could not begin until the landscape had been prepared, perhaps not for another six months.

"What is taking so long?" I wanted to know.

"Your Majesty, I am not God," Mique protested. "It takes time for a mere mortal to create the streams and the lake and the surrounding moat that the plan requires. I beg your patience, madame."

"We've had this conversation before, Monsieur Mique. Patience is not one of my virtues. I have not developed any more since last we spoke."

"We shall do our best, Your Majesty," the architect replied stiffly and hurried away.

The work proceeded much more slowly than I

wished, and the costs mounted much more quickly. Even the king seemed concerned.

"The minister of finance has asked me to speak to you," Louis said. "You must control your spending, madame." It was the first time he had ever complained about my expensive habits. I promised that I would, but it was a promise soon forgotten.

No. 43: Everything you do fans the flames of gossip

I INTRODUCED another new style, a simple muslin dress known as a *gaulle,* and summoned my official portraitist, Élisabeth Vigée-Le Brun, to paint my portrait as I wore this pretty dress and held a rose. The result, which I thought charming, was harshly condemned. Some people seemed to believe I was posing in my undergarments and pronounced the portrait indecent. To appease my critics, I asked Vigée-Le Brun to paint another: same pose, same rose, but a traditional gown of blue silk trimmed in lace.

I ignored such fault-finding when I could. I'd gotten used to it. I would never please the traditionalists at court, so I might as well please myself. Vicious rumors sprang up like weeds, especially the notion that I had an unnatural affection for Yolande de Polignac. The lies might have been laughable if so many people had not been engaged in repeating them, embellishing them, and making them ever more disgusting. I could scarcely imagine what people would have said if they'd known the true state of my heart!

"He's back," whispered Yolande de Polignac in June.

"Who?"

"Count von Fersen! He's come back from America." She arched an eyebrow and smiled conspiratorially. "A bit thinner, perhaps, but handsomer than ever, if you can believe that's possible."

"Well, I don't believe it!" I said with a laugh that I hoped wouldn't betray the sudden quickening of my heart. "But it will indeed be pleasant to see the Swedish gentleman again. He's been gone for more than three years."

During that time I had banished all thoughts of Axel and the feelings he had awakened. But I could not keep him out of my dreams, where his visits were frequent and passionate. Memories of these dreamed encounters made me blush.

How long will it be until he calls on me? I wondered. I didn't want to reveal to him or to my friends how eager I was to see him. I decided to send him a note inviting him to my little theater, where my friends and I had been rehearsing *The Barber of Seville.*

The play, written by Beaumarchais, seemed hilariously amusing when I first saw it performed in Paris by the Comédie Française. Members of the Paris company coached us. Beaumarchais, who once served as music teacher to Mesdames Tantes, attended the final rehearsals. Now we were ready to play to our invited audience, which included the princes and princesses of the blood and a number of other ranking nobility. Naturally my husband, the king, would be there—he came to nearly all of my performances and led the applause.

On a summer Sunday afternoon the blue velvet curtains parted and the play began. I had great fun in the role of Rosine, a young lady of noble birth, and Artois in his usual debonair style played Almaviva, a Spanish grandee in love with Rosine. Doctor Bartholo, Rosine's guardian, who kept her locked up and intended to marry her himself, was played by the duc de Guise, who'd recently married Madame Polignac's enchanting young daughter. Yolande's lover, the comte de Vaudreuil, was cast as Figaro, the scheming barber who manages to get the two together. The part suited Vaudreuil well—he was an aging but stylish man and a schemer himself.

The performance was going well. Vaudreuil drew a great deal of laughter and applause as Figaro. Our acting teacher had urged us to ignore the audience and to concentrate solely on the play, but I failed to follow his suggestion. I happened to glance toward the king's chair and saw Axel von Fersen seated next to Louis. At that moment everything vanished completely from my head; every word of Rosine's speech was forgotten. Doctor

Bartholo—the duc de Guise—cleared his throat and repeated his line. The prompter, standing offstage, loudly whispered the line I was supposed to say. I collected myself and, turning away from the magnetic force of Axel's presence, finally spoke the line, stumbling badly.

The play continued without other obvious mistakes, but I had to work harder than I ever had to remember my lines. The other actors surely noticed my lapses, but I hoped they hadn't deduced the reason for it. They were my friends, but they were also gossips.

When the velvet curtains closed at the end of the last act, the applause was enthusiastic. We took our bows and then went out into the audience, still in our costumes, and greeted the king, as was our custom. That done, I moved on to my other guests, pretending I had only just noticed Axel's presence.

"My dear Count von Fersen, what a pleasure to see you again!" I said cordially, but not too cordially, and held out my hand. *My God, how handsome he is!* His features were leaner, more chiseled than when I'd last seen him, the freshness of his early youth replaced by a sophisticated maturity. *Can he hear how fast my heart is beating? Can Louis?*

"An even greater pleasure for me, Your Majesty," he said with cool formality. He kissed my hand, holding it a moment longer than the little ritual required.

I glanced at Louis, and at that moment saw him for what he was: a shy, fat, awkward man, fond of me but not passionate, respectful but unwilling to accept my advice.

A man whose only true enthusiasms were hunting and making locks at his private forge. A kind man with whom I had almost nothing in common. My husband. I turned back to Axel with my most charming smile.

"Allow me to congratulate you on your delightful performance this evening," he was saying. "I had not realized that you were such a gifted actress."

I thanked him, pressed his hand the slightest bit before drawing mine away, and invited him to join us for a supper at the Petit Trianon. He accepted, and I drifted off to greet my other guests. Nothing important had been said, but everything had been communicated between us.

Yolande, who had witnessed that little scene, smiled knowingly. "What did I tell you?" she exclaimed when I returned to my dressing room to change from Rosine's costume to a simple muslin gown. "Isn't he utterly magnificent? I think his experiences in America have truly made a man of him."

"I would not have thought he needed any improving, but you're right—he's magnificent! And surely married by now."

Yolande laughed. "Apparently not. 'Adored by many, committed to none,' I hear. It makes a fine motto, doesn't it?"

"Well then, perhaps it's our challenge to find him a suitable wife!" I said merrily—my acting lessons made it possible—and I linked my arm with hers.

Count von Fersen, much celebrated for his distinguished role in the American Revolution, immediately became a part of my intimate circle at the Petit Trianon, recounting stories of how Rochambeau had convinced General George Washington to stealthily move the French troops south to Virginia.

"Yorktown turned out to be the final battle of the war," Fersen told a group of rapt listeners. "The Americans were victorious, but they could not have succeeded without the French." As a result of his own contributions, Fersen proudly wore the medallion of the Society of the Cincinnati, presented to him by General Washington. His listeners clapped.

Besides entertaining us with his war stories, Fersen had a fine baritone voice, and our friends often asked him to sing while I accompanied him on the harpsichord. We asked him to read poetry to us, allowing him to choose the poems. I swear that every woman was in love with him, and every man admired him. Because he was a foreigner, he was not caught up in court intrigues, and therefore he had no enemies. Everyone liked him.

The attraction between us grew stronger, harder to resist. It thrilled me, but I struggled against it, finally convincing myself that I could enjoy his attentions and his sincere affection with a clear conscience and without compromising my reputation. I wanted only to be near him. *Just to talk,* I reasoned. *Nothing more.*

I believed I had succeeded well in hiding my feelings from my husband, who always seemed oblivious, and from my dearest friends, even Yolande. But not from everyone. Louis's cousin Philippe, the duc de Chartres, seemed to have a sixth sense about such matters, maybe because he himself was constantly involved in romantic intrigues and so assumed everyone else was too.

"Ah, dear cousin," he said, addressing me in an overly familiar tone that I found offensive. "I see that your handsome officer has returned at last from foreign shores. I'm sure he must seem even more attractive to you now than he did before." Chartres smiled.

I should have simply ignored him, dismissed him with a haughty sniff to show my disdain for his remarks. Instead, my temper flared. I felt the blood rush to my face. And he now knew that his words had hit their mark.

"What impertinence!" I cried. "You may consider yourself unwelcome at the Petit Trianon."

"Take care, my dear. That's all I wish to say. Everything you do fans the flames of gossip." He bowed, bestowed on me his lizard smile, and walked away. I hoped, unrealistically, that I had seen the last of the duc de Chartres.

No. 44: You must protect your virtue

MY ATTRACTION to Axel von Fersen refused to disappear. I expended a lot of effort searching for ways simply to be in his presence, and more effort disguising my feelings, even—or perhaps especially—from him. Progress on my idyllic village was a temporary distraction.

By summer the moat surrounding Le Hameau had been dug, and the artificial lake was filling with water. Foundations for the queen's house and two or three other buildings had been laid. Monsieur Mique had left me with drawings of his plans and a portfolio of Monsieur Hubert's sketches of the various buildings to be constructed.

"I would enjoy giving you a tour of Le Hameau as it will be someday," I told Axel. "But your imagination will be required."

I invited several of my friends to join our little expedition, for the sake of appearances. But somehow—I can't say exactly how it happened—Axel and I found ourselves separated from the rest of the group; their voices drifted farther away, in the direction of the Temple of Love. For the first time we found ourselves alone. We gazed at each other for a long moment before Axel opened his arms and I stepped into them. Seconds ticked by as we stood motionless, locked in a silent embrace. But there was nothing tentative when his mouth found my lips, nothing hesitant about my response to his kiss. Desire rose in me like hunger in someone denied food for far too long.

"My darling Antoinette, you must know that I adore you," he murmured. His fingers lightly traced the line of my chin as he held me close. "I have adored you, and no one but you, for at least a thousand years."

I'd been resting my cheek against his chest, but now I lifted my head and smiled up at him. "A thousand years? Really?"

"You insist upon an exact count of the days since I first saw you at the masked ball in Paris? That's when I fell instantly in love with you. And I had no idea who you were. I simply believed you were the most beautiful and the most charming woman I had ever met! That was what—nine years ago? And all this time I have loved you, thought of no one but you, dreamed of you, yearned for you—"

"And asked another woman to marry you," I interrupted.

"The one has nothing to do with the other, my darling. I don't expect to marry for love—no one does." He took off his jacket and spread it on the ground. "Come, dear Antoinette, sit here with me."

There was nothing I wanted more—but I was uneasy. "Someone will surely find us."

Axel sat down, leaning back on one elbow and stretching out his long legs. He gently pulled me down beside him. "No one is looking. Even the birds in the trees are being discreet." I thought he must be right—the voices of our friends had disappeared, with only occasional trills of laughter floating back to us. I allowed myself to lie wrapped in his arms, his kisses becoming more ardent on my lips, my ears, my throat. I'd never experienced such passion. My husband rarely kissed me, and his caresses were methodical, dispensed dutifully as though he knew what was expected of him and did it to please me.

Swept by desire that carried me to the edge of complete surrender, I yielded to Axel's touch. Then I realized that I had to stop, *now!* With the greatest effort I pulled back from that precipice and leaped to my feet.

"My dearest love," he pleaded. "Come to me."

"I can't, Axel. I can't betray him." I began frantically brushing off my skirt.

Axel rose and rested his hands lightly on my shoulders. "I understand, my darling. You're right to stop me from making love to you. And I was wrong to take such liberties. I beg you to forgive me. But you'll never stop me from adoring you."

Minutes later, when I had composed myself, we caught up with the others. Yolande looked me over carefully, no doubt noting my flushed face, smiled her mischievous smile, and looked away. She undoubtedly knew, and if she did, so would others.

"Work will begin soon on the water tower," I reported briskly to my friends, who seemed unaware that Fersen and I had been missing for some time—or maybe they were only pretending to be unaware. "I'm thinking of calling it Marlborough's Tower."

"What an odd name, dear sister!" commented Artois, interrupting his flirtation with one of the youngest ladies. His wife was not with us. She never was.

"It's inspired by the song Madame Poitrine always sang to my little Louis-Joseph when she nursed him. Something about 'Marlborough is going to war.' Do you know it?"

"I know it well, madame," said Fersen. He began to sing:

Malbrough s'en va-t-en guerre.
Mironton, mironton, mirontaine
Ne sait quand reviendra . . .

"Malbrough—Marlborough, in English—is a soldier who goes off to war and leaves his lady love behind, gazing out of her tower and awaiting his return. In later verses a page brings word that Malbrough is dead, and there's a funeral. It's quite a sad song, really."

My friends insisted on learning every verse—there were a dozen—and ended with the gentlemen proposing toasts to my son's wet nurse, Madame Poitrine.

Before our group returned to the Petit Trianon for refreshment, Axel contrived to brush his fingertips along the back of my neck one more time.

The utmost discretion was necessary in my relationship with Axel. I did not want to cause my husband pain in any way or create a scandal. It would have been easier—and I could have deceived myself more easily—if Louis had taken lovers, as his grandfather did, as Artois and practically all the men at court did, and as a number of the women did as well. But Louis showed no interest whatsoever in having a mistress.

I was inflamed with love, caught in the fevered grip of passion, swept away with emotion as well as desire. I had never before experienced this kind of love, and I hadn't realized what a great emptiness had occupied the center of my life until I met my Swede. That was how I thought of him: *my Swede.*

I needed to trust someone to help arrange secret meetings with Axel. The someone I chose was Yolande de Polignac, not only my closest friend but also the royal governess to my children. Unlike the princesse de Lamballe, who made a great show of her purity and had probably never been passionately in love in her entire life, even with Alexandre, and who certainly had never had an affair, Yolande was experienced at juggling husband and lover. Why anyone with her great beauty and considerable charm had selected the aging comte de Vaudreuil for her favors was a mystery—he did know how to talk to women, but he could also be bad tempered. I knew I could confide in her.

"You must be careful," she warned. "You must protect your virtue. You are always being watched. There are many at court who would like nothing better than to catch you in an affair. Everyone believes you have a lover. They just don't know who he is."

It was Yolande who provided excuses for me when I rode off alone to meet Axel for an hour or two, or traveled incognito to a nearby village for a picnic with him, or took refuge in the privacy of my little theater in order to talk unheard and unobserved.

Axel's physical closeness was always a temptation. His tender kisses left me aching with desire, and I prayed fervently for the strength to resist. I hurried to my library and found my copy of *Julie,* the novel that my friends and I had all been reading and discussing a few years earlier. Now I read it again, to remind myself of how the heroine had virtuously renounced her love for Saint-Preux and forced herself to be faithful to her dull husband. The similarities to my own life were painfully obvious: Julie had no more in common with her husband than I had with mine. But I knew I would have to be content with knowing that Axel adored me and me alone. There was simply no other way.

I wanted more children; Louis needed sons to assure an heir. Our little Louis-Joseph was a delicate child, and if he did not survive we would have failed in our duty to provide a dauphin. For this reason, and perhaps it was the only reason, the king continued to come to my bed. He must surely have been surprised by my rapturous response, as I allowed my imagination to carry me away to the arms of my Swede.

For three months Axel and I spent countless stolen hours together, times made more intense by our knowledge that our idyll had to end. Axel made it clear that his future was in the military. He'd returned from the American Revolution covered in glory and heaped with honors. With the permission of the king of Sweden, Axel had been given command of the Royal Swedes, a regiment made up of Swedish soldiers who served the king of France. His duties would keep him away from me a great deal. At summer's end he brought me the news: "King Gustavus the Third has summoned me home to Sweden," he said, and I wept at the news.

"I will always come back to Versailles and to you, Antoinette," he promised, wiping away my tears. "And you will never be far from my thoughts."

On the eve of his departure in September, Axel and our friend Benjamin Franklin were present when the king and I witnessed a brilliant spectacle: the launching of a hot-air balloon by the Montgolfier brothers. A huge crowd had gathered at Versailles. The splendid globe of sky blue taffeta was decorated with golden suns and moons and the king's cipher, his royal monogram. A basket hung suspended beneath the balloon to carry passengers aloft, but so far, no one had gone up in such a strange device.

"The question is," said my husband to Monsieur Franklin, "what would happen to a living creature ascending into the skies? I have forbidden any normal humans to make the experiment, but I have recommended that two condemned prisoners be sent to test the problem."

The Montgolfier brothers had rejected the king's suggestion. Instead, they planned to send a sheep, which they thought physiologically most resembled a human, along with a duck and a rooster to find out what it was like to fly without wings.

The Montgolfiers set fire to wet straw and chopped wool, a mixture that emitted a great deal of black smoke and a foul smell as it heated the air inside the enormous balloon, inflating it and causing it to rise. We watched, fascinated, as the beautiful silk balloon slowly lifted off the ground with its three passengers inside the basket. It ascended faster and faster, until it was sailing high above the cheering crowds.

"Remarkable!" cried the king. "Monsieur Franklin,

have you ever seen such an astonishing sight in all your life?"

"No," said the American ambassador. "I have not. And if I weren't such an old man, I'd volunteer to go up in it the first time Monsieur Montgolfier wants a human passenger."

Axel had slipped up beside me, and his fingers brushed mine. He whispered softly in my ear, his breath warm against my skin, "Don't you wish we were in that basket, my love? Soaring up and away together?"

"Oui." I sighed as tears streamed down my cheeks. "*Oui, oui,* I do." I dabbed at my eyes. "But I'm afraid we'd have to take Monsieur Franklin with us," I murmured, and tried to smile.

After the excitement had ended, my husband and I said our formal farewells to Count von Fersen and wished him a pleasant journey home to Sweden.

"We hope your fortunes bring you this way again soon, Fersen," said my husband cordially. "Don't we, my dear?"

I nodded, smiling, unable to speak.

Three days later Axel was gone.

No. 45: You are to blame for everything

AXEL WROTE TO me often, always taking care to make his letters discreet and addressing them to Joséphine, a secret name we'd agreed upon. I missed him terribly and yearned for the joy and excitement he had brought to my life. I kept the letters at the Petit Trianon in a jeweled box with a false bottom and hid the key in my cosmetic table.

To distract myself from thoughts of him, I threw myself into the creation of Le Hameau. Construction proceeded much more slowly than I could tolerate, despite the great number of workmen toiling away. But it did me no good to get annoyed. I had plenty of other things to worry about. Chief among them were my children.

Marie-Thérèse was now five years old and known officially as Madame Royale. She was a healthy child but her temperament was serious and sometimes difficult. I dressed her in simple gowns made of muslin—mousseline—and began calling her Mousseline la Sérieuse. Her father doted on her and gave her whatever she wanted. He was by far her favorite in the family. I felt that she was becoming spoiled, reminding me unpleasantly at times of my sister Mimi, who always demanded, and got, her own way. I had resented Mimi all my life and I didn't want my daughter to turn out like her aunt.

To help Marie-Thérèse gain a more realistic and compassionate view of the world—nearly hopeless, I knew, given our circumstances—I arranged for the orphaned five-year-old daughter of one of the palace servants to become her companion, to dine with her, play with her, take lessons with her, wear the same kind of dresses, and enjoy the same privileges. In effect, I adopted this child, and I gave her the name of Ernestine.

Jacques-Armand, the peasant boy I had taken into the household several years earlier, was now nearly thirteen, too old to be the proper kind of playmate for Marie-Thérèse. I had seen very little of young Jacques since my daughter was born, but I did receive reports that he continued to do well with his studies and particularly enjoyed spending time in the Potager du Roi, the king's kitchen garden, tending the fruit trees.

Not surprisingly, my little Mousseline pouted endlessly when Ernestine joined our household, and she complained to her governess and to her father and to anyone else who would listen about my cruelty in forcing her to share. "I suppose you will do the same to my brother the dauphin when he's older and make him share?" she demanded, stamping her foot.

"If he turns out to be as haughty as you, indeed I will, my darling," I promised her.

My most earnest hope was that frail little Louis-Joseph would survive to be haughty. My son seemed delicate and often suffered minor illnesses that were a great worry to me.

Eight months after Axel and I had parted so painfully, he was back at Versailles. This time he accompanied an unexpected visitor, King Gustavus III of Sweden, traveling incognito. I'd had no warning of the visit; suddenly I received word that "Count de Haga" and his small entourage were on their way from Paris. Like my brother, King Gustavus chose not to stay in luxurious accommodations at Versailles but at an ordinary inn in the town. Naturally I was delighted to see Axel and ached to spend every moment in quiet intimacy with him, but there was much to be organized for the entertainment of our royal visitor. Night after night I arranged plays in my theater, ballets and concerts, little suppers in the gardens, and a dance at which the guests were required to dress entirely in white.

My passion for Axel, which I thought I'd succeeded

in damping to glowing embers, again burst into flame. While doing all I could to keep everyone pleasantly occupied, I was torn between my wish to be alone with Axel and my determination not to yield to my desire. There was a danger that my hunger for his love would become obvious and feed the court's thirst for scandalous gossip. Rumors of Axel's numerous affairs abounded—that was to be expected. But lately I'd also heard reports that he'd been considering candidates for the official position of Countess von Fersen. I'd expected that too—inevitably, he would marry—but the idea was painful.

We managed at last to slip away together for a delicious hour alone in my dressing room at the theater. Between kisses Axel took both my hands in his. "I've come to a decision, my darling," he said. "I can never have you as my wife, though you're the one woman in all the world I've ever loved with all my heart and who I know truly loves me. And so I've made up my mind that I shall never marry."

It was what I much desired to hear, though I had no right to ask it, and I confessed the depths of my feelings for him. "Were it not for my husband, I would pledge myself to you without reservation—my body, my soul, my very life. But I cannot betray Louis, and I cannot break my sacred vows." I went on, "There are many in this court who think nothing of living a life of deceit. They honor neither themselves, nor their wedded spouses, nor their lovers. I cannot do it. You have my heart, dearest Axel. But my loyalty is to King Louis."

And so on that day in my dressing room at the theater we pledged our hearts. "Forever," we said, and sealed the pledge with a passionate kiss.

How ironic, then, that on that very night my husband chose to come to my bed for the first time in weeks. The reason, I'm sure, was that our son had fallen ill yet again and we were both worried half to death about him. And how ironic that two months later, long after I had endured another painful parting from my beloved Swede, I confided to my closest friends that I was once again pregnant.

Our second son, Louis-Charles, was born on Easter Day, March 27, 1785, and named in honor of my favorite sister, Carolina, who was to be his godmother. This little boy was so sweet, so adorable, so robustly healthy, that I called him my *chou d'amour*—my "love cabbage," my sweetheart. As usual, everyone speculated on the true identity of the father. Artois was always the gossips' prime candidate, especially since his name was Charles. How insane people were to think such a thing!

In May Axel returned to Versailles for a short visit. I introduced him to my new infant. "The king is his father, but this child was conceived out of my love for you," I whispered to Axel, and his eyes filled with tears.

At the king's request Axel accompanied us to Paris when we took Louis-Charles to Notre-Dame. But I hated having him see the way I was received by the Parisians.

"Why is this happening?" he asked, clearly distressed by the surly stares that greeted us. "Why is there silence when there should be deafening cheers to celebrate the birth of a new prince?"

"Because," I said sadly, "they hold me responsible for the shortage of bread, for France's desperate financial situation. Madame Déficit, they call me. 'You are to blame for everything.' I think they are beginning to hate me."

I turned away so that he would not see my pain.

No. 46: So much money should not be spent on a foreigner

MY HAMLET WAS finished now, not only a dozen thatched cottages around the newly created lake but a real farm a short distance away with cows to provide my family with milk and cream, butter and cheese. A farmer and his wife were hired to look after the animals, including sheep, goats, ducks, a pig and her piglets, as well as the cows. I was happy to have a refuge in an ideal kingdom where I was the beloved queen with no worries. My children were enchanted. Le Hameau offered a perfect escape from a world that was becoming too hard to bear.

"You may give the animals their names," I told Mousseline and her companion Ernestine. The girls bestowed the names of Blanchette and Brunette on the two Swiss cows and made wreaths of flowers to drape over their horns in a little naming ceremony.

I wanted fruits and vegetables on my table that had been grown in my own gardens, fish caught in my own ponds, chickens taken from my own hen houses. I loved the sight of my daughter and Ernestine picking ripe strawberries and helping to gather eggs. A little goat followed them devotedly, and the girls each had a white rabbit to lead on a ribbon.

Unlike the Petit Trianon, built for the pleasure of the former king's mistresses, Le Hameau was mine, created especially for me. The Petit Trianon allowed me to entertain my friends in a style far removed from the suffocating formality of the court at Versailles, but Le Hameau took that simplicity a long step further. The dining room in the queen's house was more intimate than the one at Petit Trianon, and kitchens and a warming room assured that meals could be served just as elegantly. There were separate rooms for billiards and backgammon, and a sitting room done entirely in Chinese style. Blue and white ceramic pots filled with flowers were arranged around the doorways and along the steps of the outdoor stairs. Lilacs bloomed in the spring, and in the summer the scent of roses, my favorite flower, filled the air.

I loved this retreat, and I left it only when I absolutely had to. The heaviness that had weighed on my heart for so long lifted when I was in my little hamlet. I could dress as I pleased and wasn't required to change my gown half a dozen times a day for one ceremonial event after another.

Even before Le Hameau was complete, I acquired another palace to accommodate my growing family. Saint-Cloud, overlooking the Seine, would require considerable remodeling to make it suitable for my children, and the work would cost a great deal of money. Renovations were also needed at Versailles, which had been neglected for many years by Louis's grandfather King Louis XV. Versailles looked shabby when I arrived, and now it was shabbier still.

These necessary expenses—and I did believe they were necessary—triggered a flood of resentment. "So much money should not be spent on a foreigner," members of the court complained to the finance minister.

A foreigner! I had been married to the king for nearly fifteen years and borne him three children. I had lived in this country longer than I had lived in the country of my birth. I had not traveled out of France, or even very far from Paris and Versailles, in all that time. I had dedicated my life, my very being, to France. But in the eyes of many French I was still, and probably always would be, *l'Autrichienne.* They had even taken to calling my beloved Petit Trianon "Little Austria," and the story circulated that I planned to turn it over to Emperor Joseph.

I was accused of many things by my growing crowd of enemies. Pamphleteers in Paris spread cruel rumors about me that contained not a single grain of truth. The king ordered the broadsides to be kept from me, but someone—

I blamed the duc of Chartres—sent me a collection of the most vicious, concealed in a book illustrating the latest fashions. Madame Campan and I were enjoying a cup of tea together one afternoon as I casually leafed through the book and came upon a poorly printed pamphlet with a hideous drawing. The writer condemned me for smuggling money out of France and into the Austrian treasury—a lie, of course.

Silently I passed the offensive pamphlet to Madame Campan. She glanced at it and then at me. "Are there more of these?" she asked and reached for the book.

"I don't know," I answered. I felt quite ill, but I continued turning the pages, and one after another the pamphlets tumbled out. The writers argued that I was selfish and extravagant, cared nothing for the poor and hungry, snubbed the rich and powerful, mocked the etiquette of the court, dressed indecently, dressed my children indecently, committed adultery with women as well as men.

"Nothing but slander!" Madame Campan cried and snatched them from me, stuffing them into the stove.

I rose unsteadily and went to lie down on my bed.

There was no sense to these people, no reasoning with them. They would believe about me whatever they wanted to believe. I decided it was best to ignore them. If they chose to despise me, nothing would change their minds. How much worse it had become since those early, innocent days, when I was merely condemned for riding astride and refusing to wear stays!

No. 47: It is not your role to defy accepted fashion

ONE OF THE MOST distressing incidents that trampled my reputation in the mud involved an outrageously expensive diamond necklace.

I no longer had any interest in acquiring diamonds. Not only did I have more diamond necklaces, earrings, and hair ornaments than I could ever wear, but my taste now ran to much simpler jewelry. There may have been a time when I might have been pleased to own such an ornate piece, but that day was long past. When the royal jeweler approached me and tried to sell me a ridiculously ornate diamond necklace originally ordered by King Louis XV for Madame Du Barry—some 540 diamonds weighing 2,800 carats, set in a series of garish loops and pendants—I refused. It would have suited the vulgar Du

Barry, but it certainly did not suit me. Furthermore, the price was shocking; it would have outfitted several ships for the French navy.

"We need ships more than diamonds," I told the jeweler. I sent him on his way and considered the matter closed.

But unbeknownst to me, Cardinal Rohan, a member of one of France's oldest and most respected families, had fallen under the influence of a clever charlatan. Despite his lofty office of grand almoner, in charge of the royal charities, the cardinal was known to be dissolute—he owned a brothel. He was one of my least favorite people at court. The charlatan called herself the comtesse de la Motte-Valois and claimed to be an intimate friend of mine. In fact, she was not—I didn't even know her. But by various forms of trickery, including my forged signature on a letter, she convinced Rohan that I actually wanted this expensive necklace. She persuaded the cardinal that my husband had refused to buy the diamond necklace, and that if Rohan procured it for me, his status at court would increase dramatically. The foolish cardinal took the bait and swallowed the hook.

Cardinal Rohan arranged to buy the necklace from the royal jeweler, promising that I would pay for it! Then he handed the necklace over to Motte-Valois, who was supposed to deliver it to "her dear friend, the queen." But she did not. Instead, she pried out the diamonds and took them to England to sell.

Meanwhile, Rohan waited with growing impatience for me to wear the necklace in public as acknowledgment of my gratitude to him. Naturally, this did not happen. Once the facts and forgeries were uncovered, Rohan was arrested. So was Motte-Valois. Both were imprisoned in the ancient fortress of the Bastille.

Months later, after a trial, Motte-Valois was branded and sentenced to life in prison, but to my dismay, Cardinal Rohan was found innocent, and the charges against him dismissed. The most incredible and distressing part of the whole affair was this: nearly everyone believed I was the guilty one! They believed I was recklessly extravagant. They believed I loved diamonds. Some even believed the cardinal was one of my lovers! Therefore, by this logic, they were certain I must have been behind the plot. I knew what people were saying: *the queen should have been thrown into prison.* The cardinal was innocent, the fake *comtesse* was innocent, and the bad queen was guilty, guilty, guilty! Even my dearest friend, Yolande, seemed to doubt that I was not in some way complicit in the scheme.

I felt insulted, surrounded by enemies, completely exhausted by this horror. I was also pregnant again.

On July 9, 1786, I gave birth to my fourth child, a fragile daughter we named Sophie-Hélène-Béatrice. Every day I feared for Sophie's life, worried about the delicate health of Louis-Joseph, and spent hours on my knees praying for them both. My husband was no longer merely fat but almost grotesquely obese. I too had grown overly plump, my waist so tightly squeezed by stays I could scarcely breathe. My thirtieth birthday was approaching, an age at which I had always believed any sort of desirable life was over, an age at which I had decided I would no longer wear pink gowns or feathers in my coiffure.

At this unhappy moment my oldest sister, Mimi, who had always been our mother's favorite, who got everything she ever wished for, arrived at Versailles for a month-long visit. I had not invited her; she had simply announced that she was coming. It was hardly a surprise that Mimi objected to nearly everything I was doing.

"Antonia," she said severely, "what can you be thinking? Have you lost your senses? Country-maiden muslin dresses on the one hand and outlandish hairstyles on the other! Why are you so determined to defy the accepted fashion? That's not the queen's role! And those excessively costly parties you do so love to give! You've alienated half the court by refusing to invite them, and there's plenty of talk about the displeasure of ordinary citizens at the way you spend money as though it falls from trees."

I forced a smile and kept my voice level. "You sound more and more like Mama," I said. "Nothing I did ever pleased her either."

My remark did not stop Mimi. She condemned my spending on the Petit Trianon, my theater, Le Hameau, and Saint-Cloud. She reproached me for the way I was bringing up my children. Nothing escaped her critical eye and her sharp tongue. I avoided her as much as possible, refused to argue with her, and wept with relief when at last she left.

I carried on, though I was sick at heart. Baby Sophie seemed to grow weaker. The dauphin showed no signs of improvement. I asked Vigée-Le Brun for a portrait of me with my children, Marie-Thérèse, Louis-Joseph, Louis-Charles, and the infant Sophie in her cradle. But Sophie, my poor little angel, died before the painting was finished. My husband and I retreated to the privacy of the Grand Trianon to mourn, and the artist returned to alter the painting, removing the infant Sophie but leaving the empty cradle. What a sad, sad picture! For weeks I was nearly overcome by melancholy.

Then I received a piece of news that brought a glimmer of joy to my dark days: Axel had been appointed official liaison between the courts of France and Sweden. He would need a place of his own during his official visits to Versailles. With Louis's approval I arranged alterations in the rooms adjoining my apartments and offered them to Colonel von Fersen, commander of the Royal Swedish Regiment. I knew the gossips would give us no peace, but I didn't much care—Axel always behaved with complete discretion, and I had sworn never to break my vow of fidelity to my husband. At least Axel and I would have time together whenever he was at Versailles. We could talk. He would understand. My life would become more bearable.

His rooms were ready, but Axel did not come. He was still far away, involved in another war and, it was rumored, with another woman. And it seemed this affair was serious.

Part III

Rules for Madame Déficit
1789

No. 48: Give up your expensive gowns, your balls, your parties

THE YEAR 1789 began with one of the most miserable winters in memory. Heavy snows brought Paris to a halt. The Seine froze solid, and bitter cold caused many deaths. Following years of devastating harvests, there was no grain, nor was there water to grind it into flour or fuel to bake it into bread. Thousands suffered from hunger. The people could hardly blame me for the weather, but they did blame me for the lack of bread.

Doesn't she powder her hair? Doesn't that powder contain flour—flour that could be made into bread? Isn't she in some way profiting from the shortages, and from our misery?

The chief of police warned me that I would no longer be safe in Paris, and so I couldn't attend the Opéra or the Comédie Française. Scandal sheets and crude posters with obscene drawings continued to trumpet my many sins. The fierce hatred against me grew stronger day by day, and I knew no way to stop it. Nothing I said or did made the slightest difference.

No one seemed to notice that I was working hard to reduce my expenditures. I stopped ordering luxurious *robes* and sent my well-worn gowns out to be repaired and refurbished with a bit of lace and some new ribbons. I gave up the balls and parties my friends once enjoyed at the Petit Trianon and Le Hameau and closed my little theater.

I should not have been surprised when my new frugality began to affect my friendships. Yolande de Polignac, who had been my closest confidante for so long, now seemed to be keeping her distance. Had she been my dear friend only when it benefited her? Was it all about what she could get from me? Puzzled and hurt, I turned to other, less amusing but perhaps more sincere friendships, like Louis's shy, sweet sister Madame Élisabeth and my serious-minded mistress of the wardrobe, Madame d'Ossun, who had served me quietly and well for years.

Rather unexpectedly, my husband began to turn to me for advice and consolation. "What do you think, Madame Antoinette?" the king asked more and more often. "I don't know what to do."

He too tried to institute economies, eliminating useless positions at Versailles and Fontainebleau and the other royal palaces, but that created resentment and accomplished little. I now understood that it was not the enormous staff of servants that resulted in people going hungry. And it wasn't my taste for gowns and jewels, brilliant parties, and beautiful gardens. There were many causes of the misery, but it was our financial support of the American Revolution that had run up huge debts and finally pushed France to the brink of bankruptcy.

The country's finances continued to spiral downward, and nobody, not even the king, knew how to improve the situation. Finance ministers came and then were sent away, but whatever plan was suggested—taxes on land, for instance—was always shouted down by the wealthy aristocrats. The result was chaos and turmoil.

The current finance minister finally persuaded the king to summon the Estates-General, a general assembly with representatives of three groups: clergy, nobility, and commoners. This body had not met in nearly two centuries. In all this time the clergy and the nobility had avoided paying taxes, letting the burden fall entirely on the working people of France. Louis believed it was time for everyone to share in the burden. He was sure the representatives of each class would be reasonable and follow his wishes in how this could be accomplished. "Twelve hundred men will come together for the good of the country," he told me proudly. "It will be a festive occasion."

I summoned Rose Bertin and ordered her to create a splendid new gown for me. "It is important for the members of the Estates-General to see their sovereigns at their best," I told her. "No matter what scandalous rumors my enemies choose to spread about me, I intend to show them that I am still their queen." It was a role I had to play, and I thought I was ready for it.

The deliberations would open with a High Mass on May 4. Early that morning, a procession of nearly two thousand people began to form at the Church of Notre-Dame in the town of Versailles, preparing to walk to the Church of Saint-Louis, a distance of less than a mile. Bands played on street corners, and crowds that had been gathering since dawn jammed the streets; people leaned out of upper-story windows and climbed trees for a better look.

The enormous procession began to move. Heralds in purple velvet blew silver trumpets to announce the approach of the Blessed Sacrament, carried by the archbishop of Paris. The silk canopy over it was borne aloft by Louis's brothers and two nephews. Next came the twelve hundred members of the Estates-General, all wearing their traditional dress. The clergy, representing the first estate, was resplendent in robes of brilliant silk: bishops in purple, archbishops in violet, cardinals in red. The second estate, the aristocracy, was turned out in black velvet jackets richly embroidered in gold, and white silk stockings. They stuck elegant plumes in their hats and fastened swords to their belts. Last came the third estate—farmers, shopkeepers, doctors, lawyers, and ordinary workers. These commoners were required to wear plain black cloth suits and untrimmed hats; swords were forbidden. It made for a grandly dramatic procession, the simple garb of the third estate providing a sober background for the glitter and brilliance of the other two groups. The contrast seemed quite pleasing.

Suddenly one of my ladies exclaimed, "I can't believe my eyes—the duc d'Orléans is walking with the commoners!"

The former duc de Chartres, my husband's cousin who'd recently inherited his father's title of duc d'Orléans, had often been part of the group who enjoyed my hospitality at the Petit Trianon. But as he became more pompous and condescending, I grew to heartily dislike him and made it a point not to invite him. "He sees himself as the champion of the people," I said sharply, "since he can't be king."

A hundred Swiss Guardsmen in their bright red coats followed the members of the Estates-General. Behind them the royal falconers were mounted on high-stepping white horses, each man carrying a hooded falcon on his wrist. More silver trumpets announced the approach of the king, wearing a suit of cloth of gold with diamond buttons. I rode in a gilded carriage, dressed in the regal *grand habit de cour* created by Madame Bertin, cloth of silver glittering with some of the finest diamonds in my collection.

As the procession made its way through the narrow

streets, I heard the traditional cries of "*vive le roi!*—long live the king!" But as I passed by, I was greeted with silence. No one shouted "*vive la reine!*—long live the queen!" as I had a right to expect. I swallowed hard and stared straight ahead as my open carriage inched forward. It was just as it had been in Paris, a long, slow humiliation. Then, as we passed along the avenue in front of the royal stables, a group of shabbily dressed women surged forward and began to wave their fists and to shout in my face in an insolent manner, "*Vive le duc d'Orléans!*"

Spectators lining the streets recognized the duke in his black velvet and plumes among the plain dress of the third estate and took up the cry. "Long live the duc d'Orléans!" The roar grew louder until it was almost deafening. When I realized that the crowd was cheering for him instead of for me, I understood the insult intended. I was so stunned I nearly fainted. My legs grew so weak that when my carriage stopped in front of the church, I scarcely had the strength to climb the steps. The princesse de Lamballe hurried to support me.

I reached the violet-draped throne placed to the king's left and sank into it, trembling. "*Merci,* madame, I'm all right now," I whispered, though indeed I was far from all right. But I had to continue to play my role. I had to pretend to ignore the insults.

Almost immediately a noisy disturbance broke out at the entrance of the church. The great doors had been flung open to admit the first and second estates, but the members of the third estate were directed by the ushers to enter by the side door, as etiquette demanded. The commoners took offense, and their complaints grew louder.

"Will nothing satisfy these people?" Louis muttered. "They're fortunate to be included." Their peevish protest seemed to bother my husband more than the affront I had suffered.

Nor was that the end of it. The bishop's sermon that day was a direct attack on me. I struggled to keep my composure as he criticized the excesses of the king and the royal family, describing my pleasure-seeking life at the Petit Trianon and Le Hameau to drive home his point. I glanced at the king. He was asleep!

Unbelievably, Louis somehow dozed through the entire sermon. He awakened with a start when the members of the third estate burst into applause and raucous cheers for this impertinent bishop and his unseemly words, applause that etiquette strictly forbade in the presence of not only the royal family but also the Blessed Sacrament.

When the offensive event was over at last and we were safely back at the chateau, Artois insisted that I must not attend the opening convocation the next day. Provence took the opposite view. Louis—as always—could not make up his mind, taking first one position, then the other, then swinging back again. No one asked my opinion.

I held up a hand to interrupt the argument, but they ignored me until I raised my voice. "I intend to go," I said firmly. "I can't let them see how much they've wounded me. I'm their queen, their sovereign, and I shall be there."

And so I was, though I felt so ill I thought I would not be able to endure it. For this occasion Madame Bertin had dressed me in a cloak of purple satin over a white satin gown embroidered with diamonds, and my friseur arranged a plume of white ostrich feathers and a band of diamonds in my hair. I carried a jeweled fan. Was that a mistake? Did they want me to wear sackcloth and carry a broom? I don't know. I had prayed for matters to go well on that important day, but my prayers went unanswered then and through many days that followed.

King Louis had made a concession to the third estate by allowing twice the traditional number of delegates to attend. But he insisted that each order had to meet separately, discuss the issue at hand, and then cast a single vote—twelve hundred members, but only three votes would be cast. The result was always the same: the first and second estates voted together to defeat the third estate. Dissatisfaction among the commoners grew more clamorous.

"It was a sham! A sham!" they shouted. The third estate members had a louder voice than they'd had in the past, but no more power. And they were furious.

No. 49: Do not listen to scoundrels

SOMETHING MUCH more important than the national debt weighed as heavily as stone upon my heart. The little dauphin, Louis-Joseph, lay deathly ill, his small, thin body covered with sores, his spine twisted, so weak he could not walk or even leave his bed. My son was only seven, and yet he looked like an old man. I wept whenever I saw him, but still I couldn't admit to myself that he was dying. I left the men to their useless debates and spent every moment with my son, and I was with him when the end came on June 4.

We gave our poor little dauphin a simple funeral and laid him to rest at the Church of Saint-Denis among the tombs of his ancestors. Yet while our hearts were breaking, an air of jubilation was sweeping through Paris, not because the terrible conditions had improved, but because people had convinced themselves something momentous was about to happen.

To escape the tumult, my husband and I took our other children and, with Élisabeth, retreated to our palace at nearby Marly for a week of private mourning, away from the turbulence of Versailles.

Vicious pamphlets continued to appear, accusing me of such unnatural acts that I could not imagine what sort of person was capable of inventing such vileness. One charged me with scheming to poison my husband so that I could put my lover—Artois, again!—in power. But the rumor that laid me low was the claim that I had poisoned my own son.

"They said I poisoned him because I feared the dauphin might grow up to favor a revolution," I sobbed to Madame Élisabeth.

"Do not listen to scoundrels," she said, doing her best to comfort me.

But nothing did.

No. 50: You must flee

WHILE I GRIEVED, the third estate went about its work. It defiantly declared itself a National Assembly, independent of the other two estates, and swore to provide France with a new constitution. Though nothing really shocked me anymore, I was surprised to learn that the marquis de La Fayette was among the leaders. He had renounced his title and, with the help of an American named Thomas Jefferson, who had succeeded our friend Benjamin Franklin as ambassador, prepared a document called the Declaration of the Rights of Man, which included the right to revolt. To think that I had once welcomed Monsieur La Fayette as a hero when he returned from the American Revolution! Now it seemed he had become corrupted by the Americans' revolutionary ideas.

Somewhere in this fog of pain and misery, I was plagued by upsetting questions: *If Axel von Fersen were a Frenchman, whose side would he be on? He too had been a hero to the Americans. And are the rumors true about a serious affair? Has he fallen in love with someone else?*

Months had passed since I'd last seen my Swede. He'd been at Versailles through the harsh winter, but with the first thaws of spring he'd gone away to Sweden, to England, to wherever his king had called him. In a court that was always churning out new rumors, one persisted: Axel had become involved with a woman named Eléanore Sullivan, the daughter of an Italian tailor, wife of an Irishman, and currently the mistress of a rich Scotsman named Craufurd. She was seven years older than Axel.

"He is said to be enthralled by her," Madame Lamballe reported. Marie-Thérèse knew we were friends and may have suspected more.

I put aside my pride and sent Axel a message. *I need you,* I wrote. *Things are very bad here. The king needs you as well.*

I will come to you at once, he replied. And he did.

I took comfort from Axel's presence and his quiet strength as Louis tilted first one way and then the other. Sometimes the king wanted to compromise. Sometimes he wanted to come down hard on those who were agitating for limiting the power of the monarch.

"Send a few of the leaders of the third estate to that

new invention, the guillotine," Tante Adélaïde suggested. "It will be a lesson to the others."

In the end he seemed unable to muster the will to make any sort of decision.

The bread shortages grew steadily worse. Mobs responded to every rumor. Violence broke out. People began to wear cockades made of blue, white, and red ribbons in their hats, to show that they were on the side of those who opposed the monarchy. I was frightened, and I tried to hide my fear from my children. How could it possibly get any worse?

But nothing prepared me for the terrible, sickening events that were to come. Artois brought us the news: a mob had stormed the Bastille, and the ancient prison fortress had fallen.

"They came by the thousands, armed with anything they could find," Artois said, his voice breaking. "Many of them were women; some even brought their children. The fools thought they'd find guns and powder, and secret caches of grain. They believed the cells were filled with enemies of the king, and they were bent on freeing them. The governor of the Bastille hung out a white flag of peace, but the mob ignored it and commenced attacking from all sides. It was a horrendous scene. The fighting grew more intense—the mob didn't seem to care how many of their number were killed or wounded by the defending soldiers. They climbed onto the roofs and broke into the dungeons and released the prisoners, though they found only seven, madmen and forgers, not the hundreds of victims of injustice they'd expected."

We listened in stunned silence, hardly knowing what to say or do.

The king sat with his face buried in his hands. Axel stood gazing out of a window. Artois, who had been pacing agitatedly as he spoke, now sank into a chair. "Finally the Bastille fell," he continued. "There was no hope for it. The governor and his officers were arrested and led away, but the mob would not let them go. Half a dozen men seized the governor and beat him dead, cut off his head and hoisted it on a pike. 'Blood, blood everywhere!' a man who witnessed it all told me. He said the mob had managed to level the fortress until not a stone was left standing," Artois finished grimly.

We continued to sit as though we were under a spell.

Axel turned away from the window and broke the silence. "You must flee," he said. "All of you. None of you will be safe here. You are only twelve miles from Paris, and the road that carried you to the Opéra and the Comédie Française runs in both directions. A mob can be here in a matter of hours. La Fayette is in charge of the national guard, but he appears to have little control over his men. Your only salvation is to leave, and as quickly as possible."

"Where do you suggest we go, Fersen?" Louis asked, blinking as though he'd just been awakened.

"To Metz. It's two hundred miles to the east, and it's well fortified. But it will not be easy to reach it safely,"

Axel warned. "It's not just Paris that's in an uproar. Riots are taking place everywhere. On my journey here I saw for myself that people in the countryside are up in arms. They fall prey to the most scurrilous rumors. They call it the Great Fear."

I turned to my husband with a pleading look. *Let him agree to this,* I prayed silently, but I could see that he was already dubious. The discussion grew more heated. Provence, who had not said much, argued that the king should stay. Artois disagreed.

"I'm taking my family and leaving for the Swiss border," Artois said. "I've already given my servants the orders to begin packing. There's no time to lose. I urge you to do the same, Louis. Believe me, you and your wife and your children are in very great danger."

I thought Louis was about to agree, but then he wavered. "I depend upon the love and loyalty of my people," he said. "In the end all will work out for the good. I shall stay."

Axel stared at him. "But what about Antoinette and the children?"

"I will not leave my husband," I interrupted before Louis could reply. "My place is at his side." *Even if he's wrong.*

The next day Artois left with his family. The princes of the blood and their families soon followed. My former tutor Abbé de Vermond, who had been my reader and confessor for many years, got ready to depart. Provence remained, and so, we heard, did the treacherous duc d'Orléans, who had begun to call himself Philippe Égalité. *What nerve!* I thought.

And now the comtesse de Polignac, my close friend and for the past few years my children's governess, began to talk seriously of leaving. The path of our friendship had sometimes been uneven, but Yolande was still dear to me, and I loved her children almost as much as I did my own.

At first she'd refused to consider it. "I'm staying here, madame. My loyalty to you requires it."

But I urged her, "You must go, and go now. I'm terrified of what's happening, and I'm afraid it will get much worse. It would be a mistake for you and a tragedy for your family if you let your affection for me stand in the way of your good judgment." Finally she agreed.

We embraced when the time came for parting. Yolande, disguised as a maid, would ride on the outside of the carriage like a servant. Under other circumstances we might have joked about it, but now we were all weeping. "Adieu, adieu!" I sobbed.

"Go!" the king urged her. "Don't waste another minute!"

"But you, too!" Yolande pleaded. "Surely you must leave and save yourselves!"

I shook my head and repeated what I'd told the others: "My place is here, for the sake of the king and the dauphin."

Through a blur of tears I watched my dear friend's

carriage drive away. *How many more painful farewells must I endure before this terrible time is over?*

At the end of July King Gustavus III recalled Axel to Sweden. He was leaving reluctantly, for he believed we were in the gravest danger.

"And so, once again, a farewell for us." I sighed. The day was hot, and storm clouds threatened, soon covering the sun. Lightning forked across the sky. Axel was holding my hand. We had ridden out to Le Hameau to steal an hour or two alone—there were so few members of the nobility who had not yet fled from Versailles that we didn't worry about rumors and gossip. As the first drops of rain began to fall, we took refuge in the queen's house.

I felt sad, and there were many reasons for my sadness. For one, I was aware that I had lost my youthful beauty. I'd grown plump; my once perfect pink and white complexion had faded; my hair was no longer as thick and reddish blond as it had been when Axel and I first met, fifteen years earlier. Yet Axel was handsomer than ever, the years adding distinction and elegance to his good looks. I had little in my life to be happy about—two of my beloved children lay dead, my husband seemed unable to pursue a sensible course of government, the monarchy was shaken to its very bedrock, I was most heartily despised by the people.

And what about Mrs. Sullivan? In all the time Axel had spent with me, I had not asked him that question. He was free to do as he wished, and I was not. I knew that he'd had many women over the past fifteen years, but was Eléanore Sullivan different from all the others? I could not bring myself to ask.

We gazed out at the rain falling gently on Marlborough's Tower, not saying much, simply being together. Axel began to hum the little song Madame Pointrine had sung to Louis-Joseph years ago.

Malbrough s'en va-t-en guerre.
Mironton, mironton, mirontaine
Ne sait quand reviendra . . .

"Please, don't sing that!" I pleaded. "It's such a sad song! And now I fear that it may become true at any time—that you're not coming back!" I began to weep quietly.

"Surely you don't believe that, Antoinette," Axel said, bringing my hand to his lips. "I won't be gone long this time. King Gustavus won't keep me more than a few months."

I was thinking of Mrs. Sullivan, not of the Swedish king, but I kept silent.

Axel knew what was on my mind—as he often did. "You're thinking of Eléanore, aren't you? She's a good friend, and I can assure you that she and Craufurd are your loyal supporters."

"But do you *love* her?" I couldn't stop myself from blurting out the question.

"My dearest Antoinette, there are many different kinds of *love*. Please remember that you, and you alone, own my heart. You always have and always will. That hasn't changed, and it will not change."

I understood what he meant by different kinds of *love*. Certainly the passionate *love* I felt for him was entirely unlike the tender affection I had for my husband. But understanding did not entirely remove the sting of jealousy I suffered for the *other kind of love* that Eléanore shared with Axel. Still, I looked into Axel's eyes and saw that I was deeply adored. "Dearest Axel," I said. "I can ask for no more than that."

A few days later my Swede was gone, promising to return as soon as his responsibilities allowed. *Ne sait quand reviendra . . . I don't know when he'll come back.*

No. 51: Your presence is demanded in Paris

I PRAYED THE king would change his mind and decide that we too must leave, and quickly. He did not. Instead, we tried to continue some semblance of life as we had always known it. For almost twenty years, nearly every hour of my day had been conducted according to unbending rules of etiquette. I'd found it terribly tedious, but suddenly, as the rigid structure was crumbling all around me, I longed for some of that old dependability.

I spent most of my time with my children: Louis-Charles, the new dauphin, was four and a half, and Marie-Thérèse—Mousseline—nearly eleven. With Madame Polignac gone, the children required a new governess to oversee their households and their education. I chose Madame Tourzel, a sensible and loyal woman. The children quickly came to love her and her daughter Pauline, though the governess herself was strict with them; Louis-Charles called her Madame Severe.

They had their tutors and their daily lessons, and in a peculiar way their days seemed almost normal. But I was fearful for their lives, as well as for my own. I had heard that my husband's cousin the duc d'Orléans—now Philippe Égalité, the darling of the commoners—wished to see me dead; he was said to be making plans to assassinate me. Nearly as frightening was the rumor that I was to be arrested, charged with adultery (with Artois, with Yolande de Polignac, with anyone and everyone they could think of), and sent off to a convent after a severe whipping. But in spite of these threats I managed to get up every morning, go to Mass, and spend time with my children as the weeks passed.

I kept most of my jewels in a box, ready to carry with me, and I advised Madame Tourzel, "Do as I have done, and be ready to leave at a moment's notice, if that becomes necessary—as I'm sure it will be."

But the king refused to budge, still insisting that he didn't want to abandon his subjects. "I'm the father of a large family," Louis told anyone who would listen. "All Frenchmen are my children, even when they misbehave. They'll come to their senses eventually, and I must be here, waiting patiently, to lead them, as a father must."

Even those who agreed that we should leave could not agree on where we should go. Metz, which Axel had recommended and where Artois had taken his family, was too far. Compiègne wasn't far enough. So we did nothing.

Axel returned from Sweden at the end of September and took a house in town rather than staying in his apartments at the chateau. "This will allow me to summon aid, should your family require it," he explained.

A week later, I understood. A mob composed mostly of women gathered at the Hôtel de Ville in Paris, demanding bread. From there they began to march to Versailles, the mob growing bigger and more unruly as it went. Thousands upon thousands marched through the night, in pouring rain, along roads slippery with mud. They covered the twelve miles from Paris and reached the chateau around dawn, screaming not only for bread but for my entrails, which they promised to make into cockades. They called for "the baker and the baker's wife"—Louis and me—determined to bring us back to Paris. They wanted us to guarantee they would have the food we were deliberately withholding, perhaps to starve them to death, perhaps to enrich ourselves.

Surely they were not all women who marched and shouted; at least some were men disguised as women. They easily overcame the royal guard and murdered two of our loyal soldiers, cut off their heads and mounted them on pikes before they stormed toward my bedroom, shouting my name. I was almost too terrified to move, but

I threw a cloak over my sleeping shift and fled through a secret passageway to the king's apartments. Madame Tourzel was already there with my frightened children.

The crowd filled the marble courtyard, screaming over and over for the baker and the baker's wife. I sat trembling while Louis paced. "Listen to them!" he exclaimed. "They're demanding that we come out on the balcony."

"They're insane," I muttered. "The insanity of the mob. But we must do it, monsieur."

"I'll go," said Louis. "You stay here, Antoinette."

"No," I said, "we'll go together. The children too." I knelt down and spoke soothingly to Mousseline and Louis-Charles, "Don't be afraid, darlings. They don't want to hurt you."

I prayed that I was right.

The four of us stepped out onto the balcony and faced the roiling, maddened crowd, their faces twisted with hatred. Little Louis-Charles, his eyes wide with fear, clung to my hand, whimpering. Thérèse stood on tiptoe and whispered, "Maman, they're dressed in rags! Look at them! They're almost naked!"

"They're very poor," I explained.

The crowd had begun chanting, "The queen! The queen! We want the queen!"

I turned to my husband. "Take the children. I'll stay here."

Mousseline grabbed her father's hand and tried to tug him to safety. Louis-Charles hung back, insisting bravely, "I want to stay with Maman." But Louis picked him up and carried him away.

I stood alone on the balcony, having no idea what would happen next. My legs trembling, I swept a low curtsy, as a queen does to her loyal subjects. That gesture seemed to calm them, to give them a moment to come to their senses. They grew quiet.

Monsieur La Fayette appeared suddenly at my side. I wanted to slap him, but when he reached for my hand and kissed it, I clenched my teeth and allowed it. "We of the national guard are doing what we can to control the crowd," he said, "but my men are far outnumbered."

"Vive la reine!" someone shouted from below, and others took up the cry. But I didn't trust them. They could turn against me in an instant.

"Madame, they demand that you and the royal family come to Paris," La Fayette said. "I will escort you."

I glared at him. "Do we have a choice, Monsieur La Fayette?" I asked mockingly.

"No, madame, you do not."

I hesitated. As he said, we had no choice. "All right," I agreed.

I hurried to my apartments to pack and was aghast at what I found. I had locked the doors before I fled, but they had been broken down. Once inside, the mob had erupted in fury. They'd stabbed and slashed at my bed. With broomsticks and muskets and whatever else came to hand, they'd smashed the big gilt-framed mirrors hanging on every wall. The glittering shards lay scattered everywhere.

My self-control deserted me, and I stood among the ruins of my once-elegant apartments and howled like a madwoman.

That afternoon, the king and I and our children, along with Madame Élisabeth, Madame Tourzel, and Pauline, climbed into a carriage and joined the disorderly procession to Paris, accompanied by hundreds of our attendants and servants. We moved slowly, with many stops, while the mob surged around us, pressing their faces to the carriage windows, taunting us, screaming over and over, *"Vive la nation!"* That traitor La Fayette rode beside us. "For your protection," he repeated, though I could see that he offered scarcely any protection at all.

Late that night we arrived at Tuileries Palace, where I had often stayed after a night at the Opéra or a masked ball. But this was different. The palace, I saw at once, was dirty, strewn with rubbish, virtually uninhabitable. Where were all our attendants to sleep?

I was angry, frightened, and exhausted, but now strangely calm. Help would come, I was certain. Axel would see to it. Count Mercy would get word to Emperor Joseph, and my brother would send us aid. This nightmare would come to an end—I would awaken, and all would be well. For now I must remain in my role as queen, behave like a queen, never let these people forget that I was their queen, but also remind them that I was their friend.

No. 52: You may not leave the palace without permission

TUILERIES WAS a prison disguised as a palace, and I was now a prisoner pretending to be a queen. Somehow, in such strange circumstances, I managed to keep up the charade, though I never quite convinced myself it was real. Our people found places to sleep and eat. The rooms were cleaned and painted, and many of our possessions were brought from Versailles. All of my finery was carefully put away under the direction of the comtesse d'Ossun, mistress of the wardrobe. I called in Madame Bertin to refurbish my gowns—there was no thought of replacing them. Léonard, my hairdresser, paid regular visits. Madame Tourzel and Pauline made sure the children, including little Ernestine, continued their lessons. Ernestine had become like a sister for Mousseline, and the two girls spent all of their time together. I was glad they had each other.

We resumed the ceremonies that defined our lives—the *lever,* the toilette, the *coucher.* We ate our *grand couvert* in public, as we always had, and soon there were card parties and entertainments in the evenings. But everything was on a smaller scale, a miniature version of our lives at Versailles.

The biggest difference: we could not leave. Louis was not permitted to hunt, and that was a sore trial for him. We attended Mass and went for walks in the gardens, always surrounded by guardsmen who listened shamelessly to our conversations. People who called themselves *citoyens*—"citizens"—hurled insults of every kind, especially at me. We were prisoners, and it was clear that the people of Paris wanted it that way.

Axel gave up his house in the town of Versailles and took up residence not far from Tuileries, resigned his commission in the Swedish army, and promised to do whatever he could to help us. What a blessing it was, after the howls of hatred from the market women who wanted to murder me, to hear my dear Axel describe me as "an angel of goodness"! I adored him for saying it.

All this time, thoughts of escape were never far from my mind. My friends often proposed schemes for me to get away, since I was the clear object of the hatred, but I always refused. I would not leave without Louis. I was the king's wife, and my duty was to remain at his side, no matter what he decided.

But Louis could not make up his mind to flee, even though in the summer of 1790 we had a real chance. To escape the heat of the city, we were allowed to stay at Saint-Cloud, my palace outside of Paris, as long as we returned to Tuileries every Sunday. Louis was given permission to ride without guards for several hours each day.

"Suppose, then, he were to ride off one day and not come back?" Axel suggested. "You could bring the children to a meeting place you've agreed upon."

I seized on the idea. "Madame Tourzel and Élisabeth will go there separately, along with our attendants."

"And I will arrange for a large coach to meet you there, and you will flee together. It will be hours before your absence is noticed," Axel assured us.

Louis listened to the plan. "But what about Mesdames Tantes?" he asked bleakly. Adélaïde and Victoire were elderly—Sophie had died several years before—and not able to make such a flight. "I cannot leave them. They've been like mothers to me!"

And so we abandoned the plan.

I understood how he felt. I'd received word of my brother Joseph's death in February. I mourned him, not only because he was the brother I loved best but because that was one fewer person I believed I could count on to help us. I had never been close to my brother Leopold, who succeeded Joseph as emperor, and Leopold had recalled his ambassador Count Mercy d'Argenteau, on whom I had relied for the past twenty years. That left Axel von Fersen, and I now depended on him more than ever. I counted on his practical advice and his concern for my husband and children as well as on his continuing love for me.

Axel was convinced that we must find a way to escape, and he would not give up trying to persuade us. "It's still possible, Antoinette! But with every day that passes, your chances of success get smaller, and one day they will disappear entirely. It will be too late."

Still Louis could not make up his mind to take action—not even when Mesdames Tantes on their own decided to leave for Rome, and the authorities allowed the two old ladies to go.

At the end of October we returned from Saint-Cloud. We had enjoyed an illusion of freedom there, but at Tuileries there was none.

The National Assembly notified me that the royal children—*my children!*—belonged not to me and Louis, but to the nation, and must be brought up as the nation saw fit. If Louis were to die, the assembly ruled, I would not be allowed to serve as regent. That duty and honor would go to Provence, and if Provence were to die, then to the next surviving royal relative still living in France: the duc d'Orléans—Philippe Égalité!

"Never, never, never!" I cried when I learned of the provisions being made for my son, all without my consent.

It was clear to me, if it wasn't to Louis, that we had to get Louis-Charles out of the country. It was the only way to assure that he would one day occupy the throne and rule France, once this upheaval was finished, order restored, and the monarchy preserved.

"Then you must act now," Axel told us bluntly. "If you are intent upon saving your son, you must take your children and leave at once. Without the king, if necessary. It will be difficult if not impossible at this point to escape with the king."

"I should have fled when you first advised it more than a year ago," Louis said morosely. "Just hours after the fall of the Bastille, you urged me to go to Metz. I wanted to, but Provence was against it. I should not have listened to him. I should have listened to you, Fersen."

I rose and went to stand behind the king, placing my hands on his shoulders to lend him strength. "We made a promise to stay together," I told Axel firmly. "I intend to honor that promise."

"You are a courageous woman, madame," Axel said.

"Is it not too late to try, then?" Louis asked, peering at him anxiously.

"I shall do everything in my power to make it possible, monsieur," said my Swede, and he glanced at me. I hoped my husband didn't notice, or didn't understand, the look that passed between us.

My love for Axel had deepened over time, and never more than during this time of crisis. Many nights I lay awake wondering what my life would have been like if, by some miracle, I had found myself married to Axel instead of to Louis, who'd always been more like a brother than a husband. Of course that was impossible under any circumstances, but I still allowed myself to dream.

Now I pressed my hand to my mouth and turned away. Axel left the room quickly.

No. 53: Do nothing to arouse suspicion

WE BEGAN IMMEDIATELY to plan our escape. I ordered a large armoire to be stocked with all the things we'd need, such as new clothes for myself and the children. The armoire would be sent to a sympathetic friend in Brussels and kept there until we reached our destination.

Madame Campan, my first lady of the bedchamber, disapproved of this. "I'm afraid what you're doing is dangerous," she said. "Surely the queen of France can find gowns and linens wherever she goes."

"Perhaps so, madame. But I want everything arranged, and I need your help."

I sent her in secret to visit Rose Bertin and other dressmakers, ordering a gown here, another there, half a dozen chemises from one shop and another half dozen from a second, slippers and gloves somewhere else—not enough from any one source to arouse suspicion and never saying for whom she was making these purchases. Her sister helped us by sewing some of the children's clothes herself, using her own children as a guide for the correct sizes.

"I will send for you as soon as we arrive," I promised Madame Campan and her sister.

Most important, we needed a traveling coach suitable for the difficult and dangerous journey. The royal carriages were not large enough and could be recognized easily, so none of them would do. But before we ordered a new berline, Louis and I had to decide who would make the hazardous journey with us. Madame Tourzel insisted that she must come along to care for the children. Louis's sister Élisabeth would make six. Our servants would travel in a separate carriage.

Axel then placed an order for a berline to be built for a friend, "Baronne de Korff." According to the story Axel told anyone who asked, Madame Korff was a widow who planned to travel to her late husband's home in Russia accompanied by her two children, their governess, and a valet. Axel knew someone on whom he could rely to provide passports and identity papers for the travelers.

Axel outlined his plan to Louis and me as we huddled together in the king's apartments during the dark days before Christmas. "Madame Tourzel will assume the identity of the baroness and dress in an unadorned gown of good quality. The king will travel as her valet and Madame Élisabeth as a maidservant. The dauphin must be disguised as a girl, and he and Madame Royale should wear simple dresses. And you, Madame Antoinette—will you consent to play the role of the governess with as much skill as you once displayed in your theater?"

"Certainly," I said, warming to this idea. "And will you travel with us as our coachman?"

"Only part of the way," Axel said. "There is still much to discuss and critical decisions to be made. You have not yet settled on your destination."

I favored Switzerland, but my husband disagreed. Louis believed with his whole heart that the people of France would eventually come to their senses, the monarchy would be restored, and we would return to Paris in triumph as the rightful rulers. "Therefore, we must not actually leave France," he said, "but only reach a safe place near the border."

He finally settled on the town of Montmédy, about 180 miles east of Paris. This was only the first of many disagreements. But Louis was still the king, and he expected to be obeyed.

No. 54: You must go tonight

WE ARGUED AND debated every piece of our plan to escape. Axel thought it better not to travel with a large armed escort. "That will simply draw attention to you, which is the last thing you want," he reasoned, but the king would not agree. Nor could we settle on the best route to follow from Paris to Montmédy. Even once those critical decisions were made, the details proved complicated and had to be carried out in complete secrecy—hard to accomplish with so many people involved at so many stages. It was a long journey under the best of circumstances, and we all understood that a lot could go wrong.

While we waited for everything to be ready and the time to be right, my husband, my children, and I lived surrounded by danger. Guards seized a man in the gardens carrying a knife. Probably quite mad, the man confessed that he planned to attack me while I was out walking. The king's spies later uncovered a plot to poison me. I asked my doctor to prescribe an antidote, but he warned that someone might poison the antidote itself! Madame Campan became convinced that the sugar I used to sweeten my drinking water could easily be poisoned, and she changed the contents of the sugar bowl several times a day. I was never sure who could be trusted and who might be a spy in our midst. My nerves were constantly on edge as we encountered one delay after another.

Our new clothes had been finished and the armoire packed and sent to Brussels. The berline was ready, outfitted with every convenience, including storage for food and ways to prepare and serve it. There was even a commode for relieving ourselves. Axel had secured all the necessary documents for Baronne de Korff and her companions. I entrusted the box containing my diamonds, rubies, and pearls to Léonard, my loyal friseur, who was to keep the jewels safe until we were all reunited. Everything was ready. Still, my husband hesitated.

Meanwhile, the anger that had simmered all around me for months was rising to a boil. I pretended a calm I certainly didn't feel. The longer we delayed, the more people began to suspect that we were planning an escape. Axel tried to be encouraging, to show the grim picture in a better light. General La Fayette, who had so far done his best to protect us from the most vicious of the attacks, seemed to be losing his authority over the guardsmen. One of my wardrobe women was suspicious of the armoire sent to Brussels and reported it to the authorities. As a result, our guards were put on high alert. But when weeks passed and we had not attempted anything, they relaxed their vigilance and again took to napping throughout the night.

Then on Sunday, June 19, Axel came to Tuileries looking worried and exhausted. "It's too dangerous to delay any longer," he warned. "You must go tonight."

"But it's Sunday!" Louis protested. "It's out of the question for me to make my escape on the Lord's day!"

Axel stared at my husband in disbelief. He turned to me, but before he could speak, I held up my hand. "Will not tomorrow night do just as well?" I asked.

Axel hesitated for an instant. Then he bowed. "As you wish, Your Majesties," he said. "Tomorrow, then."

The next day, the twentieth, Axel returned in the afternoon to rehearse the details one last time. "Everything is in order, monsieur and madame," he told us. "Just before midnight I will be waiting with an ordinary carriage along the Seine, close by the Pont Neuf. I'll be among other carriages for hire, where I'm unlikely to attract notice."

Louis urged him to be cautious. "If something should go awry, Fersen, *je vous en prie,* get to Brussels as quickly as you can. Perhaps from there you can find a way to help us."

"Until we meet again," Axel said, kissing my hand as we parted.

"Oui," I said, my voice husky with tears I couldn't shed. "Until we meet again."

It was late afternoon. I collected myself and hurried to the children's apartments, where Madame Tourzel was playing a game with Louis-Charles. Marie-Thérèse was bent seriously over a book. "I've decided to take Madame Royale to the gardens of the Folie Boutin," I told the governess.

"And I, Maman?" Louis-Charles asked, immediately losing interest in his game and rushing to take my hand.

"Another time, my *chou d'amour,*" I told him. "Come along, Mousseline," I prodded my daughter.

One of the delights of Paris, the Folie Boutin gardens were privately owned by a member of the nobility. They were only a short distance by carriage, but getting there meant running a gauntlet of jeers and catcalls by the market women.

"Look straight ahead and pretend you don't hear them," I reminded Marie-Thérèse. "But if you hear a kind word, be sure to acknowledge it."

"I never hear a kind word," my daughter said sadly. "Only ugly ones."

Once we were safely inside the walls, walking about among the colorful blooms where everyone could see us, I said quietly to Marie-Thérèse, "What I am about to tell you must be kept secret. You must not be startled by anything unusual in our routine tonight, anything out of the ordinary that happens. Everything has been carefully worked out, and now we must trust that all will go according to plan."

Marie-Thérèse looked at me thoughtfully. I still regarded her as a child, but in fact she was twelve and a half, almost a young lady.

"Will you tell me the plan?" she asked.

"Only that we are leaving tonight, and that the journey will be long."

"Are you going to tell Louis-Charles?"

"No," I said. "He's only five. He wouldn't understand."

"That's true, Maman," she said. "But he would invent all kinds of fanciful tales and tell them to everyone, just to pretend he really *does* understand. I wouldn't say the least thing about it to him, if I were you."

I had to hide a smile. My daughter had a way of expressing herself that often sounded old beyond her years. And she was quite right about her brother: the dauphin didn't deliberately lie, but he could not be depended upon to adhere strictly to the truth. His habit of inventing fanciful tales, as Marie-Thérèse had described them, was troublesome. I had instructed Madame Tourzel to do her best to put an end to this sometimes enchanting but often provoking habit.

"Who will escape with us?" she asked.

I named those who would be in our party.

Marie-Thérèse frowned at me. "And what about Ernestine?" she asked.

I hesitated. "There is barely room for the six of us," I explained. "I wish we could take all of our friends, but we cannot."

"She is like a sister to me," my daughter reminded me sternly. "May she not ride in the cabriolet with the servants? We can find her a nice disguise, I'm sure."

"Ernestine will be safe," I promised her. "She can leave Paris with one of the other families fleeing for Brussels, and we will meet her later on. All will be well, I assure you." I wished I felt as confident as I sounded, but my daughter seemed satisfied, at least for the moment.

We tried to enjoy our walk in the gardens, no doubt our last for some time, and then climbed into our carriage for the unpleasant drive back to Tuileries, our prison for only a few more hours.

No. 55: Trust that all will go according to plan

THE EVENING dragged by, each minute seeming longer than the last. Madame Tourzel saw that the children said their prayers and went to bed. Provence and his wife dined with us, as they often did, and we parted fondly, promising to meet eventually in Brussels. At about eleven o'clock, when the last twilight of midsummer was fading, we went through the motions of the *coucher,* the king in his bedroom and I in mine, as we did every night, even as prisoners. That night could be no different.

I lay sleepless and beset with fears until darkness was at last complete, not even a moon. I rose and dressed in a plain brown-striped gown, a black cloak, and a black hat with a veil, suitably dull attire for the governess of a widow's children. By then Madame Tourzel had awakened the children and was persuading Louis-Charles to put on the specially made dress. He wouldn't be happy about that and was no doubt demanding an explanation.

One by one, at different times and by different doors, we slipped out of the palace, walking past drowsy guards who paid little attention to such ordinary people. One by one we made our way to the bridge by the Seine. I was the last to arrive and found Axel leaning on his elbows on the stone wall by the river, whistling Madame Poitrine's little tune as if he hadn't a care in the world. A few other drivers lounged nearby with carriages for hire. For their benefit we kept up our play-acting.

"Madame Korff, I am at your service," Axel said, bowing to Madame Tourzel and ignoring me.

Madame Tourzel, who now found herself cast in the role of baroness, acknowledged his greeting. I, playing the part of governess, clutched my son and daughter tightly by the hand. Marie-Thérèse nodded knowingly, but the dauphin, pulled from his bed, put into a dress, and led out into the street in the middle of the night, could scarcely contain himself and his curiosity. Madame Tourzel had told him he was taking part in a play, and we let him continue to think that.

"You must be quiet, Amélie," I warned my son, using the feminine name we'd decided to give him.

He began at once to protest. "Why are you calling me that?"

"It's a play," his sister reminded him in a stern whisper. "Remember? You are to pretend that you're a girl, and not a dauphine but an ordinary girl. And every time we call you Amélie and you respond properly, you will earn a toy soldier."

"And what am I to call you?" he asked her. "I've forgotten."

"Agläié," she said. "A pretty name, don't you think?"

"But why is Papa dressed like a servant?" he demanded as we crowded into the carriage.

"You mustn't call him Papa—he's our valet, Monsieur Durand. And I will not answer any more questions until the wheels of the carriage are turning. Every time you ask a question, Amélie, you will lose a toy soldier. Do you understand?"

I had begun to think that toy soldiers, always a helpful bribe, were not going to work well in this situation. What little girl collects toy soldiers?

Axel, perched in the coachman's box, flicked the reins and set out on an indirect route through dark, narrow streets where we were less likely to attract attention. I was uneasy when we were stopped at the customs barrier and asked to show our papers, but the officials merely yawned and, after glancing at the passports belonging to Baronne de Korff and her party, waved us through. Six miles beyond the city gates we found our handsome green and yellow berline waiting for us. In minutes we were on our way. Several servants and bodyguards followed in a cabriolet. It was one o'clock in the morning.

The berline was very large and very heavy, and therefore very slow, even with half a dozen strong horses. If we moved steadily we could make good time, but the horses had to be changed at each *poste,* at intervals of fifteen miles. At the first *poste* Axel left us. If it had been up to me, I would have gratefully accepted his offer to accompany us all the way to Montmédy, but Louis had decided otherwise. And so there was another parting.

I had endured so many partings from Axel; separation was the story of our love. Out of that depth of feeling he was putting his life at risk to save me and my family, and he asked nothing in return. While the horses were being changed, fresh ones put in the traces, the others led away to rest, we shared a rare moment together. "I will always be there for you, Antoinette," he whispered. "*Toujours, mon amour.* Always, my love."

"Always, my darling," I replied, and went to join my husband.

Louis checked his watch. It was now past two. We could not help wondering what was happening at Tuileries, if our absence had been discovered, if we were being pursued.

On we rolled through the dark and sleeping countryside.

The roads were rough and jolted us badly. The hills were steep, and we often had to get out and walk while our overloaded berline labored to the top. With every mile we traveled, every hour that ticked by, we were farther from our prison in Paris and closer to safety. As the sky began to lighten, our spirits lightened too. I began to feel a little easier.

That afternoon we were to meet with a troop of some forty dragoons under the leadership of the duc de Choiseul. The duke was the son of the French foreign minister who had been responsible for arranging my marriage to the dauphin. According to the plan, he was to be waiting at a *poste* with his men, but one thing after another slowed us down—broken harnesses, the slow pace of the berline—and we would be very late for the rendezvous.

"I'm sure Choiseul will be there," the king said.

I'm not so sure, I thought. I knew the young Choiseul; he was loyal, but he lacked experience, and he could be impatient and impetuous. I said nothing, hoping I was wrong.

But I was not mistaken. When we reached the *poste* in the late afternoon, there was no sign of Choiseul. He must have decided that our plan had failed.

"What do we do now?" we wondered. No one knew. None of us had any experience in making such decisions. Louis and I discussed the situation. We couldn't ask questions of anyone; that would have surely aroused suspicion. There was a chance we might be recognized. Finally the king gave the order: "We shall press on to the next *poste* and pray that help awaits us there."

But in one hamlet after another, the soldiers we expected did not appear. Failure marked our path. And then the unimaginable happened. A young postmaster in one of the little villages peered into the carriage and recognized "Monsieur Durand," the valet, from the king's likeness on the fifty-*livre* note. The postmaster sent word ahead and sounded the tocsin, the alarm bell summoning the citizens. As we entered the town of Varennes-en-Argonne, a wretched village of only a few handfuls of inhabitants, we were surrounded by an angry mob armed with pitchforks and whatever else they could grab.

"C'est fini," I breathed. "It's over. We're finished."

No. 56: End the charade

I FELT READY to collapse, but for the children's sake I knew I had to show strength when I had none.

"Perhaps it is not over yet," said Louis, trying to sound optimistic while everything was falling apart around him. "I am their king. Surely they will listen to me."

But they didn't. They might have torn us apart if it had not been for the good efforts of the mayor of the village, a Monsieur Sauce, who escorted us to his shop—he was also a grocer, a supplier of candles and soap. It was nearly midnight. We had been traveling with scarcely any stops for nearly twenty-four hours. The children were weeping, exhausted after only snatches of sleep.

The mayor led us up narrow wooden stairs to the plain rooms where he made his home above the shop.

"You are welcome to rest here," he said. "I'm obliged to keep you under guard while we send word to General La Fayette in Paris that we have detained you."

When he had gone, I turned to the mayor's wife, a sympathetic woman in a threadbare dress. *"Je vous en prie, madame,"* I said. "I beg you to allow me to feed my children and help them wash their faces. And it would be kind of you to provide us with clean linens so that they may lie down and sleep."

The good woman curtsied respectfully and hurried to assist us. The dauphin was soon sleeping soundly; my daughter struggled to stay awake to show her support for me, but I persuaded her that she too must try to sleep.

And so we waited. The night passed. Perhaps help would yet come. Weren't there supposed to be soldiers all along the way to protect us from just such an event? Axel would have seen to that. We talked little. There was nothing to say.

Madame Sauce prepared us a simple meal of omelettes with cheese and sausage from her larder and brought a flagon of wine. I was unable to swallow so much as a mouthful, but the king was ravenous, as always, and consumed my portion as well. Louis-Charles was convinced that all of this was still part of a play and did his best to continue in his role as Amélie.

"The play is over, my son," his father told him gently. "It's no longer necessary for you to act your part."

A thought occurred to me: if I could persuade the kindly Madame Sauce to persuade her husband in turn to let us be on our way, maybe we could yet be saved. As we sat side by side through the long hours, the woman and I spoke of many things, our children in particular, until I finally found it in me to ask her, "Madame, can you not convince Monsieur Sauce to let us go? You would both be contributing to restoring peace and tranquility to France."

I'm sure my words touched her deeply. She began to weep, and as the tears ran down her cheeks, she shook her head sadly. "*Bon Dieu,* madame, it would be the destruction of my husband. I love my king, but I love my husband too, as I know you understand, and he would be answerable."

And I did understand. Below the windows of the humble room where we sat, the crowd grew larger and angrier. "To Paris!" they shouted. *"Vive la nation!"*

We delayed as long as we could, always hoping for the arrival of the soldiers who would rescue us. One of my waiting women pretended to be taken with a violent colic and collapsed on the bed, moaning with pain. "I cannot leave with my faithful servant in such a state of suffering," I told the mayor. "I implore you to give us time to bring her to recovery."

But Monsieur Sauce saw through the pretense, apologized, and refused. "I don't believe that she is truly ill," he said.

I was determined we would not leave. When the king's arrest papers arrived, I snatched them out of the hands of the startled mayor and ripped them to shreds. "How can you treat the king of France in this manner!" I shouted.

My husband admonished me. "I beg you, madame, this man is doing his duty as he sees fit."

But I threw the papers on the floor and stamped on them. Louis merely shook his head as I raged.

In the end, no troops arrived. Louis feared that even if they did, there would be a great deal of bloodshed. "I cannot accept that," he said. "We must give up and return to Paris. It is our fate."

A fast courier had ridden off to Paris to inform the men in charge that we'd been captured. While we waited for the next step, I had time to think. I realized that I was no longer the same person I'd been when we had left just two days earlier.

I called my daughter to me and spoke to her in a way that I never had before. "Marie-Thérèse," I said, "I want you to listen to me very carefully. For some time now I have been keeping notes in a journal, making a record of my life. I'm afraid I no longer have the heart for it. You are twelve years old. You are thoughtful and observant. You have always been my Mousseline la Sérieuse. I am asking you to continue my story. Will you promise to do that?"

Marie-Thérèse's eyes widened with concern. "I will, I promise you, Maman. When the time comes, I will do this for you."

"The time has already come, my darling," I said. "You must begin now."

We embraced then, and our tears mingled as I pressed my daughter close to my heart.

Part IV

Instructions to Madame Royale 1791

No. 57: Be as much like your grandmother as you possibly can

I, MARIE-THÉRÈSE-CHARLOTTE de France, Madame Royale, promised to continue my mother's story. I was six months short of thirteen years of age when she passed me this great responsibility and I accepted it.

I begin my part of her story soon after my mother's outburst in the mayor's rooms. My father was shocked by her fury—her temperament was much fierier than his. I had always been closer to my father than to my mother because he never disciplined me and she did. As a small child I often resented her strictness, and I was embarrassed much later to be reminded that I once told Abbé de Vermond I wouldn't mind if she died. What an *enfant terrible* I must have been! But as I grew older, Maman and

I grew closer. Her anger didn't surprise or upset me—as long as it was directed at someone else.

Toward evening, two dozen national guardsmen arrived in Varennes to escort us back to Paris. We again climbed into our berline. Our bodyguards were gagged and bound to the outside of the carriage. Two officials named Barnave and Pétion rode with us—to keep us from bolting, I suppose—and the berline was wretchedly overcrowded. I had to sit on Madame Tourzel's lap; Maman held Louis-Charles. Barnave was good-looking and suave and seemed enthralled by my mother, who maintained her most regal air throughout the ordeal. But Pétion was another sort entirely, ugly and coarse, and he amused himself by pulling my hair and making crude remarks to Tante Élisabeth, the most pious soul imaginable.

The day was hot and dry. Clouds of dust rose from the road and drifted through the open windows of the carriage—we weren't permitted to shut them—and it clung to our clothes and choked us. Word had spread of our capture, and crowds gathered all along the way to watch us pass. Uncouth peasants reached in and tried to touch us, sometimes shouting filthy insults in our faces.

"I refuse to let them see how I feel," Maman muttered, though she was clearly miserable and seemed ready to drop from fatigue. "I am still their queen, and I shall present myself as one."

For four days our berline crept over the rutted roads, and finally entered Paris. We drew up in front of Tuileries

Palace, exhausted and filthy, surrounded by thousands upon thousands of staring people. Before this awful time they would have removed their caps out of respect, but that was a thing of the past, and they kept their heads insolently covered. I understood: they hated my mother with a twisted rage, generally felt sorry for the king, and for some reason adored my little brother. Only the dauphin received smiles and a few cheers. I was ignored.

Never had I wanted a bath so badly! Maman was often laughed at because she bathed nearly every day, but I loved those baths she allowed me to take in her tub at the Petit Trianon. How I yearned for that, once we had crawled stiffly out of our berline and dragged ourselves into the palace that was again our prison. Madame Tourzel carried my brother off to his room to put him to bed.

I heard Maman's shriek when she entered her apartments, and I ran in after her. The rooms were a complete wreck. The furious Parisians had broken in and destroyed everything, ripping apart the draperies, slashing the upholstery, smashing the mirrors and china. The destruction here was even worse than it had been at Versailles.

Maman stood in the midst of the ruins, pulling at her hair and sobbing. "Oh, how they must hate me!" The thin silk of her gown was dark with perspiration and caked with grime. Her damp hair clung to her neck. Her eyes were red with weeping. She looked terribly ill. "They torment me beyond endurance." Her voice sounded flat and wooden.

I rushed to her and threw my arms around her. "Dearest Maman!" I cried.

Outside her windows—several panes had been broken—we heard the wearisome chant, *"Vive la nation! Vive la nation!"*

I was very afraid. What was going to happen to us? I was trying to be strong for my mother, trying to be a brave woman like her, but my courage was draining away and I began to tremble. "Are they going to kill us, Maman?" I asked in a voice like a little girl's. I felt ashamed of my weakness and my cowardice. "Are they?"

"I don't know, Mousseline," she sighed, using my childhood name. She took my hand and drew me down beside her on a sofa that had been slashed. I picked at the stuffing that spilled out. Crude words had been scrawled all over the walls. I stared at them, not comprehending their exact meaning but understanding that they must have been rude insults.

"Why did you call me Mousseline when I was young?" I asked, allowing her to stroke my hand. "I've forgotten."

"Because I liked to dress you in pretty little gowns made of mousseline—muslin. And I began calling you Mousseline because you had a beautiful laugh, fine and light, and everything about you was fine and light and lovely. As it still is."

I leaned my head on her shoulder, and I felt her lips brush my hair. But suddenly she stood up, appearing rigidly determined. "I want a bath! And I think you must as well, my dear Marie-Thérèse. You can no longer afford to be fine and light, and so I'm taking back that name. You are no longer Mousseline. You must now use the name you were given, the name of your grandmother, the empress of the Holy Roman Empire, a woman who was as strong as iron. From now on, you must be as much like her as you possibly can!"

I was surprised and comforted by the return of my mother's firmness. I hoped that I would be able to live up to her expectations. The stories my mother told me about my grandmother made her sound formidable, though not always lovable. I prayed that I had inherited some of her strength. I would need it in the days ahead. We still had many trials to endure.

No. 58: Try to stay alive

ONE BY ONE OUR friends learned of the failure of our attempt to flee, and they began to return to Paris. Madame Lamballe was among the first to visit us. She brought a little spaniel as a gift for Maman. Our trusted servants had been arrested and many of them mistreated, but eventually most of them were released and returned to us. At last we felt it was safe to ask Madame Campan to come back as well. But Ernestine, who had gone away to Brussels with one of my mother's friends, did not come back, and I missed her very much.

You would be surprised by the changes, I wrote to her in one of my frequent letters. *It is now forbidden to address the king and queen as Majesty. And the usual signs of respect—standing in the presence of the king; uncovering one's head—are forbidden as well.*

Disturbing things were happening all around us. The people of Paris were so terribly angry. They marched by the thousands to the Champ de Mars, a great open space, to sign a petition demanding an end to the monarchy. Madame Tourzel told me that most of these people could not even sign their names but instead put an *X* on the sheets of paper presented to them. They wanted no more king or queen, but who would then rule them? The National Assembly prepared a new constitution that declared the king was no better than anyone else. They were to have a new government.

Maman was furious. "Nothing but scoundrels, lunatics, and beasts!" she complained bitterly, but Papa said he had no choice and must go through a ceremony, swearing an oath of loyalty to this new government. "They are demolishing the monarchy, stone by stone," muttered my mother while we waited for my father to return from the Champ de Mars.

Much later, he came to Maman's apartments, where she was writing letters and I was reading. His face was so white that I thought he must be ill. And he was weeping—I had never before seen my father weep. My mother rose to greet him, exclaiming, "My God, Louis!" She helped him to his usual chair and wiped away his tears with her own handkerchief.

"All is lost," he sobbed. "There is nothing for me now but humiliation."

Outside the palace I could hear joyful shouts and cheering, a few cries of *"vive le roi!"* but far more of *"vive la nation!"* My mother got down on her knees and laid her head on my father's lap. They had forgotten I was there, and I hardly knew what to do. My mother raised her head and noticed me. "Leave us, Marie-Thérèse, for heaven's sake!"

I did as she commanded, but I shall always remember the sight of my parents holding each other, cloaked in sadness.

Sometimes Maman talked about fleeing to Vienna. She spent hours every day writing letters to her friends and relatives, trying to get someone to help us. "There's not much we can do to help ourselves," she told me, "except to try to stay alive."

She used a complicated cipher that took hours to compose. First she wrote out what she wanted to say, and then she rewrote the letter using the secret code before burning the original. The letter might be intercepted by enemies, but it could be understood only by the person who received the letter and used the same cipher to read it. She spent every day at this task, but no help arrived. "I do not understand *why,*" she muttered, over and over.

My brother was off with his tutor, but my mother liked to have me by her side, even when I was supposed to be concentrating on my lessons. "Please stay with me," she said. "I need you, Marie-Thérèse."

One day I did something I should not have done and that I wish to this day I had not. My mother had gone out with Madame Campan, leaving me alone. I was to be studying a history lesson. She'd left a letter on her desk only half transcribed into cipher. I thought it must be another plea to my uncle Emperor Leopold, in Vienna. Why I chose to walk boldly to her writing table and to read what she had written, I cannot say. It was mischievous of me, but once I saw to whom the letter was addressed—not to *my dear brother Leopold* but to *my dearest Axel*—I could not help myself. I read on.

I love you more than I can say, she'd written, *and I cannot bear to think of not writing to you or receiving your dear letters, even though it brings much danger to both of us to do so.*

I can hardly begin to explain my feelings when I read this letter. Count von Fersen had been a visitor to Petit Trianon ever since I could remember. He even had rooms in the chateau for a time. I knew that he was a good friend to my mother, and to my father as well, and he had arranged our escape. I believe to this day that if he had stayed on as our coachman, he would have gotten us safely to Montmédy. Everything would have been different, I'm sure of it.

But this letter stunned me.

I walked to the window and stared out into the garden where a gentle rain was falling. *Is he my mother's lover?*

My father loved my mother—I had seen them on the day he wept in her arms. Then I thought of the tall, handsome gentleman who had dressed as a coachman and arranged for us to escape, and I understood that Axel von Fersen loved her too.

Now I knew that she loved him as well. She loved them both.

No. 59: Take good care of your mother

THE END OF 1791 was a bleak time for my family. It was very cold. My thirteenth birthday, Christmas, and New Year's Day were all observed solemnly. No one could find it in themselves to celebrate these occasions, though we tried to make the holidays happy ones for Louis-Charles.

My parents worried constantly that one or all of us would be poisoned. The pastry cook had been overheard saying, "It would not be a bad thing if the king's days were shortened." The head cook, however, was sympathetic to us and warned us to eat only roasted meats, avoiding soups and other prepared dishes. A trusted servant brought bread and wine from the outside, but we always pretended we had eaten the food from our own kitchens. Papa hated this. Sometimes he sent Madame Campan to nearby patisseries, always a different one, to buy him the cakes and sweets he loved.

The poisoning plots were foiled. My mother grew thinner and thinner. My father grew fatter and fatter.

On a cruelly cold day in February with the snow frozen so hard that it crackled under foot, I sat reading in Maman's apartments with her little spaniel, Mignon, curled in my lap. Maman as usual was writing letters. Mignon suddenly growled and then leaped off my lap and began to run in circles, yelping madly.

At that moment a stranger, muffled in a greatcoat, scarf over his mouth and wool cap pulled down to his eyebrows, appeared in Maman's apartments, accompanied by a huge dog. The stranger bent down and whistled softly, and Mignon, at first terrified by the big dog, ran to the stranger, her tail wagging. The stranger quickly removed his cap and scarf and gloves and knelt before my astonished mother, kissing her hand.

"Axel!" Maman cried, and at once she burst into tears. "I never dreamed I would see you again."

It was easy to read my mother's expression. But I could not help but observe the look on the count's face. In the six months since he'd last seen her, on the night we fled from Paris, she had changed greatly. She had once been very beautiful—that was obvious from the paintings of the vibrant young queen who had loved to ride all day and dance all night. I remembered when her hair was thick and blond, always done up by Monsieur Léonard in the latest fashion. Now it was faded and turning gray. As a little girl I had dreamed that one day I would be as beautiful as my mother. But now she was thin—gaunt, even—and her skin, which used to glow with beauty and health, was deathly pale and drawn. At that moment I saw my mother as Count von Fersen must have: old, worn, and haggard. He appeared shocked, and shaken. To his credit, he recovered quickly.

His disguise and forged papers had gotten him over the border from Belgium. "And the soldiers who are guarding you did not suspect a thing—though perhaps Odin here gave them pause."

The enormous dog moved to the door and stood as a sentinel. Mignon jumped back into my lap and eyed the intruders warily.

The count showed Maman a sheaf of papers from King Gustavus of Sweden. "My king has vowed to come to your aid," he told her. "He has considered invading France by way of the coast of Normandy. But more than that, he believes he can help you and King Louis escape. He is working on what he considers a foolproof plan. You would agree to it, wouldn't you?"

My mother sighed wearily, as she often did in those days. "I would, with never a second thought, if it meant that my children would be safe and the dauphin would then one day be king. But I don't believe you can persuade my husband to accept such a plan. He has given his word, over and over, that he will stay." She hesitated and looked at Axel von Fersen sadly. "As before, he and I are together until the end, whatever that may be."

The count nodded. "King Louis is an honest man, and a good one," he said. He took my mother's hand and held it.

I had, of course, been present all along. I felt like an intruder, and I was wondering what to say or do when my mother turned to me and said, "Marie-Thérèse, do go and tell your father that we have a distinguished visitor, and ask him to join us here."

"Oui, Maman." I picked up Mignon and prepared to leave.

"Marie-Thérèse!" she called after me. "Not a word of the identity of our visitor!"

"C'est entendu, Maman," I said. We knew that spies were everywhere.

I left them and hurried to the king's apartments. Papa received me fondly, as he always did. Unlike my mother, who was so thin she looked as though she might snap in two, my father was so fat that he looked as though he might burst out of his waistcoat and breeches. "Ah, my dear Thérèse!" he said, glancing up from his journal with a smile.

I delivered my message. "But who is it I'm to meet?" he asked.

I shook my head. "I don't know. He has a very large dog. I think Mignon is frightened."

"A dog?"

"*Oui,* Papa," I said.

"Then let us go together."

I accompanied him back to the queen's apartments, and I saw the warmth with which he greeted the count. My mother signaled that I was to leave them, and I did.

I don't know exactly what was said among them. The next day my parents talked for a long time privately, after the Swedish count had gone. I wondered if he had stayed the night, and if he had, where he had slept. He returned to dine with my parents. I was called in later. "Bid farewell to our friend Count von Fersen," Maman instructed.

I saw the look of suffering in her eyes, and I did as I was told, murmuring the prescribed phrases.

"You are as beautiful as your mother was when I first met her," said the count. "I beg you, Madame Royale, take good care of her." Then he kissed my hand gallantly, and I was sent away to my own rooms below the queen's apartments.

But I could not sleep, and around midnight I rose and went to my window, which looked out over the front courtyard. A tall man in a greatcoat and scarf with a cap pulled low on his brow was making his way to the main gate, followed obediently by a huge dog. A guard opened the gate to let them pass. The man stopped and turned to look up at the window above mine. He touched his fingers to his lips and sent a kiss toward that window, where I imagined my mother was standing and watching. A moment later he walked through the gate. It clanged shut behind him.

I wondered again: Had they once been lovers? Were they lovers still? I cannot say for certain—I can only guess. But I had seen with my own eyes my mother's unswerving loyalty to my father. She refused to leave him, even to save herself.

No. 60: Pray it does not happen

IF I HAD NOT MADE a promise to my mother to continue her story, I surely could not bring myself to describe what happened in the weeks and months that followed Count von Fersen's farewell visit.

Against his will, my father, the king, signed papers declaring war on Austria, the very people my mother counted on to rescue us. The French had always disliked the Austrians and mistrusted them, part of the reason why my mother had become the object of their hatred.

"From my very first day in this country there have been those who called me *l'Autrichienne* so that it sounds like 'the Austrian bitch,'" my mother told me. "In the beginning it was the jealous courtiers and people like Madame Du Barry who wished for my downfall. Now the common people have turned against me. They blame me for everything that has gone wrong in France. And I have done nothing to deserve their hatred."

But the Austrians were not coming to rescue us. My mother's brother Emperor Leopold died in February, and his son Francis became the new Holy Roman Emperor. Francis had never met my mother and cared nothing about her and her family. The French people believed Francis was after more of their territory, and they refused to understand that all of the queen's sympathies were with the French. To them, she was still the enemy they had always despised. There seemed no way to convince them they were wrong.

Worse was to come. "I've had a letter from Fersen," she told the king in a voice choked with despair. "There is no longer any possibility of rescue from that quarter. King Gustavus the Third of Sweden has been assassinated."

My father sank deeper into gloom. During those dark days he barely spoke—not even to me. Sometimes a week passed without one word from him.

On June 20, 1792, exactly a year after our foiled attempt to escape, an angry mob of filthy, brutish people forced their way into the Tuileries gardens, brandishing pikes and axes, searching for the king and queen. My brother and I were with our mother and heard them shouting vile language as they stormed the doors of the palace. Louis-Charles buried his face in our mother's skirts. I was terrified, much more frightened than I had been in Varennes, where I had not truly realized what was happening. Now I did.

"Maman," I cried, "they're going to kill us! Where can we go?"

But my mother remained calm. "Hush, now," she whispered. "This will end soon."

I didn't believe her. I was sure we were about to be butchered. When it seemed the attackers would soon be upon us, my mother grabbed us each by the hand and half dragged us through a secret door concealed behind a drapery. We ran to my father's apartments and fell into one another's arms, thanking God that we were all safe.

But I was startled to see my father wearing a strange drooping red cap, too small for his large head. It looked foolish on him.

"The *bonnet rouge* is the symbol of the revolution," Papa explained mildly. "They came here shouting their slogans. I agreed to wear it." He shrugged. "Why not, if it satisfies them?" He pulled it off and tossed it aside. "But they're gone now."

"Next they will be happy only if you dress like the *sans-culottes*," said Maman angrily.

She was referring to the shabby, baggy trousers worn by the workingmen of Paris in place of the elegant tight-fitting knee breeches and silk stockings that our men—the men of the nobility—usually wore. The trousers, along with a short jacket, wooden sabots, and *bonnet rouge*, had become the uniform of the revolutionaries. The thought of my father in such a costume might once have made me smile. But I hardly ever felt like smiling anymore.

There were new rumors every day. The one that most terrified Maman was not that the revolutionaries wanted to kill her but that they wanted to take Louis-Charles away from her *now*—not at some later, unspecified time—to raise him with their own philosophy in which there would be no more king, no more monarchy. Because of this fear, there were always whispers in our family of some new plot to escape. We had been prisoners at Tuileries for nearly three years, and I often thought that if I could have just one day—even a single hour!—at Le Hameau with my mother and her friends, I would never ask for another thing.

The summer was hot, and the palace was stifling. We no longer went for walks in the gardens, where insults were hurled at us, nor did my mother suggest a carriage ride to the Folie Boutin. I attended Mass each morning with my mother and father and Tante Élisabeth. One day, kneeling beside my aunt in the chapel, I murmured, "I have the most terrible feeling that something dreadful is about to happen."

"Then pray that it does not," she said, never taking her eyes from the pages of her prayer book.

My mother shared my sense of doom. She believed

that the palace was going to be attacked again. The mobs had grown larger and their aims more deadly. My father insisted the loyal Swiss Guards would defend us—"to the death," he said. But if the handsome guardsmen were killed, what then would happen to us? Our lives were in constant danger, and I did not want to die.

My parents were more worried than they let on—that was clear when my father didn't have his *coucher* on the night of August 10. The sky could be falling, and the king always had his nightly ceremony. I could not remember a single time when he had not. But that night there was no *coucher.* And my brother and I were told not to sleep in our usual rooms.

"I had beds made up for you close to the king's apartments," Maman told us. "I will not leave you."

But sleep was nearly impossible, especially when church bells all over Paris began pealing. I knew what it meant: the bells were calling the people to arms. Louis-Charles tossed restlessly on the cot next to mine. I remembered the little song that his wet nurse, Madame Poitrine, used to sing to him when he was an infant, and I sang the verse about the lady climbing her tower as high as she could go:

Madame à sa tour monte,
Mironton, mironton, mirontaine,
Madame à sa tour monte
Si haut qu'elle peut monter.

Soon my brother was sleeping peacefully in the midst of the clangor. I listened to his steady breathing and occasional sighs. After a time I drifted off to some restless place between sleep and wakefulness. But just as dawn was breaking with blood-red streaks across the early sky, everyone was up, tensely waiting for the awful thing we knew was coming.

No. 61: Remain calm and composed

We did not have long to wait for something dreadful to happen. One of the king's attendants informed him, "We're surrounded by at least ten thousand strong, far more than the Swiss Guards can control. Something must be done to rouse the loyalty of the national guard."

The arguing went on and on about what should be done. Everyone had a different opinion. Finally the king, pale as death, went out alone to face the crowd and found himself the object of insults—"Fat pig!" He returned quickly. His pallor was gone; now he was red-faced and sweating. He sat mopping his brow with a handkerchief.

We listened to the roars outside our windows: *Down with the tyrants! Death to the king! Death to the Austrian bitch!*

"Surely there are enough loyal troops to defend us," my father said, trying to rally us. "The Swiss Guards are loyal and well trained and courageous."

"But fewer than nine hundred in number," Tante Élisabeth reminded him.

"We cannot count on the national guard," my mother said. "La Fayette's men have proved themselves undisciplined and untrustworthy."

My mother and my aunt glared at each other. They had once been close friends, but now they disagreed about practically everything. My father looked helplessly from one to the other.

We could hear the pounding on the main doors of the palace, and the shouts grew to a roar. There were thousands of revolutionaries out there, throngs of furious *sans-culottes* from the outer districts of Paris. Newly arrived troops from Marseilles were leading them, singing at the tops of their voices:

To arms, citizens!
Form your battalions!
Let's march, let's march!
May a tainted blood
Irrigate our furrows!

We understood perfectly that *tainted blood* referred to the blood of the king and queen and all those loyal to them.

One of these loyalists urged us to flee to a building close by where the National Assembly was meeting. "You will be safe," the nobleman said. "The mob would not dare attack you there."

My father leaned one way, then the other, changing his mind several times. Tante Élisabeth was for it. My mother was against it. Finally, someone convinced Papa. "Let us go, then," he said and stood up to leave.

The princesse de Lamballe and Madame Tourzel were allowed to come with us, but most of the others, including Pauline Tourzel, were ordered to stay behind. "Don't worry," my mother assured them. "We'll be back soon enough."

I wanted to believe her, but I heard the princess's grim prediction to the governess: "We're never coming back."

We followed my father out of the palace and hurried across the broad courtyard with an escort of armed guards. The mob pressed so close we could smell their foul breath. I felt as if we were about to be crushed by their terrible rage. Maman tried to protect Louis-Charles with her body until a tall man stepped forward, scooped up my brother, and carried him above the heads of the crowd until it was safe to hand him back to my mother. In her haste, she lost one of her pretty silk slippers.

They herded us into a sort of pen and left us standing under the burning sun for hours with scarcely anything to eat or drink while the assembly debated what should be done with us. We heard gunfire and screams inside the palace. The mob had broken into the royal apartments and wreaked havoc, plundered the wardrobes of my parents and dressed mockingly in the royal finery. They trampled on my mother's elegant gowns and my father's handsome cloaks and argued over the scraps to take as souvenirs. Screaming obscenities, they smashed every mirror—just as they had at Versailles.

I tried to imitate my mother, who seemed determined to remain calm and composed, but when Pauline Tourzel and the other ladies found their way to us, bedraggled and frightened, I couldn't stay calm any longer. "Oh, my dear Pauline!" I cried. "Don't let us ever be separated again!" And my brother, Louis-Charles, who loved Pauline better than anyone except Papa and Maman, clung to her passionately and would not let her go.

"We were fortunate not to have been murdered," Pauline said, trembling from her ordeal. "Many others were. People were mowed down with musket balls; Swiss Guards were hacked to death with knives; servants were hurled from windows; cooks were slaughtered in the kitchens; washerwomen were stabbed and clubbed in the laundry." Madame Tourzel held Pauline and stroked her hair.

Consigned at the end of the day to a former convent where we were given just four cramped rooms to accommodate the group of us, we waited uneasily for the National Assembly—the former third estate—to decide where we were to go next. But the local government, the Commune de Paris, stepped in, claiming we were *their* prisoners, not the National Assembly's, and ordered us taken to the Temple. After spending three years of our lives at Tuileries Palace, we were moving to a different prison.

No. 62: Learn to endure it

IT WAS A LONG, slow journey across the city, and unbearably hot. There were thirteen of us—my parents, aunt, brother, and I, along with the princesse de Lamballe, Madame Tourzel and Pauline, three of my mother's ladies, and two of my father's valets. We were packed into two carriages loaded with as many of our belongings as we could rescue from the wreckage of our apartments at Tuileries. Insults were hurled at us as we passed, and as usual the dreadful *sans-culottes* refused to respectfully remove their caps.

When we arrived at the Temple, a huge crowd had gathered. A musty old fortress with walls more than eight feet thick, the Temple had once belonged to my uncle the comte d'Artois. Attached to the palace were two ancient towers.

My mother shuddered. "I've always hated this place, had an absolute horror of it," she muttered to Madame Tourzel as our carriage rolled to a stop. "The palace is not so bad, but I tried at least a thousand times to persuade Monsieur le Comte to have those towers torn down. Now you will find they intend to shut us up in one of them."

She was right. "All efforts are being made to accommodate you in comfort," one of the commissioners assured us. "The great tower will soon be ready to receive you." Meanwhile, we were committed to the small tower, and no matter what the commissioner had promised, no one worried about our comfort. Two dozen guards were responsible for making sure we didn't escape, and if we were miserable, so much the better.

My father's bed—*the king's bed!*—had no curtains around it, and the mattresses were crawling with vermin. In the room where I was to sleep, I found pictures hung on the walls of men and women doing the most disgusting things. I stared for a moment and then turned away and bit my lip. A jailer named Rocher plainly enjoyed my shock. My father himself pulled down the offensive pictures and ordered the guard to take them away.

Rocher replied insolently, "Of course, Louis."

He had addressed my father by his Christian name! Not *Sire* or *Majesty,* as common people were expected to, but *Louis!* I had never even heard my mother call him that in public. I expected my father to explode in anger at this kind of insult, but he didn't. Instead, he merely said, "*Merci.*" With a nasty smirk, the jailer carried away the pictures.

When Rocher wasn't being openly insulting, he annoyed us in countless smaller ways: puffing on his pipe and blowing smoke in our faces; sleeping on his cot, open-mouthed and snoring, so that we had to walk past him. He sported the oversize mustache worn by many revolutionaries and sometimes chewed the ends of it.

We hated the confinement and the presence of the guards, but we did what we could to get used to this crowded new arrangement. Our captors brought a few chairs and curtains salvaged from our apartments at Tuileries. Papa was delighted to discover a library with hundreds and hundreds of books, and he seemed determined to read his way through them. Maman had a small clavichord and an embroidery frame, and some kind person brought little Mignon and obtained permission for my mother to exercise the dog in the garden.

We had arrived with only the clothes on our backs, but soon we had new wardrobes and fresh linens for our beds. Maman managed to contact some of her old seamstresses and couturiers, including Madame Bertin. Her modest new dresses and hats didn't compare with the expensive gowns and accessories she once wore, but she said, "Better than nothing, I suppose. We should be grateful for what we have."

Though I often felt sad, we struggled on day after day, always with the hope that our lives would improve. But they did not.

"You must learn to endure it," Maman instructed. And I did try.

Not long after this stage of our imprisonment had begun, the princesse de Lamballe, Madame Tourzel, Pauline, and our three ladies were taken away to La Force prison. We were all dismayed, but Louis-Charles was beside himself.

"Not Pauline!" he wailed, throwing himself into Papa's arms. "They must not take Pauline away! Papa, order them not to take her from us!"

But there was nothing Papa could do. He was not in a position to give orders. I was too despondent even for tears but sat dry-eyed and resentful.

My mother, my aunt, and I no longer had any attendants. Léonard, the friseur who had always dressed my mother's hair, had disappeared. He did not come back to us after all of Maman's precious gems had been stolen from him during our failed flight to Varennes. The one piece of jewelry she still had was the tiny gold watch her mother had given her when she left Vienna as a young bride. She treasured it as though it were the royal jewels.

The commissioner arranged for people to help us, but they proved worse than useless and not at all likable. But then miraculously my brother's former valet Cléry arrived. Cléry had been with us since Louis-Charles was born. He was now supposed to fix my mother's hair and to teach me how to do my own. It was through this faithful valet-friseur that we received scraps of news from the outside world.

We learned from him that General La Fayette had fled. He'd once been a hero to my mother during the American Revolution, her protector after our arrival at Tuileries, and then her pursuer during our flight to Varennes, but his star had fallen long ago.

We didn't need Cléry to bring us word of the blood-bath that was about to begin.

Our three friends Madame Tourzel and Pauline and the princesse de Lamballe were hauled from La Force prison to stand before a tribunal made up of the most radical revolutionaries. For some reason Madame and Pauline were spared, but my mother's dear friend Marie-Thérèse de Lamballe was not. In the courtyard outside the tribunal she was knocked senseless with hammer blows; her head was cut off—how can I continue with this?—her body stripped of all her clothing, her stomach cut open, and her intestines pulled out. The murderers paraded through Paris. Their destination was the Temple. Somewhere along the way, the rioters found a friseur and forced him to curl and powder the blond hair on the severed head and to rouge its cheeks. They were determined to show this trophy to my mother.

We heard the shouting and the drunken roars of the

crowd outside our windows. "What is it?" asked my father. "What's going on?"

One of our guards, more decent than most, explained, "I regret to say it, monsieur, but the people wish to show you the head of the princesse de Lamballe."

Outside our windows the head of the princesse de Lamballe stared hideously at us from the end of a pike.

My mother, frozen with horror, seemed unable to move. Her mouth opened as though she were about to scream, but no sound came out.

"They wish Madame to kiss it." The guard stopped and stared down at his boots. He swallowed hard and continued. "They say, 'As they were lovers in life, so they should be in death.'"

My mother fainted and lay insensible on the floor. I rushed to kneel beside her, calling "Maman!" and begging her to open her eyes.

The guards prevented the raging mob from entering the tower, but the rioting and the shrieking went on through the night. I closed my eyes and kept them shut, listening to my mother's desperate sobs. I could not forget the hideous sight.

No. 63: Like it or not, you're a Capet

IN SPITE OF ALL the horrors forced upon us, we somehow adjusted to our new life in the Temple. "We must survive until someone comes to save us," Maman reminded me nearly every day. "Only by surviving will we triumph over our enemies."

Survival, to my mother, meant maintaining a routine as though everything were normal. After breakfast each morning Papa gave Louis-Charles his lessons in reading and writing. Tante Élisabeth instructed me in mathematics, which I enjoyed. In the afternoon Maman took over with the history of France, followed by music lessons on the clavichord, though it had become jarringly out of tune. "Oh, if only I had my harp!" she lamented.

I looked forward to our single hour of exercise in the

garden. I endeavored to teach tricks to Mignon, now more precious to us than ever since the murder of Princesse de Lamballe. Even when the weather was foul, a stiff wind whipping cold rain in our faces, we had to leave our quarters while they were searched. I hated the idea of our jailers fumbling through everything we had.

"They're doing what they must," my father said. His explanation of duty didn't soothe my mother and me.

In the evening there was time for games—my father was partial to backgammon—and he loved to read aloud to us. Maman and Tante Élisabeth preferred to spend the time praying.

"Prayer is my only consolation," said my mother.

On September 21, the monarchy officially ended. The people would elect a national convention. Under the new regime, the next day would be the first day of a new year—it would no longer be September 22, 1792, but Day 1 of Year 1 of the new era.

"Hey, Louis Capet!" cried Rocher, the detestable jailer, with a leering grin. "Did you hear the news?"

My father glanced up from his book. "Are you addressing me?" he asked.

"That I am," said the vulgar fellow. "No more *King* Louis for you, my friend. No more kings, period. No more titles. From now on you're Louis Capet."

"But that is not my name. If you knew anything about French history, Rocher, you'd know that the Capets ruled France until 1328. I am a Bourbon, not a Capet."

"Well, like it or not, you're Capet now," the jailer retorted impertinently. He turned to my mother, who had been glaring at him with undisguised revulsion. "And you—you're Madame Capet. Might as well get used to it." He leered at me and made a mocking bow. "No more Madame Royale for you—Mademoiselle Capet."

I could see that my mother was about to give Rocher a piece of her mind, but my father held up a warning hand. Maman closed her lips firmly and deliberately turned away from the tormentor.

No. 64: No whispers, no secrets, no plotting

IF ONLY THE insulting name change had been the worst we had to deal with! For a few days we had the luxury—we saw it later as that—of spending our time in each other's company, without ceremony or fuss of any kind. "So this is how ordinary people live!" I remarked.

"How would I know?" Maman said. "I've never lived like an ordinary person."

I had been thinking about Ernestine. How fortunate she was to have gone to Brussels! I'd wished for her to return, but now I was glad she had not. If she'd come back to Paris, like the princesse de Lamballe, she might have been murdered, her head carried around on a pike. So many of the people we knew had met terrible ends. I thought sometimes of Jacques-Armand, the boy my mother adopted before I was born. I'd seen him a few times after he had chosen to spend his time in the king's kitchen garden at Versailles and eventually was put in charge of it. Now and then Ernestine and I had visited the Potager du Roi, hoping to see Jacques-Armand in workman's rough clothes, his hands dirty, as though he had not been wearing silks and velvets since the day my mother brought him home. He was well built, blessed with thick blond curls and blue eyes and a winning smile, and he always let us pick some fruit and eat it on the spot.

"How handsome he is!" Ernestine had once sighed after he'd peeled a pear for us and sliced it with a little silver knife. "I think someday I'll marry him."

This had upset me because I was half in love with Jacques myself. "You can't," I told my dear friend. "Because I intend to marry him, and I'm a princess and you're not, and I get to choose."

Ernestine had burst out laughing and then clapped her hand over her mouth to stifle it.

"Why are you laughing?" I demanded.

"Because, Madame Royale, you'll have no choice at all. Your parents will see to it that you marry a prince, and you'll have nothing to say about it."

"I order you to be quiet!" I cried. I could be very imperious when I was young. But I knew that she was right. My parents had already been discussing the possibility that I would someday marry my cousin Louis-Antoine, the duc d'Angoulême, son of Artois, an idea that seemed very remote now that our world was crumbling around us.

Somehow Jacques had been forgotten. My mother no longer mentioned him. I calculated he would be a man of twenty-two. What was he doing, now that the chateau was wrecked and the gardens probably in ruins? Was he loyal—and was he still alive? I wondered if Cléry would be able to bring me news of him. But I had no chance to ask, for we were faced with a more serious concern.

Papa was taken away from us.

Early in October the guards, led by the loathsome Rocher, marched him off and announced that he would henceforth be kept in the great tower.

My brother began to howl at the top of his voice. "*Non, non, non!* You cannot take our dear papa from us! Oh, Monsieur Rocher, you are too cruel!"

I didn't scream at the volume produced by Louis-Charles, but I did sob loudly and plead with the man I hated. "Why? Oh, Monsieur Rocher, don't take him away, *je vous en prie,* I beg you!"

My mother wept so piteously that only a heart of stone could have refused her.

Finally, Rocher relented. "I'm under orders, you see. Louis Capet must be removed. However, I am not a monster. I'll permit you to have your dinner together once a day, but you must speak French, in voices loud and clear. No whispers, no secrets, no plotting. *Entendu?*"

We understood. We agreed to the rules. Then we set about finding ways to break them. All our writing materials had been confiscated, but sometimes we managed to discover hiding places—removing the pit from a peach and replacing it with a tiny scrap of handkerchief on which we had written a message. I spent a great deal of effort thinking up ways to get messages to Papa, and for a while we had Cléry to assist us.

A few weeks later, Maman, Tante Élisabeth, Louis-Charles, and I were moved to apartments in the great tower and permitted to join my father. In this new arrangement my brother shared Papa's room, and my mother and aunt and I had a rather pretty little room done up in striped wallpaper and white curtains and furnished with three narrow beds, a dressing table, and a chest of drawers. The cooks provided us with decent meals, and Papa had plenty of wine to drink. Most important, we still had one another, and we clung to that comfort.

As always, the challenge was to learn as much as we could of what was happening in the world outside our prison. Every evening around seven o'clock newsboys passed below the tower selling their pamphlets and shouting out the day's news. We stood at our barred windows to listen. "Even if it's not what we wish to hear, it's better than hearing nothing and imagining the worst," Maman said.

No. 65: You must forgive them

ROCHER REMINDED us as often as possible that my father would soon go to trial. The jailer always grinned with pleasure when he spoke of it. "Louis Capet will be judged! And, I'm quite sure, found guilty! Imagine that!"

On December 11, the commissioners came for Papa, led by the repulsive Pétion who had demonstrated his coarseness during our journey back from Varennes. He had since been elected mayor of Paris—I could not imagine who voted for him—and read out the decree with all sorts of flourishes, as though he were a great actor strutting upon the stage.

"Louis Capet, you will be brought before the body of legislature and interrogated."

Then Pétion turned to my mother. "Madame Capet, you will not be allowed to see the prisoner before his trial, and you may not write to the prisoner or receive any kind of communication from him." He refused to say when or if we might hope to see the prisoner again.

I cried—*wailed* is probably a better word—when Papa was led away. Somehow my father remained calm.

December 19 was my fourteenth birthday. Maman, Tante Élisabeth, Louis-Charles, and I spent most of the day weeping. Cléry was allowed to bring me a little gift from Papa, an almanac for the coming year. A new commissioner seemed to feel pity for my mother and sent a new clavichord to replace the one that had become so badly warped by the dampness of the tower that it was no longer playable. A nice gesture, but an empty one—it did not bring Papa back to us.

One by one the days and weeks passed: Christmas, New Year, the Feast of the Epiphany, festivals we had once celebrated with banquets and music and dancing. Another cold, hard winter settled over Paris. Still we had no idea what was happening to Papa. Every evening at seven we listened for the cries of the newsboys, always relieved when there was no word of the trial.

Then, January 20, a Sunday, we heard the news we dreaded most: *Capet to die tomorrow.* The terrible words rang in our ears like a curse from God. Maman and Tante Élisabeth fell to their knees and began to pray. Louis-Charles and I clung to each other without speaking.

Soon after the criers had passed on by, Rocher arrived, smirking as always. "Come, ladies," he said. "Time to bid adieu to Monsieur Capet."

Sobbing and barely able to hold ourselves upright, the four of us struggled down the gloomy stairs to my father's apartments, where Pétion had brought him earlier. It had been six weeks since we had last seen him, and I was startled and grieved by the change in him. He had lost a great deal of weight. His face, though still round, was drawn and haggard, and suffering had etched deep lines. His clothes, which no longer fit him, were unkempt, and his hair hung limp and straggly.

We rushed into his arms, and he sat down and held us in a long, wordless embrace. My mother was so overcome that she could not speak but clutched my father's hand, with Louis-Charles pressed between them. My father folded me close with his free arm, and I leaned my head on his shoulder. Tante Élisabeth crouched at his feet.

Papa tried to speak to us calmly, but we were not at all calm, and I'm not certain I heard all he had to say. He looked sadly at Maman and said in a breaking voice, "My cousin the duc d'Orléans—Philippe Égalité, as he calls himself—voted for my execution." He shook his head, bowed with sadness. "My own cousin! It's hard for me to accept."

Papa sighed deeply and continued. "I have asked them to make proper arrangements for my family, but I don't know in what way my wishes will be honored. And my children—especially you, Louis-Charles—please listen: you must forgive the enemies who are sending me to my death. It is what is required of us as Christians."

I couldn't help myself; I started screaming, "*Jamais!* Never! I'll never forgive them! *Jamais!*"

My father tried to calm me, stroking my shoulder. "Shhhh." He hushed me until I was quiet. "My darling Marie-Thérèse, you and Louis-Charles, kneel here, and let me give you my final blessing."

Obediently my brother slid off Papa's lap, I managed somehow to get control of my grief, and we knelt before him. Papa placed his hands on our heads and blessed us.

Maman interrupted. "Louis, let us all spend this our last night together. Surely, our captors will not deny us that! Just these last few hours!"

Louis-Charles was clinging to Papa's hand again, refusing to let go, his face flushed and wet with tears. But Papa remained calm, the only one of us who was, and would not agree. "I need to prepare myself to die," he said. "I must do that alone."

Finally, he rose unsteadily. He looked exhausted and yet somehow at peace. "You must leave me now. I won't say goodbye. I shall see you again tomorrow morning at eight o'clock, I promise you that."

But Maman would not give up easily. "Why not seven?" she insisted, her voice shrill.

Papa managed a tired smile. "Seven, then."

"You must promise!" Maman cried.

"I do, Antoinette. I promise. Now I bid you good night."

With great effort he detached himself from his weeping family, went into his bedroom, and gently but firmly closed the door. I thought Maman might insist that we spend the night there in Papa's study, but in the end Rocher ordered us back upstairs to our apartments. We lay down on our beds, but I'm sure no one slept. The weeping went on all night.

The next morning we were up long before daylight, waiting for Papa. But he did not come, nor did he send for us. A cold rain was falling. The hours passed. Church bells tolled the hour. We understood that he was not coming. Then in the distance we heard drumming, a silence, and then the boom of cannons and a burst of joyous cheers. I looked at my mother. Her face was contorted with grief. She closed her eyes and nodded, once.

My father was dead.

No. 66: Obey your aunt in all things

"Louis Capet" had been executed by guillotine. At the time I knew little about this new machine invented by a doctor. Because it was quick—a heavy blade in a wooden frame dropped to sever the head from the body—the guillotine was thought to be more humane than hanging or decapitation by a swordsman, who often bungled the job. I have tried many times since that day to erase the scene from my imagination: my father slowly climbing the steps of the scaffold, handing his prayer book to the priest, removing his coat, kneeling beneath the suspended blade; the gendarmes roughly placing his head on the block, the wooden collar fastened in place, the executioner releasing the blade; the terrible sound, the gushing blood. I've tried, but failed. That final scene plays over and over.

Cléry had promised to bring us my father's gold wedding ring and a packet containing strands of our hair, but he was locked up in the tower and kept there for weeks. When he was finally let go, Cléry left these items behind, hoping someone would find them and bring them to us. His hope was eventually realized.

My father was dead, but my mother, my brother, my aunt, and I were still alive. My mother was allowed to order mourning clothes made up in black taffeta, but she was refused the black curtains and coverlet for her bed that she requested.

"I remember when my own dear papa died," Maman told me. "My mother went into deep mourning and remained so for the rest of her life. She cut off her beautiful hair, she refused to wear any but mourning clothes, and she never again put on her jewelry. Her apartments were completely draped in black." I shivered as she described it. "It never occurred to me that someday I would be affected in the same way," Maman said. Her voice had grown hoarse from weeping.

Maman refused to leave our small quarters to take her exercise in the courtyard. It would have meant descending the stairs and passing the door to the rooms that had once been my father's, and that was too painful. I watched her grow thinner and paler with each day. It frightened me, but I felt helpless to change it. My mother seemed to be dead already, though somehow she went through the motions of living.

Foolishly we clung to a slender thread of hope that we might still be rescued, but hope was all we had. Some of the anger seemed to have drained out of the common people of Paris now that my father had been sacrificed to their blood lust, and Maman and Tante Élisabeth discussed in whispers the idea that we might be exchanged for some French prisoners being held in Austria. I wondered—but dared not ask—if Axel von Fersen might yet find a way to save us. I even dreamed that Jacques-Armand would suddenly appear, galloping up on horseback, leaping off his steed, storming past the guards, and carrying me away. In this dream his friends would quickly follow and save Louis-Charles and Tante Élisabeth and Maman as well. There may have been plots, surely there were some good intentions, but nothing came of any of them. And my dreams of Jacques-Armand were only that.

My mother's health had been fragile for some time, but now her situation worsened, and she was subject to frequent bleeding as well as fainting fits. My brother too was often ill with fevers and pains and coughs. I slept near them so that I could tend them during the night.

We learned that Philippe Égalité, the cousin who had voted for my father's execution, had himself been arrested and imprisoned. My mother greeted the news with the same indifference she now treated everything. "I never liked him," she said, not even glancing up from her knitting. It was as though she had lost the ability to express real feeling.

But then something happened that opened all of her wounds and produced unbearable agony. The guards reported, wrongly, that a plot to abduct Louis-Charles had been uncovered. They told their supervisors that my mother always referred to my brother as the new king. I knew that she thought of him as Louis XVII, but it was a daydream that helped her maintain her sanity. Nevertheless, the newly elected National Convention decreed that my brother must be taken away from her.

"Madame Capet, you are ordered to hand over the boy Louis-Charles Capet to our custody," said the gendarme in charge.

My mother behaved like a madwoman. I believe she would have more willingly parted with her arms than with her beloved *chou d'amour.* Louis-Charles clung to her, shrieking.

"I will not let him go!" she shouted.

"We shall take him by force, madame!" The gendarme tried to pull him out of her arms, but she held fast.

The arguing and the screaming went on. The gendarme threatened to kill her. "Then kill me if you must but I will not release my son!" she cried.

I was cowering in a corner when suddenly the gendarme spun around and pointed at me. "Seize her!" he ordered, and his men obeyed. Rough hands grabbed and held me. "Now, madame, hand over the boy, or we will kill your daughter." He snatched a fistful of my hair and held a knife to my throat. I thought I was going to faint.

My mother gasped and released her grip on Louis-Charles. "All right," she said. "I no longer have the strength to oppose you."

They seized my brother and carried him away, kicking and howling. All night we could hear his heartbroken sobs in the apartments below ours, the same closely guarded rooms where my father had been kept. All day Maman stood by the barred window and waited for a glimpse of Louis-Charles, now dressed as a *sans-culotte,* as he was taken to the garden for his exercise and later brought back again. The sobbing went on night after night, and my mother's vigil by the window day after day, for nearly a month.

August 2, 1793, was a night of suffocating heat. At two o'clock in the morning as we tossed restlessly in our beds, four officers arrived—a different group this time. The officer in charge addressed my mother: "Widow Capet, we have come to arrest you. You are accused of being an enemy of the revolution, and you will face trial by the Revolutionary Tribunal. Until that time you will be secured in another prison."

My mother stared at them, dazed and speechless.

"Where are you taking her?" I demanded. I was trembling, and my voice quivered.

The officer refused to answer.

My mother, always so modest, was forced to dress in front of them. She did as she was told, without protest. She collected a few things to take with her, embraced my aunt, and then turned to me. She seemed so calm that I could not judge if she was controlling herself—there were no hysterics this time—or if she had become entirely deadened to everything that was happening to her.

"My darling Marie-Thérèse," she said, gripping my hands; hers were as cold as death in spite of the heat. "My own sweet Mousseline la Sérieuse. These may be my last words to you. Remember to obey your Tante Élisabeth in all things. She is to be your mother now."

I looked into her eyes and tried to answer, but I could not utter a word.

"Widow Capet, come with us," said the officer.

I watched them take her away, a gaunt figure shrouded in black disappearing down the narrow stairs. At that moment I knew in my heart I would never see my mother again.

No. 67: Remember your poor mother

I HAD NO IDEA where they had taken my mother or what was happening to her. Later—much later—I learned this: She was driven under heavy guard to La Conciergerie, an ancient prison that had once been a magnificent palace on the Île de la Cité, in the middle of the Seine. There she was confined to a small cell with a miserable bed and a thin blanket. Only a half curtain separated her from guards who sat in her cell every hour of the day and night, allowing her no privacy. She was forced to perform her most intimate functions in a bucket only a few feet from these men.

A handful of kind people did what they could for their former queen. The jailer's wife, Madame Richard, tried to make the cold, damp cell habitable and brought her a pillow and some clean bed linens. When she arrived, Maman had only the clothes on her back, her black widow's dress, stained and ragged after six months. Madame Richard saw to it that she got some clothing—a sort of wrapper made of white cotton, a petticoat, and a few other things. She was not allowed to have her knitting or her embroidery, for the needles and the scissors were thought dangerous. A young maid named Rosalie Lamorlière, nearly an angel in my opinion, later told me what she could about my mother's days in La Conciergerie.

"I brought your dear mother a small stool of my own," said the maid, "and she climbed on it and hung a tiny gold watch on a nail."

"My grandmother gave her that watch," I told her. "It was her most precious possession."

"But they took it away from her five days after she came to us," Rosalie said. "She wept, as you might expect. But she wept quite often. Who could blame her?"

Dear little Rosalie tried to make my mother's pitiful life easier, bringing small bunches of flowers to brighten the fetid, stinking cell. Soon even that scrap of kindness was forbidden. The jailer and his wife, Monsieur and Madame Richard, who had been helpful and occasionally even indulgent to my mother, were taken away and imprisoned, punished for their compassion for the widow Capet. They were replaced by yet another couple, who were not about to repeat the mistakes of their predecessors.

"She kept right on hoping for rescue by her Austrian family," Rosalie said. "'They won't let me die,' Madame said. 'You'll see.' Maybe it was to convince herself."

But her family had done nothing. They didn't care about my mother, or about any of us. The only one who truly cared was Count von Fersen, and he was far away.

Day after day, still shut up in the tower, Tante Élisabeth and I clutched each other's hands as we listened every evening to the cries of the newsboys outside the tower. Our lives had become much meaner. We had only one room now and were supplied with only the barest necessities. No one could enter our room except to bring water and firewood, and little enough of that. We were not allowed candles, and our large bed sheets were taken away, lest we knot them together and somehow manage to escape through the gratings that covered our windows.

Sometimes we heard my brother's voice in the gardens below. He was put in the care of a cobbler named Simon, an ignorant ruffian who taught him to curse, using the most disgusting obscenities, and to yell slogans such as "Down with the monarchy! Death to the queen! Death to all the nobility!" Simon also taught Louis-Charles to sing, his poor little voice croaking the words of their revolutionary songs.

Oh, my poor brother! It broke my heart to hear him. He didn't understand. If it satisfied his rude guardian to hear him shout "Death to the queen!" then Louis-Charles would do exactly that. What had they done to him?

Believing my mother was somehow involved in escape plots, they moved her to an even smaller, more squalid cell into which no outside light could enter. Three men were set to guard her at all times, one at the door of her cell, one at the courtyard outside her barred and sealed window, one in the cell with her. How horrible that must have been for her! How did she bear it? Yet I knew she would not have cooperated in even the most foolproof plot if it meant leaving without Louis-Charles.

"The National Convention would not allow her the smallest comfort, not even a blanket to ward off the cold," good Rosalie told me, "and she had to spend the night in total darkness, without a single candle. I warmed her nightgown at my own fire before I took it to her, but it was not enough. She was ill and weak and exhausted. Sometimes when I went to her in the morning, she would drag herself from her cot, saying to me, 'I slept a little and dreamed of Le Hameau.' Once or twice she tried to sing a sad little song, something about 'Malbrough goes to war, and we don't know when he's coming back.'"

I knew the song, and I wept at the memories it brought me.

On the night of October 12, my mother, the "widow Capet," was taken to the hall where the Revolutionary Tribunal sat in judgment. Hour after hour they hounded her with questions, using the allegations of the awful pamphleteers to accuse her of every imaginable crime, including starving the common people and plotting to have them all murdered.

"They say she answered well," Rosalie said. "As ill as she was, she showed them her intelligence and inner strength. I think she surprised them." When the questioning ended, the guards took her back to her wretched cell. Two days later she faced the tribunal again.

From one of the brave lawyers who attempted to defend her I learned some of the worst of what my mother had to endure. "The prosecutors claimed that your brother, the little Capet, had told them his mother had engaged in acts of incest with him."

Incest? I gasped when I heard this incredible accusation. "But it's not true! I swear it!"

Had Louis-Charles said such a thing? I realized that perhaps he had indeed said it if they had told him he must. My innocent little brother who yelped obscenities beneath my window wanted nothing more than to please his captors. I had warned Maman, when we were preparing to flee from Tuileries, to tell Louis-Charles as little as possible. "He will invent all kinds of fanciful tales and tell them to everyone," I'd told her.

Maman took my warning seriously and instructed his governess to do her best to put an end to this habit of telling untruths. Clearly, Madame Tourzel had not been successful. But I could not imagine what ideas had been put into the boy's head and if he even understood what he was saying.

When my mother heard this accusation, the lawyer told me, she rose, turned to the crowd gathered in the great hall, and spoke out indignantly. "I appeal to the conscience and sensibilities of every mother present. Is there even one among you who does not shudder in revulsion at the suggestion of such horrors?"

A group of fierce market women who had sat knitting throughout the trial suddenly dropped their needles and their wool and turned sympathetically toward the accused. Some cried out, "Show her mercy, for the love of God!" There was such a commotion that the judge pounded his gavel and shouted for order. The trial continued for two long days.

No one seemed to doubt how it would end. The people demanded vengeance. The jury of tradesmen returned the verdict: *Guilty, guilty, guilty.* "We will settle for nothing less than the death of *l'Autrichienne.*"

Without uttering a word she rose and stood with great dignity while the gendarmes came to lead her back to her cell. It happened to be my name day, in honor of Sainte Thérèse. I thought of how we had once celebrated at Petit Trianon when I was a child, with feasting and music and my mother smiling and beautiful in one of her lovely white gowns. I wondered if she remembered too.

No. 68: Embrace your fate

"THEY BROUGHT the queen at five o'clock in the morning on the sixteenth of October," Rosalie continued. "'I am to die today,' your dear mother said, and I began to weep. I couldn't help myself!"

I too wept as Rosalie described my mother's last hours. "They would not allow your mother to say adieu to you and your aunt and your brother. Even the king had been allowed that privilege! Your mother sat at her table and wrote a letter to Madame Élisabeth—she believed that you too had been taken away, and that pained her—and then she lay down to rest. I tried to persuade her to eat a little, but she shook her head. 'My girl, I don't need anything,' she said. 'It's all over for me.' I coaxed her to have a little broth, to give her strength for what lay ahead, but a few spoonfuls was all she could swallow.

"She was bleeding again, and she asked the gendarme to turn away while she changed her linens, but he would not! He was under orders, he said, not to take his eyes off her for even a second. Such indecency! Then she put on the white dress with a white muslin fichu tied around her shoulders and a plain white bonnet." Rosalie paused in her recitation and looked at me. "Mademoiselle, are you sure you wish me to continue?"

I nodded. "Tell me. I need to hear it all."

Rosalie struggled for a moment, then continued in a whisper. "They bound her hands, and she hadn't expected that. She even tried to reason with them: 'You didn't bind the hands of King Louis the Sixteenth,' she told them, but they ignored her quiet complaint and, I fear, bound them even more tightly. I believe she thought she would be taken by carriage, as the king had been, but they wanted to humiliate her, you see? She was forced to climb into a tumbrel, a rough wooden cart drawn by a pair of draft horses, to La Place de la Révolution. As though she was a common criminal!"

For months before my mother had been taken away to La Conciergerie, we had listened every day to the sound of the tumbrels rumbling over the cobblestones, carrying the condemned prisoners to their final appointment with "Sainte Guillotine, the patron saint of patriots," as they called this horrible machine of death. Since my father's execution, hundreds of members of the aristocracy had met death beneath the terrible blade. The streets were always crowded with the kind of rabble who enjoyed such events.

Now her final moments had come. I've been told that she met them with courage. I believe she climbed the steps of the scaffold with a sense of relief. At last her ills were at an end, and she was ready to not only accept her fate but embrace it. Once again the drums rolled, the blade dropped, the executioner held up the severed head by a handful of white hair, and the crowd cheered their victory. Marie-Antoinette, queen of France, was dead.

No. 69: It is time for you to begin a new life

MY MOTHER'S LIFE was ended, and yet at the time I knew nothing of it. True, Tante Élisabeth and I heard the cries of the newsboys—"Widow Capet is dead!"—but we could not let ourselves believe them.

"It cannot be," my aunt insisted firmly. "Your father was allowed time to prepare his defense, and his trial lasted for days. He was permitted to make his farewells to us, even if he went off without the last one he had promised. Surely these evil people would not be so cruel as to deny your mother—and us—the consolation of a farewell embrace, a blessing!"

"But why are the newsboys shouting that she's dead?" I asked.

"They are under orders to torment us," she said. "I am sure of it. We must continue to pray for her."

I desperately wanted to believe my aunt, and I clung to the hope that my mother lived. I observed my fifteenth birthday, still not knowing her fate. But as the cold, gray days passed and spring came once again, we heard nothing more about my mother. My brother continued to shout revolutionary slogans below our window, and the newsboys announced more beheadings every day. Sometimes we recognized the names: Barnave, for instance, the official who had ridden with us from Varennes and wanted to help my mother. The duc d'Orléans—Philippe Égalité—my father's cousin who had voted for his death. Madame Du Barry, once my great-grandfather's mistress and my mother's enemy. The list of the dead seemed endless.

"The streets of Paris are running red with blood," said Tante Élisabeth, but she continued to believe my mother was alive. The officers who guarded us ignored our pleas for news of her, though I asked them at least a thousand times.

Our guards seemed to take pleasure in finding ways to treat us with increasing severity. They would not allow us fish or eggs during the Lenten fast, telling us, "None but fools believe in that nonsense." They took away the playing cards and the chess set with which we sometimes tried to pass the time. The reason? There were kings and queens in the deck and among the chess pieces! They took away Mignon, my mother's little spaniel, and broke my heart again.

In May we were awakened by the sound of the bolts being thrown open and pounding on our door. Tante Élisabeth dressed hurriedly before the gendarmes burst in. "*Citoyenne,* come with us," they ordered roughly.

My aunt embraced me and prepared to leave. "Don't worry," she said. "I'm sure I'll be back soon."

"No, citizen, you will not return," a gendarme said, and they seized her roughly.

It was the last I saw her. The next day I heard the newsman's cry, "Another Capet dies!" I did not deceive myself that she might have been saved.

And still the officers would tell me nothing.

A year passed, day after empty day, and suddenly my brother's voice fell silent. Again, there was no explanation. Louis-Charles simply ceased to exist. I became, then, the orphan of the Temple, alone in the tower, beyond despair, beyond hope. I was the most unhappy creature in the world.

But in some small ways, my captivity became less onerous. Perhaps someone felt sympathy for me, for I was allowed to walk again in the Temple gardens, and one of the officers brought me a little dog. She was ugly but clever and well behaved, and I named her Coco. Most crucially, I was allowed a woman companion, Madame

Chantereine. It fell to this goodhearted lady to tell me the truth about my family, a sad truth that I had already known in my heart but had denied. My mother, my aunt, my brother—all were dead. "Louis-Charles too?" I asked.

"Of an illness," said my companion. But she could not say what it was.

It was Madame Chantereine who arranged for Rosalie's visit and a chance for me to hear of my mother's final days. But I had been kept away so long that I had nearly lost the power of speech. And once I'd heard her story, I could no longer weep. It was as though all my tears had been shed, and I had none left.

Sometimes, I discovered, miracles do happen. On the day of my seventeenth birthday, the minister of the interior, Monsieur Benezech, presented himself in my room. I expected the usual insolence common to representatives of the National Convention, but this man was of an older generation. "I have news for you, Madame Royale," he said.

Madame Royale? No one had addressed me by my title for a very long time. "Tell it to me, *je vous en prie,*" I replied.

"Your relatives in Vienna have sent for you. In return, they have agreed to release several French prisoners. It is time for you to begin a new life."

I simply stared at him, wondering if this might be a cruel joke. But it was not. The minister explained how the exchange would take place: I was to leave immediately, traveling incognito under the name of Sophie and accompanied by several of my family's servants and by Madame de Soucy, who had once been my brother's deputy governess.

In order not to attract attention, Benezech, with Coco tucked under his arm, escorted me to his carriage in a quiet side street not far from the Temple and drove me to a remote place where a berline waited. Soon after midnight I began the long journey from Paris to Vienna, retracing the journey my mother had made twenty-five years earlier on her way to marry the future king of France. Long before dawn on December 20, 1795, the carriage rolled down the darkened streets of Paris, through the gates of the city, and toward the frontier. For the first time in six years I was free.

Though I was grateful to be out of prison, I was leaving France with much regret. It was my country, I was a Frenchwoman, and I would never cease to regard France as my home. I put my head in my hands and wept bitterly for my family, my friends, my homeland, and all that was lost.

Epilogue

WHEN I WAS VERY young, my mother used to tell me how she had sobbed when she left the Hofburg Palace in Vienna, leaving behind her mother and family and all that was familiar, bound for a country she didn't know in order to marry a young man she'd never met.

I hadn't understood her sadness. My only thought was how exciting it must have been!

Now I understand. It has not been easy. For more than two years, since I left France, I have lived at the Viennese court of my cousin Emperor Francis II. I don't much like him—he didn't lift a finger to save my father or my mother. I don't think he likes me either. The members of my party who made the long, difficult journey with me have since been sent away. The French are not welcome here, for the two countries are still at war—the war my father was forced to declare. The Hofburg has turned out to be another prison for me. A gilded cage, but nevertheless a cage. I sometimes wonder if Versailles was not a gilded cage for my mother. She lived her whole life imprisoned by rules. Sometimes she tried to break out. I believe she must have been very lonely.

Today I am preparing to leave. My uncle the comte de Provence declared himself King Louis XVIII after the death of my brother. Czar Paul of Russia has offered him refuge in one of the Russian provinces, and I am to join him there. I know nothing of that part of the world, but my future has been decided: I am to marry my cousin Louis-Antoine, the duc d'Angoulême. Antoine is the son of my father's youngest brother, Artois. My parents always hoped I would marry him. I haven't seen Louis-Antoine since we were children. I wonder what he's like now. I suppose I'll find out soon enough.

My uncle Provence has written to me: *My dear Marie-Thérèse, the monarchy will soon be restored, the Bourbons will take the throne, and as the wife of the duc d'Angoulême, you will someday find yourself queen of France.*

Should that be my fate, I hope to do honor to the title. But my biggest hope is that the world will someday come to understand Queen Marie-Antoinette-Josèphe-Jeanne, to admire her for the good that she did, and, most especially, to forgive her for her wrongs.

Marie-Thérèse-Charlotte de France
Vienna, May 1798

Historical Notes

THERE IS NO HAPPY ending to this story.

Marie-Thérèse left Vienna and began a lifetime of wandering. In June of 1799 she married her cousin Louis-Antoine, the duc d'Angoulême. That same year Napoleon Bonaparte, a young military officer, declared himself emperor of France. Bonaparte was in and out of power until his defeat at Waterloo in 1815 and the subsequent restoration of the House of Bourbon. Provence ruled as King Louis XVIII until his death in 1824, when Artois ascended the throne as King Charles X and Artois's son Louis-Antoine became the dauphin. Marie-Thérèse was now titled Madame la Dauphine.

In 1830 by means of an elaborate deception Louis-Philippe, son of the duc d'Orléans—who called himself

Philippe Égalité, voted for the death of his cousin King Louis, and was then himself executed—now came onto the scene. Louis-Philippe replaced Charles X, declaring himself king of the French. Before being coerced into signing the abdication papers, Marie-Thérèse's husband held the title of King Louis XIX for less than a half-hour, and she was queen of France for those same few minutes. Rather than live under the usurper's rule, Marie-Thérèse, her husband, and her father-in-law went into exile one more time.

Louis-Antoine died in 1844. The marriage was childless and has been described as an unhappy one. In the years after she left the tower, Marie-Thérèse lived at various times in Russia, England, Scotland, France, Prague, and Italy. Another revolution ended Louis-Philippe's reign in 1848. In 1851 Marie-Thérèse died at the age of seventy-two at her small palace outside of Vienna. She ended her life as a sad and bitter woman. It's not hard to understand why.

One more unhappy note: Axel von Fersen died in Stockholm in 1810, beaten to death by a revolutionary mob. He kept his promise to Marie-Antoinette, the love of his life, and never married.

Author's Note

"Let them eat cake."

The French people were starving; there was no bread; and Queen Marie-Antoinette, dressed in expensive silks and diamonds and with her hair in a towering pouf, flicked her jeweled fan and pronounced the famously disdainful sentence.

That's how the story goes. In fact, she never said it. Arguments have raged for years about the source of the story—exactly who said what, the definition of *cake,* the circumstances under which the words were uttered, and if they were even uttered at all. The often-repeated remark is part of the myth of Marie-Antoinette as the cruel queen whose behavior sparked the French Revolution.

But was she as heartless as she is usually portrayed? I wondered about that, especially after I saw Sofia Coppola's 2006 movie *Marie Antoinette.* I was curious about who this bad queen really was and what she did that made her one of the most hated queens in history.

To answer my own questions, I read biographies and tried to learn about her, her family, her friends, and her life.

I visited Vienna, where she spent her childhood among brothers, sisters, and tutors under the critical gaze of her domineering mother.

I traveled to Versailles, where she went as a young bride to marry a boy she'd never met. I waited until the dozens of tour buses had left the parking lot, and in the hour or two before the enormous chateau was closed for the night, I walked through nearly empty chambers, including the spectacular Galerie des Glaces, the Hall of Mirrors. I walked around the Petit Trianon (it was closed for renovation), looked in at the little theater where she and her friends had put on plays, and strolled the lovely grounds of Le Hameau to imagine her delight in living what she believed was a simple life.

In Paris I visited the Grand Palais, where more than three hundred objects and paintings had been assembled to tell her story—including the seating chart for the young dauphine's wedding supper and a reproduction of the infamous diamond necklace. Leaving that exhibit area, visitors descended a spiral staircase to a lower level and confronted an enormous shattered mirror. It was a stunning reminder of the destruction caused by the mobs as well as a symbol of the end of the life she knew, and it took my breath away. Beyond that powerful image lay a long, darkened gallery with an exhibit of the vicious pamphlets and caricatures expressing the hatred focused on the queen.

Finally, I peered into the cell at the Conciergerie where Marie-Antoinette spent her final weeks.

The more I read about her and the more I retraced her steps, the more she came alive to me as a flesh-and-blood person, seriously flawed, but not evil. She was not responsible for a single death. She may have worn her diamonds and called upon her couturière to make another fabulous gown when the people were going hungry—a serious mistake on her part, certainly, but not a crime. She was extravagant to a fault, but it was not her extravagance that brought France to the brink of ruin. She felt entitled to every luxury, but she did not perform the horrible deeds often blamed on her. And neither she nor her husband, an inept king who had no idea of how to govern, deserved to die.

The Bad Queen, like my other novels, is a work of historical fiction. I'm often asked if the books I write about famous queens—Bloody Mary, Anne Boleyn, Catherine de' Medici, and now Marie-Antoinette—are "true." The answer is that they are based on the known facts. But as anyone who has studied history has learned, the facts are often debatable or simply unknown. Many times there is no proof, just speculation and educated guesswork. The history in all my books is as accurate as my research can make it. I have not invented a single character in this novel. I have woven the actual historical figures and the known facts into a fictional framework. Much of the dialogue is based on quotations—translated from French, of course—found in historical accounts.

But I have used my imagination to bring certain events to life; I've also chosen to let Marie-Antoinette tell her own story, expressing her thoughts and feelings in a voice that I hope is much like hers. That is what makes *The Bad Queen* a work of fiction rather than a biography.

Carolyn Meyer
Albuquerque, New Mexico
2009

Bibliography

Chapman, Martin, et al. *Marie-Antoinette and the Petit Trianon at Versailles* (San Francisco: Fine Arts Museums of San Francisco, catalog, 2007).

Erickson, Carolly. *To the Scaffold: The Life of Marie Antoinette* (New York: Morrow, 1991).

Fraser, Antonia. *Marie Antoinette: The Journey* (New York: Random House, 2001).

Levron, Jacques. *Daily Life at Versailles in the Seventeenth and Eighteenth Centuries* (New York: Macmillan, 1968).

Weber, Caroline. *Queen of Fashion: What Marie Antoinette Wore to the Revolution* (New York: Holt, 2006).